Alien Main

Alien Main

T. L. SHERRED
and
LLOYD BIGGLE, JR.

DOUBLEDAY & COMPANY, INC.

GARDEN CITY, NEW YORK

1985

Library of Congress Cataloging in Publication Data

Sherred, T. L.
Alien main.

I. Biggle, Lloyd, 1923–   . II. Title.
PS3569.H4345A79   1985   813'.54

ISBN: 0-385-19358-0
Library of Congress Catalog Card Number 84-1503

First Edition

ABOUT THE AUTHORS

LLOYD BIGGLE, JR., is one of America's foremost Science Fiction writers. His numerous stories have appeared in all the leading Science Fiction magazines, as well as in many anthologies, and his novels have been translated into a dozen foreign languages.

T. L. SHERRED is well known in the Science Fiction field for his black humor and his inventive story devices. He is the author of ALIEN ISLAND and has appeared in the groundbreaking anthology AGAIN, DANGEROUS VISIONS and in the SFWA HALL OF FAME.

Foreword

A few days before yesterday a structural defect permanently removed any desire or capability to write.

The things of merit in this book belong to Lloyd Biggle.

I'm very grateful for Lloyd's taking over to finish this book and it never would have been finished if he hadn't done all the work.

T. L. SHERRED

Lefkir Bonrin suggested that I keep a personal log. "Eventually Earth will have historians again, Kera Jael. They'll want to know what happened. Right from the beginning."

But that was two long centuries after the real beginning and a full Earth year after my own beginning, which happened when I was a Fifth Level 'cad, a student at the Space Academy. In the way of twenty-two-year-old females, I was then much more concerned about my own future than with my family's past. My introduction to Earth came at a Visual History horror session: I watched Earth destroy itself.

Lefkir Bonrin was a dry little pedant of the type that leaves no mote of information undissected. His Visual History course was one of the academy's most severe scourges, ranking just below Astro Math and Nucleonics and several notches above Space Survival. He believed that every space captain should be a dedicated scholar, and he considered me a scholastic wastrel because I thought education was something to be used, not embalmed. Further, I'd had the temerity to tell him so.

On that particular day he was preoccupied with abstruse points concerning the philosophy of governmental operations, and when Lefkir Bonrin made a point about world governments, he contemplated *all* world governments—analyzed, compared, and classified in all of their permutations. After the first twenty-five or fifty, this can be downright soporific, and we unfortunate victims of his evening class, with a full day of hard work behind us, were dozing our way through a boring analysis of world government conferences on Sprenard 486N92R5 when it happened—dozing with wide-open eyes fixed hypnotically on the screen where Sprenard's politicians were making their preposterous gesticulations to the accompaniment of Lefkir Bonrin's droning commentary.

Suddenly his voice changed. "This is one extreme," he announced. "Now I'll show you the opposite. Here is Earth 938G24F7—one of the Regez Anlf's three failures."

The petty political histrionics were replaced by an enlarging space view of a lovely water-blue world frosted with the fluff of white clouds. The viewer carried us through a rapid succession of increasing magnifications until it focused on a city.

It was a magnificent city of Class Four or perhaps even Class Three culture. Its foundations may have been rotted by degeneracy, but none of that was visible from space. It lay shimmeringly beautiful in the morning sun without the faintest clue that it teetered on the brink of obliteration. For a suspenseful moment we contemplated the confidently proud splendor, the towers and spires reared high, the orderly veins of traffic radiating to the city's horizons, the comic clusters of scurrying transportation microbes, the buildings of all descriptions arranged in a miraculous patchwork mosaic that only high civilization can achieve. Each increment, large or small, was its own monument to genius and work and aspiration.

Suddenly a grotesquely misplaced sun filled the screen, and the city dissolved in its death glow as the nuclear storm—a monument of a different sort to that same genius and work and aspiration—broke over it with the fury of a smashing, incandescent cosmic fist. Towers and spires toppled, streets were obliterated by spilling debris, and the writhing landscape vanished in a convulsive eruption of smoke and dust.

Another filter clicked in, and the viewer plummeted to record a city's death throes. The revelation that there were people down there came as a shock, though I could not have said why. Those unfortunate enough to survive the pummeling force of the explosion were undergoing the shredding agony of incineration in the hideous afterglow of lethal radiation. Even in death and torment, Earth's people looked surprisingly human.

Then the realization hit my innards with an impact that had me gripping the arms of my chair to keep from leaping to my feet. This was the planet Earth, and I was watching my ancestors die.

When I could wrench my gaze away, I turned to look at Lefkir Bonrin. He stood in his accustomed place at a little lectern at one side of the screen, a shrunken huddle of the academic robes that he preferred to the usual professorial smock. His normal posture was one of communicating with higher mentalities, none of whom he expected to find in his classroom. On this day, nothing was normal. He kept his eyes on his students, studying one after the other as though he were taking roll.

I turned again to the horror scene. The catastrophe had almost run its course, from obliterated city to pulverized town to masticated village to seared countryside, before I realized that Lefkir Bonrin's gaze now was fixed intently on me. The expression on his wrinkled face suggested that I was a particularly repugnant fact that he'd been unable to classify.

We discussed the incident afterward—we of the Fifth Level's 3rd Echelon. The founders of the Space Academy had the inspired idea of placing the campus in space—since we 'cads had to be trained in adaptability to extreme conditions, and it is far easier to simulate various gravities in space than to simulate 0-gravity on a planet. After terminal and the day's final meal, my echelon liked to group-walk a section of the heavy promenade, the long high-gravity corridor that encircled the academy's outer perimeter, and then jump into the 0-grav tank, where we orbited slowly within the translucent shell that enclosed the campus. As we wheeled below the stars—soft blobs of light that seemed to circle about us—we meditated or performed the day's mnemonic chores. Or sometimes we joined hands in a circle so we could float together and talk.

The night that Lefkir Bonrin showed us the destruction of Earth, we needed to talk. It did not require the sage comments of the several geniuses among us to make us aware that the awesome destruction of a world had no obvious connection with the dry Visual History presentation that had preceded it, and this was baffling. Lefkir Bonrin's mind was as systematic as a star chart. He was not given to sudden shifts and deviations. He never hurried, never drifted an iota from the inexorable logic of the historical course he was laying out for us.

Our echelon pondered this while floating in slow rotation in the 0-grav tank. Seri Drak was of the opinion that the old historian's mind finally had cracked—a development he had been predicting for more than a year. Seri considered himself the echelon's unofficial psychologist. "Old Lefkir must have a perverted taste for catastrophes," he said. "Did you notice that he stopped talking when the holocaust started? He forgot that he was supposed to be teaching. He stood there by the screen and drooled."

Ef Hirgla interrupted before Seri could launch into his exposition of Lefkir Bonrin's psychoprofile. Seri's psychoprofiles were intolerable immediately after meals. "Nonsense," Ef Hirgla said. "Lefkir Bonrin just put the holocaust in for shock value. All the faks use the same shoddy technique. When they think they've caught more than half of a class sleeping, they dial something to wake us up. Actually, it's their teaching that puts us to sleep, but the computer has no remedy for that. Each fak has his own perverted preferences—old Vekklo has sprung that scene of Rezlian swamp monsters on us three times this term."

"You're both being silly," Morro Senyi said, tossing her head. Morro was the echelon's number one genius and also its number one beauty. She was the only female in the academy who could look both alluring and intelligent in a fatigue smock. She was addicted to tossing her head when we were in the tank—she liked to watch her long hair float in 0-gravity. She tossed it now and said, with her most infuriating supercilious smile, "Lefkir Bonrin never does anything without a purpose. He's plotting something, and I know what it is. Day before yesterday, Seri made that stupid remark about scenes of violence arousing people sexually. Lefkir Bonrin has decided to test the theory. Actually, he's trying to seduce Kera Jael. Didn't you notice him staring at her? Probably he's already found out that nothing else will arouse her, and this is a last resort. He had to spring it on the whole class to make certain that she would see it."

Seri Drak leaped to my defense—he leaped literally, somehow managing to propel himself across the circle at Morro Senyi—and in the ensuing argument and fracas the echelon broke up and finished the float in small groups. I refused to dignify Morro Senyi's insult by protesting it. She had always disliked me because I envied her intelligence more than her beauty.

She was right in one respect. Lefkir Bonrin's presentation of the destruction of the planet Earth certainly had something to do with me. I knew that for a certainty because of the way he had looked at me, but I considered it his problem and no concern of mine. 'Cads never lost sleep over fak motives except when we were waiting for our term ratings to be posted. I'd almost forgotten the incident when he finally sent for me.

The summons arrived in the middle of a Nucleonics exam, and I signed out cheerfully and headed for the fak common. Even a session with Lefkir Bonrin, for whatever cause, seemed preferable to Nucleonics. I stopped being cheerful when I found his office empty. A records tek shooed me along to the director's conference room, and that seemed downright ominous.

But the man seated with Lefkir Bonrin at one end of the long conference table was not the director. I recognized him instantly. He was Naslur Rayl, the Regez Anlf's Third Secretary, who directed outworld exploration and trade. More than that—he ruled it absolutely, and any 'cad would have regarded him with trepidation. He was our future employer.

The two of them had their heads together over a reader screen, and they did not look up until I reached them. They were a grotesque study in contrasts. Lefkir Bonrin, in his bulky academic robes, looked shrunken and wrinkled. Naslur Rayl, wearing the ultimate in skimpy day suits, had the full robustness of a former athlete, which he was. His handsome face was one of the best known in the Regez Anlf because it was always prominently on display at political functions.

But the scowl that Naslur Rayl turned on me was somewhat removed from the expression with which he charmed fellow politicians and constituents. It suggested that he and Lefkir Bonrin together had finally succeeded in classifying me and weren't pleased with the result.

"Sit down, Kera Jael," Lefkir Bonrin said. "Do you know Naslur Rayl?"

"Not personally," I said, keeping my voice steady.

Naslur Rayl relaxed his scowl long enough to chuckle. "We'll have to remember," he told Lefkir Bonrin, "that this is the great-granddaughter of Dana Iverson *and* Ken Jordan *and* Lee Lukkari. The combination might even be genetically inflammatory."

"Who," I asked, "are Dana Iverson and Ken Jordan and Lee Lukkari?"

Lefkir Bonrin's scowl took on a flavor of incredulity. "Are your family traditions so feeble that you don't know the names of your own great-grandparents?"

"Probably they never used their Earth names at home," Naslur Rayl said. "Why should they? Only scholars would be interested, and only linguists could pronounce them." He turned to me. "We have a tale to tell you, great-granddaughter of Dana Iverson, Ken Jordan, and Lee Lukkari. Your great-grandmother, Lecz Lukcarinz, is known to my departmental file concerning the world Earth 938G24F7 as Lee Lukkari. It is customary, in our contacts with outworlds, to simplify our names, and that of the Regez Anlf, into something more easily pronounceable in a local language. Your other great-grandparents, Ken Jordan and Dana Iverson, were natives of Earth 938G24F7. When they escaped the holocaust and claimed their Regez Anlf citizenship, their Earth names were as unpronounceable to most Regez Anlf citizens as ours would have been on Earth. They modified them into more acceptable patterns, as Lecz Lukcarinz had done in her Earth contacts."

I must have looked skeptical, because he grinned and pushed the reader screen toward me. "Convince yourself," he said. "We want you to read this before we talk."

It was true, of course. My great-grandmother, Lecz Lukcarinz, had used the name Lee Lukkari on Earth, and naturally my other great-grandparents, Earth natives, had borne Earth names when they fled Earth. I shall use them here, because this report is for Earth; and, in my other great-grandmother's tradition, I shall modify Regez Anlf names to make them more accessible to Earth natives. I already have. Lefkir Bonrin and Naslur Rayl would recognize themselves in this report but not their names, and I am Kera Jael only on Earth. I cannot promise consistency. There may have been many such transliterations used in that long-ago contact between the Regez Anlf and Earth, but Regez Anlf records do not refer to them, and few Earth records survive.

I read Naslur Rayl's report. It was only a summary, and much of it was dimly familiar to me. The Regez Anlf, following its normal practice, had contacted the planet Earth and offered trade. The Regez Anlf is a trading association of worlds. It makes itself known to an outworld only after careful study and when it is convinced that the relationship will be mutually beneficial. Its objective is to obtain luxury products, exotic foods, and perhaps raw materials unique to the world contacted. In return, it pays in metals or materials or whatever is rare and highly valued on the outworld.

The outworld receives a bonus benefit without charge. An alien association spurs a world's technology, its culture, its civilization, its psychology. This costs the Regez Anlf nothing and works to its advantage as much as that of the outworld, because the outworld will aspire to Regez Anlf membership. The Regez Anlf has grown and prospered and become great simply because its very existence constitutes a challenge to the outworlds with which it trades.

Contact with Earth followed that pattern. Lee Lukkari trained for it, and then, as captain, she took the cruiser *Kayta* to Earth. In accordance with standard Regez Anlf procedures, she secured a mind link with a native. When mind-mating between cruiser captain and outworld native succeeds, that native becomes the Regez Anlf's representative on his world.

The mind-mating with the Earth native was successful. The native was Ken Jordan, and he became the Regez Anlf's representative. His principal assistant was an Earthwoman named Dana Iverson. Working in consultation with Lee Lukkari—who had returned to the cruiser *Kayta*, which she had left in solar orbit on the opposite side of the sun—Ken Jordan saw to the construction of an Earth base and recruited a staff.

He began trading, buying Earth products that would appeal to the Regez Anlf and paying for them with gold. The report described the products Ken Jordan bought for shipment to the Regez Anlf, and I smiled as I read the list: coffee, tea, candy, marmalade, cheese, olives, spices, anchovies, bacon, whiskey, beer, cigarettes, cigars, wines, rum, furs, exotic woods, silk, linens, worsted, folk art, music boxes, toys.

There was a special tradition in my family concerning one of those products, Irish whiskey. When Ken Jordan escaped to the Regez Anlf, he somehow managed to acquire a quantity of it, and every child born into the family had its health and future toasted in Irish whiskey as long as the whiskey lasted. We were a prolific family, unfortunately, and the last of it vanished while I was still a child. Or perhaps Ken Jordan found other excuses for toasts. I have a childhood memory of another, much stranger one: "Here's to beer!" I grew up wondering what beer was. Finding it on the list of exotic Earth products, I still wondered. If Ken Jordan also acquired a quantity of that Earth commodity, it had been consumed long before my time.

Of course there'd been no further shipments after the holocaust.

The Regez Anlf's contact with Earth had been successful, Ken Jordan proved to be a remarkably efficient local manager, and the trade was proceeding with unusual smoothness. And then, for no reason that anyone had been able to figure out—not Regez Anlf officialdom, not the study teams aboard the *Kayta*, not even Ken Jordan and Dana Iverson—Earth had suddenly erupted into nuclear warfare. The Regez Anlf withdrew its trading mission, evacuated all Earth employees who wanted to go, and placed Earth on its permanent embargo list. No Regez Anlf ship had approached it since then.

I finished the summary and pushed the reader aside. Lefkir Bonrin and Naslur Rayl were watching me intently.

"Did you learn anything?" Naslur Rayl asked politely.

"A little," I said. "It's the family legend cluttered up with facts."

"Does the family legend report that your great-grandparents always wanted to return to Earth?"

"It does," I told him. "It also reports that their children applied repeatedly for permission to visit Earth. So did their grandchildren. It's my mother's consuming ambition. She's always been bitter because the Regez Anlf refuses to lift the embargo. She studied the records meticulously, and she was certain that life survived there. So she wanted to return."

"To do what?" Naslur Rayl asked caustically. "Walk in the radioactive footsteps of her ancestors?"

"Isn't that reason enough?" I asked him.

"Your mother is one of the Regez Anlf's most distinguished captains," he said, "but Regez Anlf captains are trained to establish and supervise trading contacts. Even if life survived on Earth, there certainly is nothing there to trade for. There won't be for centuries. So why visit Earth?"

"My mother feels that the Regez Anlf was responsible for Earth's destruction," I said.

Naslur Rayl leaned forward with a jerk. "Why?" he demanded sharply. "We went there as peaceful traders. We bought a highly select list of products and paid for them liberally. Earth nations had been preparing for nuclear warfare for decades before we arrived. The war that destroyed Earth certainly was none of our doing, and it was costly to us. It wiped out a promising trading contact."

"My mother feels that the Regez Anlf was responsible," I repeated stubbornly.

Naslur Rayl slumped back in his chair and studied me querulously. "That's silly. It contradicts all the evidence. Why would your mother think that?"

"I don't know. She studied the records at every opportunity, and she believed that the Earth war would never have happened if the Regez Anlf had timed its contact differently."

"I see." Naslur Rayl leaned forward again. "Your ambition is to be a cruiser captain?"

"It's another family tradition," I said proudly. "On the Regez Anlf side, it goes back nine generations. My mother, and her mother, and her mother's mother—"

"Is it also your ambition to return to Earth?"

"I have given no thought to that. Captaincy comes first."

"Naturally a great-granddaughter of Lee Lukkari and Dana Iverson and Ken Jordan could not consider returning to Earth under someone else's command," he said dryly.

"Naturally," I agreed. I was not going to let them bait me.

"Lefkir Bonrin agrees with your mother," Naslur Rayl said. "He has studied the Earth records for four decades, and he has adduced proof that the Regez Anlf contact with Earth unbalanced a stable situation and precipitated a nuclear war. He will present his conclusions to the Council tomorrow, and I expect the Council to agree with him."

He paused and scrutinized me intently. "The Regez Anlf has had just three failures in nine hundred years. If its procedures were the cause of one failure, they may have caused all three. Unchanged, they may cause others in the future. This will have to be investigated carefully. Where Earth is concerned, the Council's acceptance of Lefkir Bonrin's report will automatically commit the Regez Anlf to make such restitution as it is capable of. I must be prepared to present the Council with a plan. We have reviewed your record, and we are impressed. So I am hoping that you'll agree to return to Earth."

"Of course," I said. "As a cruiser captain—"

He shook his head gravely. "A cruiser captain is trained for trading contacts. Our second emissary to Earth will need a training so unusual and so exacting that a special program will have to be devised. If you go, you'll go in command of a highly skilled team of volunteers instead of a spaceship. The Regez Anlf is about to commit itself to the rebuilding of a world."

2

Lefkir Bonrin made his presentation; the Council accepted his conclusions and committed the Regez Anlf to the rebuilding of Earth.

Then politics intervened.

Good politics, Naslur Rayl said, was the lubricant that kept civilization in motion. Bad politics was the sand in the lubricant. The Council vote was merely a declaration of principle, and I quickly learned that it was far easier for a politician to espouse a principle than it was for him to vote the funds necessary to practice it. More than two Earth years passed before I finally set foot on the sadly overgrown Earth base once trod by Lee Lukkari, Ken Jordan, and Dana Iverson, and in that interval Naslur Rayl sifted a monstrous quantity of sand.

Once the Regez Anlf committed itself to the rebuilding of Earth, the next logical step would have been to order a survey. In order to rebuild a planet, one ought to discover what's there to rebuild. For one reason or another, the shifting sands of bad politics buried the necessary funds—for survey ships or anything else. I was left marking time, but marking it is not the same thing as wasting it. I passed those two years in intense training with the two fellow members of what Naslur Rayl called his Reclamation Team, his RT. There was plenty of money for training, because it could be siphoned out of various educational budgets, including that of the Space Academy.

All of the members of the RT were space orphans. That label was a mark of distinction at the Space Academy—most of the 'cads were. Elsewhere, it was applied contemptuously. Space orphans who had the misfortune to grow up among grounders often had scarred childhoods and lifelong complexes because of the ridicule their status attracted.

We were the children of spacers, and we rarely saw our parents. Either we grew up feeling abandoned and unwanted, or we achieved a rare self-reliance that eminently suited us for careers as spacers. It was inevitable that the three principals Naslur Rayl selected for the lonely job of rebuilding a world would be space orphans. It was equally inevitable that all three of them would possess the explosive combination of genes that Naslur Rayl had commented on. We were cousins; we had known each other from childhood, and all of us were descendants of Lee Lukkari, Ken Jordan, and Dana Iverson.

"I'm making you team commander," Naslur Rayl told me. "Will you have any difficulty in giving orders to two older male cousins?"

"I don't see why I should," I said. "I've been ordering them around all of my life."

The failure of the politicians to provide survey funds meant that no one had the slightest idea of what we should train for, least of all ourselves. Further, the Space Academy offered no program of study or training in making restitution for Regez Anlf blunders or rebuilding worlds. Lacking so much as an inkling of what skills and techniques we would need or what tasks might confront us, Naslur Rayl devised a special course of study with a thoroughly practical objective. He wanted us taught to survive on a world that had destroyed itself with a nuclear holocaust.

"That's your first and most important problem," he said. "To survive. I can guarantee that you won't accomplish much if you aren't able to do that. The environment will be hostile. It may be lethal. You can't expect the human survivors—if there are any—to make you welcome. If any tradition of the Regez Anlf survives, it's more likely to be remembered with bitterness and hatred than with affection. We precipitated a war, and then we ran out on it. You may have the problem of rebuilding a world whose inhabitants will distrust and resent everything you do. And you can't operate by building a secure base and sitting in it, as Regez Anlf traders do only too often. You'll have to come to grips with two problems—the environment and the human population. Both are likely to need a lot of rebuilding."

The horrendously difficult task of healing a world population descended from holocaust survivors, in whatever condition we found it, and thereafter maintaining its good health, was handed to my cousin Wiln Marra, who had been training as a med tek. My cousin Morl Klun was assigned a problem just as formidable. He was the family rebel. He had rejected family tradition and enrolled at a university instead of the Space Academy, and his special interest was primitive societies. Since most of the worlds of the Regez Anlf scrupulously protected and preserved those primitive societies that had chanced to survive their civilization's early excesses, he had ample material for study without outworld training. Naslur Rayl attempted to pluck him from his university anthropology classes with an order, and Morl Klun ignored it until it had been softened into a polite invitation. Then he joined us enthusiastically; but when he found out what was expected of him, he disgustedly discarded all of his textbooks. Primitive societies, anywhere in the galaxy, develop according to long-recognized principles, but no one knew or dared to guess what kind of evolution might have occurred with high-technology societies that had rendered themselves primitive through nuclear warfare.

In addition to being the group's commander, I was the technologist. My job was to devise the means of rebuilding Earth within guidelines Morl Klun laid down as compatible with the primitive cultures that survived, while Wiln Marra kept everyone healthy.

Each of us trained the other two in our specializations while the Space

Academy was training all three of us in survival. Its method was to plunge us into every kind of hazardous condition it could devise, one after the other, on the theory that nothing could kill us if it couldn't. Several times it came perilously close. With the barest minimum of supplies and equipment to sustain us, we were dumped into every environmental purgatory that a dozen worlds could supply. We rotted in jungles and thirsted in deserts and soaked in swamps and froze on windswept tundras, and we had more than a few adventures with monstrosities of flora and fauna that took malicious resentment at our intrusion.

Between such expeditions, Lefkir Bonrin took it upon himself to create a special academic purgatory. We found it more hazardous than Naslur Rayl's jungles and deserts and swamps and tundras. He stuffed us with the history of Earth, and he wasn't content until he'd convinced himself that we knew everything that the Regez Anlf knew. My one pleasant recollection that came out of this ordeal concerns the day I handed him a recently discovered family heirloom, a holograph manuscript by my great-grandmother, Dana Iverson, that contained her eyewitness account of Earth's history from the Regez Anlf's arrival until her departure during the nuclear war.

"Half of what you've been teaching us is wrong," I told Lefkir Bonrin brightly.

This wasn't true, but the manuscript seriously undermined several of his favorite premises. He had to choose between starting over or giving up, and he chose to surrender. This effectively terminated all of our training. At that point the project seemed doomed and our two years of grueling work wasted; but Naslur Rayl's good politics finally provided lubrication, and he got his appropriation.

He held a sparsely attended reception for us. It had been a long time since Lefkir Bonrin's report had twitched the Council's conscience, and the only members who bothered to attend were self-important politicians who were still protesting the expense. Naslur Rayl's determination to see the project through had never wavered, but his two-year ordeal had left him somewhat daunted. His unlimited support now had a cost ceiling. "Expenditures within reasonable limits" was the expression he used.

A great-uncle honored us with a family reunion, and forty-nine descendants of Lee Lukkari, Ken Jordan, and Dana Iverson—all the members of our far-flung family who weren't too distant to attend—gathered to give us a proper send-off and make speeches about our dramatic return to whatever might be left of our ancestral world. It was a somber gala occasion. At least there was no hedging in the pledges of family support, but—as Morl Klun pointed out—the family wasn't expected to pay for our trip.

Naslur Rayl's "reasonable limits" included a cruiser for support and our own choice of supplies and equipment.

"My mother should be the cruiser captain," I told him.

He nodded thoughtfully. "She should. But it might take half a year or more to extricate her from her present assignment and bring her back here. By that time, the unspent portion of the appropriation would revert to the treasury and have to be voted again. Under the circumstances, don't you think—"

The cruiser *Hadda* was immediately available, and we took it. We then spent days in selecting supplies and equipment and calculating quantities. When finally we reported aboard the *Hadda*, its captain, Ilia Sonal, welcomed us with appropriate ceremony and invited us to her quarters. Her manner was cordial enough, but she regarded us with a coldly calculating curiosity that I found repelling.

"First, the question of command," she said. "I am ordered to support you. This means that I come under your orders when I place the *Hadda* in an access orbit to the planet Earth 938G24F7. From that moment, your mission takes precedence."

"Within reasonable limits," I suggested. I suspected that she had friends and supporters among the bad politicians.

Her smile dripped icicles. "There are basic Regez Anlf regulations that can't be violated under any circumstances. I can't land this ship on an outworld except in dire emergency, for example, and it would have to be the ship's emergency, not yours. I can permit a limited number of crew members to land on missions that you devise, but you will have to convince me that the missions' objectives are important, that your plans for accomplishing them are sound, and that the lives and health of the landing parties will not be jeopardized. On the other hand, you are to have unlimited support with topological and engineering and scientific and supply functions. We've taken on special staff in an attempt to anticipate your needs in those areas. As I understand your mission, you won't know what to expect until you get there, and your approach will have to be one of trial and error. So we really can't consider specifics about your support until you decide what you want to do and what you'll need." She paused. "This is taking a lot of verbiage to describe a simple situation. You are in full charge of the planet operation. I have no authority to tell you what to do, or what not to do, or how anything should be done, or even to make uninvited suggestions. I will support you as fully as possible within the limits imposed by Regez Anlf regulations and sound operational procedures."

That ended the conversation. I was in a thoughtful mood when she summoned an aide to show us to our quarters. Like all Regez Anlf captains, Ilia Sonal had been trained to make contact with a high-technology outworld, establish trading relations, and prepare the way for bringing that world into the Regez Anlf. She was accustomed to having full command of her area of operations. The Earth mission had to be an unwelcome and boring sidetrack as far as her career was concerned. Once she'd placed her ship in Earth orbit, there would be little for her to do on an assignment that might stretch out for years. Further, her sphere of authority was limited. The glory, if such a thing were possible from an assignment to rebuild a world, would fall to those who took the risks and made the decisions, but the captain of the supporting cruiser would garner a full share of the blame for failure. I was wondering whether Ilia Sonal might pose more of a problem than the Earth natives.

I asked the others to come to my quarters as soon as they were settled, and we talked about it. Neither of them foresaw any difficulties.

Although the three of us had our inflammatory genes in common, we also had sufficient genetic dilution to be totally unlike each other. Morl Klun was a small, wiry type—shorter than I am—full of energy and always grinning. His green-tinted complexion and hair resulted from the fact that his mother was the cruiser captain who opened trade with the world of Qlarnf and found a mate there. The Qlarnfians refused to join the Regez Anlf because that would have required them to submit to outside authority, and I suspected that this same trait made Morl Klun the family rebel.

Wiln Marra was Morl Klun's opposite—tall, blond, plain-looking, sturdy in build but gawky in manner, with the unnatural pallor of a scholar. Our strenuous training had toughened all of us, but not even the desert exercises had altered his pale complexion. He had to wear protective clothing to keep from blistering. For a med tek, he was ridiculously shy in personal relationships.

I stood between the two of them in appearance—being of medium size, with light brown hair—and also in outlook. I was the practical one. Morl Klun's nature took ridiculous swings between elation and gloom. Wiln Marra considered the whole universe to be in a perpetual state of catastrophe, but he was grimly determined to view it from the bright side. I tended to be suspicious of everyone, but since most people deserve to be suspected, that was only evidence of my practical nature.

Our reactions to Ilia Sonal were typical. I regarded her with suspicion.

Morl Klun asked cheerfully, "Why worry?"

When I was younger, I'd envied him his curly hair. He brushed it aside now—he'd always been carelessly proud of it—and his grin broadened. "Look. Her authority stops at the atmosphere. Below that she has only a limited veto power. Let's treat her politely until we land, and then we can start giving her orders. If she won't cooperate, we can appeal to Naslur Rayl, can't we? He'll have to back us up."

I hadn't told them what Naslur Rayl had said to me in a last, private conversation. "If you have problems with your cruiser captain, use your priority code and let me know. I'll simply send another ship to relieve the *Hadda*. I'll do this without question the first time you ask. If the replacement ship has been on station long enough to justify relief, I'll do it without question the second time. If there's a third time, people here will begin to wonder whether the problem is with you rather than with the captains, and that would bode ill for your mission. You also should keep in mind the fact that a replacement ship might not be immediately available. So try to get along with the *Hadda*'s captain."

I said, "Only a major crisis would justify an appeal to Naslur Rayl. I'm worried about the dozens of minor things we'll have to cope with day after day."

Morl Klun shrugged and asked again, "Why worry? She can't refuse to give us the technical support we request. She can't refuse to send down the supplies we requisition. If she has the right to veto crew landings, so do we. I don't want untrained spacers mucking about on our world. We not only shouldn't request that, we should forbid it."

" 'Reasonable limits' are subject to expansion or contraction," I said. "My hunch is that hers are permanently contracted." I turned to Wiln Marra. "What do you think?"

He murmured dreamily, "I wonder how old she is."

Both of us stared at him furiously, and his only reaction was to blush. Without a doubt, he was smitten. As a youth he'd had an embarrassing knack for falling tumultuously in love with older females, but I'd hopefully assumed that he'd outgrown it.

"I suppose it isn't your fault if your glands keep malfunctioning," I told him. "But don't start using them for brains. Any cruiser captain is likely to be old enough to be your mother. You ought to know that, since your mother *is* a cruiser captain. Why don't you go back to your quarters and prescribe some medicine for yourself?"

He blushed again. "I merely wondered—she seems very competent."

"She *is* competent," I said. "If she weren't, she wouldn't be a cruiser captain. Keep your mind on your work."

Morl Klun was grinning at him. "The nice thing about being a med tek is that you're able to look at an attractive female and persuade yourself that you *are* keeping your mind on your work. Is her complexion a trifle pale? What medicine should one prescribe? Could she stand losing a little weight? If so, from where? One could spend an entire afternoon contemplating that problem, taking a little off here, putting it on there—always viewing the subject analytically in medical terms, of course. And then—"

Wiln Marra got to his feet angrily and stomped out.

"I wonder," I mused.

"About the advantages of being a med tek? They probably work equally well from the female point of view."

"I'm wondering whether you two dudheads are going to give me more trouble than the most obstinate cruiser captain."

The fact that we had so little to do made it an uneasy voyage. We'd completed all of the anticipatory planning we could think of and speculated endlessly about every potential problem we could imagine and how to deal with it. Ilia Sonal insisted that we take our meals with the ship's officers, and this led to daily social crises that somehow got negotiated without open enmity. Wiln Marra really was very bright and capable, but throughout the journey, he behaved in Ilia Sonal's presence like a tongue-tied moron. Morl Klun's notion of helping Wiln Marra's romance along was to bait the captain and shatter her aplomb. He began comparing Space Service rules, hierarchy, and etiquette with the social customs and taboos of an obscure tribe of primitives that he certainly invented, though he claimed to have studied it on the world of Witisil. He speculated, in Ilia Sonal's presence, as to whether a cruiser captain's role in the ship's sexual relationships approximated that of a tribal chief, and he began to ask sly questions about sexual initiation ceremonies. Ilia Sonal was not amused, but she permitted no flicker of emotional reaction to cross her lovely, cold face. She seemed determined to prove that a cruiser captain did not have emotional reactions. I finally told Morl Klun, privately, to desist. I didn't care how much he ruffled the *Hadda*'s captain, but his banter made Wiln Marra seethe with anger and threatened to destroy the Reclamation Team's harmony before we commenced operations.

Eventually we reached Earth.

I have seen many worlds from space. Some looked beautiful, some forbidding, some enigmatic, some nondescript. The planet Earth was not nondescript. It was all of the rest, and more, and I studied it for long minutes before I understood why.

It was mine. It was my ancestral home, and now it had been given to me to make what I could of it. I knew it intimately in the way that one can nostalgically familiarize oneself, through photos, room plans, and family memoirs, with an ancestral home never visited. I had immersed myself in all that was known about the world that once had been—its geography, its meteorology, its topology, its mineralogy, its oceanography, its geomorphology, its ethnology, its sociology, its economy, its technology—the complete list. I had fondly pondered both beauties and blemishes with all of the introspective objectivity one might devote to any ancestral home when contemplating essential alterations and repairs.

But all of that concerned the Earth of two hundred years before. I would not know how much of this planet I was studying from space was terra incognita until I landed. But it was mine, and I was eager to take possession.

Ilia Sonal stood beside us, a slight frown on her face. I suspected that she resented the lovely blue globe with its shroud of white as much as she resented us. She handed me the scientific staff's initial appraisal: no electromagnetic wave activity had been detected; infrared filters and heat sensors had picked up no population clusters of humans or large animals; the scientists thought it unlikely that there could be any surviving human civilization with a culture of Class Seven or below; there were in actual fact no signs whatsoever of any surviving human population on the area of the planet being surveyed.

Ilia Sonal read the report with me, leaning over my shoulder and smiling slightly. It would have pleased her if we'd decided to pack up and go home. "I assume," she said primly, "that you'll want a number of survey and scientific studies made before you land."

"Just two," I said. "General radioactivity and atmosphere. We'll do our own local check as we descend."

I admired the high art with which she concealed her disapproval, though I knew that her expertise came from long practice—she disapproved of so many things. There was no ripple of expression on her face. "Where do you plan to land?" she asked politely.

"At the old Regez Anlf base," I told her. "First business is to see whether it's still functional."

"I'll order the tests," she said.

However much she disapproved, she was grudgingly aware that she had just become my subordinate as far as the planet Earth was concerned, and she was too well trained in command procedures to perform at anything less than top efficiency.

Burluf Nori, the ship's chief topologist, came to me for instructions.

"Start your spiral at the old base," I told him. "That's where we'll start from. When you hit the east coast, move west and south."

"And north?" he asked with a smile.

He was an elderly man, old for the Space Service, quiet, disposed to gruffness, but he had the competence that only enormous experience can bring in a difficult line of work. Charting primitive populations on a global basis is an enormous task, requiring an endless tedium of data collecting and exacting evaluations.

"My first concern is our immediate neighborhood," I said. "If we have neighbors, we want to find them before they find us. We have to plan our first contacts with care. Beyond that, you have a world to cover, and you know best how to manage it."

The planet tested much as we'd anticipated. The rains of two Earth centuries had washed the atmosphere and cleansed the land. There was a scattered residue of hot spots, but the world was no longer radioactive. We could land safely as long as we took the standard precautions.

Ilia Sonal formally celebrated our departure in much the same attitude with which she'd greeted us on arrival. We had a final discussion concerning procedures. The *Hadda* would remain in close orbit until scientific and technical studies had been concluded and our initial supplies had been platformed down to us. "Close orbit," to Ilia Sonal, was an orbit approximating that of the planet's lone satellite. She'd decided to position the *Hadda* on the opposite side of Earth from its moon and work from there. Such an unreasonably remote orbit was certain to impair the efficiency of her support, but Morl Klun told me not to fuss—the further away she kept the *Hadda*, the wider my own sphere of authority.

She politely wished us good luck, and I politely thanked her for her cooperation: past, present, and—hopefully—future. We exchanged salutes. Wiln Marra was staring at her in mute admiration, and I wanted to kick him. She'd deliberately togged herself out in dress uniform, and the contrast with us, in our floppy protective suits, was ludicrous. She even handed us onto the ramp of our landing craft, smiling graciously at each one as she did so. I wondered whether we would ever meet again except by communicator viewing screen. I also wondered whether she might be wondering the same thing. The ramp closed; we dropped into space and slowly drifted away from the *Hadda*.

Our destination was the old Regez Anlf base. Ken Jordan had supervised its construction on Peche Island, in the Detroit River, which he had purchased from the Canadian government with Regez Anlf gold. There was no evidence that the Canadian or any other Earth government still existed, but the base was intact—we'd observed it from space—and its power unit was still operating efficiently. I activated its navigational signal and got a strong and clear response. I homed in on it and headed us Earthward.

"What if there aren't any people?" Wiln Marra asked suddenly. "Can we rebuild a world without people?"

"There'll be people," I said confidently.

"All the test results were negative."

"Tests from that distance haven't any significance except for picking up gross facts about population concentrations or high-tek civilizations. Burluf Nori's low-level survey will tell us where the people are."

He wasn't convinced, but I was too interested in the changing scenes on our viewing screens to argue with him. We plummeted toward Earth, dropping through the cloud cover so rapidly that we caught no more than an occasional glimpse of the countryside around the old base; but we knew what we would find there—the dead remains of two sprawling cities that had once faced each other proudly across the broad river that had been an international boundary. The remains were certainly still there, but a rampant growth of forest almost completely obscured them.

There was a moment of hesitation as the landing craft hovered over the base waiting for long-unused controls to respond. Then our craft inserted itself through the protective field, and we landed. I scrambled out the moment the ramp went down; my two cousins trod on my heels, as eager to set foot on Earth as I was, but the three of us halted abruptly at the edge of the ramp.

The base occupied the entire island, which was an Earth mile long and half a mile across at its widest. The transparent dome, turquoise-tinted in the gathering dusk, enclosed the island, curving back to the landing port at the top. Dome and force field had protected the base against the nuclear holocaust and—later—even the weather, but vegetation already growing there had been left to work out its own patterns of survival. In the absence of air currents, trees had seeded themselves about their own roots, and crowded groves dotted the base. Underbrush was rank, and a strange, prickly, waist-high vegetation with knife-sharp leaves grew everywhere. The buildings looked to be in good condition except where a tree had fallen into one of them. There were no cleared spaces, no streets, not even any footpaths, and the ship had come to rest in a thick clump of the prickly vegetation, which pushed up around the ramp and encroached upon it.

Morl Klun dashed back into the craft for a survival kit's machete, and he slashed a path through the weeds all the way to the edge of the dome. We followed him and stood looking northward across the Detroit River to the forested shore where the mighty city of Detroit had once stood. Some of its debris was still visible in the shallow water. I wondered whether my great-grandfather and my two great-grandmothers had once stood at this very spot and looked out on a vastly different shore. The trees were lovely, but they exuded an excruciating loneliness. We saw no signs of any kind of life.

We turned back, finally, and I could hear the communication unit beeping long before we reached the landing craft. It was Burluf Nori calling. He had left the *Hadda* immediately after we did to begin his topographical survey, and he had followed us down.

"I've located a human settlement," he said. "The cultural level seems a bit obscure—I have a feeling that we'll have difficulty in applying our usual parameters to this world, and the forests are going to make direct observation difficult. I'm guessing Class Seven optimum, but it may be as low as Class Eight or Nine."

"Where is it?" I asked.

"Look north," Burluf Nori said, chuckling. "Maybe you'll see it. The diffusion is almost at the water's edge. I'd guess that your landing was observed, and the observer spread the news. The entire community seems to have gathered along the river."

3

Future Earth will view the old Regez Anlf base as a monument and a prized tourist attraction. Many of those who read this will have visited it; others will have read descriptions and seen photos. They will know it better than I, for they will have seen it as I never have—as the garden spot that my great-grandfather, Ken Jordan, intended it to be.

He was a remarkable man—a man of strange whims that always turned out to have an inexorable logic behind them. Future visitors may marvel at the facilities he built for a hundred or so Regez Anlf employees: bowling alley, swimming pool, restaurant, office building, various types of residences. He built for the future and also for his own convenience—the office building contained four bars. He had the entire island landscaped and splashed with exotic touches, one of which was a clump of palms, a tree almost as alien to the base's latitude as it would have been to one of the Regez Anlf worlds. By the time of our arrival, that clump of palms was threatening to make a forest of itself.

The trees survived because of the dome and the force field that protected the base. These were products of Regez Anlf technology and would be almost as difficult to explain in nontechnical terms as my great-grandfather's predilection for palm trees.

I sent a routine message to the *Hadda*, informing Ilia Sonal that we had arrived safely and found the base intact, and I asked her to platform down an initial stock of supplies. By the time I emerged from the landing craft, Morl Klun and Wiln Marra had hacked a path to the nearest building. I did not join them immediately. I stood looking at the overgrown landscape and trying to envision the base as it had once been, with sweeps of green lawn and bright flowers and artfully placed shrubs.

The building my cousins had selected at random turned out to be a residence hall. I expected to find it strewn with signs of the frantic departure that must have occurred when the Regez Anlf personnel fled from a world wracked by nuclear warfare, but there were none. The small apartments were decorated and furnished strangely, even incomprehensibly, to our alien eyes, but clothing and personal effects were arranged neatly except where time or vermin left remnants of rotted or devoured fibers in heaps below the empty hangers. The departure had been so abrupt that the young Regez Anlf employees had not even been permitted to return to their quarters for their most valued possessions.

We chose sleeping rooms on the top floor of the building, and I sat in the window watching the far side of the river fade into darkness. I was waiting for the humans I knew were there to emblazon the night with some mark of their presence—a light, a fire—but there was nothing. When my cousins joined me, we talked far into the night about the apparent coincidence of finding a surviving community literally within hailing distance of the Regez Anlf base.

"After all of that strenuous preparation," I said, "it'd be ironic if the job turned out to be simple."

"It can't be a permanent community," Morl Klun said confidently. "Not in that forest. Whoever or whatever they are, they have to earn a living. Permanence means agriculture. These people will be rovers, hunting for what they can catch and gathering what food they can find."

"Then they may be gone by morning," I suggested.

"That's possible. It's even probable if they actually saw our ship land. They may have left already. This base probably has a sinister reputation as a magical island. The arrival of the magicians would be a signal to any primitive tribe to cut and run."

"We'll have to go after them," I said. "What's the probable impact on them if we put the landing craft down in their midst?"

"They'd be either awed or terrified. Most likely they'd run away. If they stayed, it'd be to worship us."

"Is our mission going to be enhanced by our being worshipped?" I asked.

"Hardly. We don't want to rebuild Earth by passing periodic miracles. We want to help the natives do their own rebuilding. It'd be a bit difficult to work with them if they thought we were gods." He paused. "There should be usable boats in that boat tunnel. If there are, I'd recommend a less miraculous approach."

"Even a powered boat might defeat our purpose," Wiln Marra said.

"What's the likely reception if we paddle over there quietly?" I asked Morl Klun.

"Almost anything. They may make us welcome. They may try to kill us and eat us. Or they may try to kill us and eat us after they make us welcome." He grinned cheerfully. "Therein lies the fascination of studying primitive societies."

"It sounds like an easily requited fascination," I said.

Wiln Marra spoke earnestly. "Naslur Rayl said that our first task was to survive. But if we make a habit of always considering our safety first, we'll risk nothing and accomplish nothing."

"With our protective equipment, we surely can face any primitive tribe without worrying about how hungry it is," I said. "Let's sleep on it and decide what to do in the morning."

But I could not sleep. I lay awake most of the night, thinking and planning.

The platform loaded with supplies arrived sometime during the night. It came to rest in another thick clump of prickly weed. We hacked a path to it, and then we decided to leave the unloading until later. We followed the previous day's path to the edge of the dome and looked across the water. Wiln Marra aimed his binoculars at the north shore.

"Nothing," he said finally. "No natives. Nothing at all resembling a boat."

"Let me look," Morl Klun said. "Primitive boats don't always resemble boats."

But he was unable to detect any trace of the people we knew had been there, and neither could I.

We cut a path to the boat tunnel. Several small boats had been pulled onto a dock and overturned. One large boat was still in the water and two had sunk at the dock—victims of time rather than adversity. The large boat would have been difficult to use without its engine, and we would have distrusted an Earth engine that had not been used for two hundred years even if it had run. We were equally skeptical about the small boat motors that hung on a rack.

"Never mind," Morl Klun said. "We don't want a motor. Not now. Let's try this."

He indicated a metal boat that was overturned on the dock. We slid it into the water and satisfied ourselves that it was still watertight. While Morl Klun went to select the gear he thought we'd need, and Wiln Marra went for a med kit, I chose three oars from a pile beside the dock. When they returned, we launched our mission to rebuild a world in as inauspicious a manner as could be imagined—we awkwardly propelled ourselves through the boat tunnel and nearly capsized twice before we reached the river.

We quickly discovered that the wide, peaceful-looking water had a treacherous current, and all three of us had to work furiously to keep from being carried far downstream. Shallows on either side were strewn with rubble—the bleached bones of the two cities that died simultaneously in the holocaust. Downstream, the water parted to embrace a large, wooded island. Directly to the east was the lake from which the river emerged. Both river and lake teemed with fish, and the largest broke water with enormous splashes.

We finally made our landfall, pulled the boat into concealment, and then moved along the shore looking for a path. It was awkward going. The trees encroached on the water's edge, and the rubble in which they were rooted made the footing treacherous. The path we finally found had not been used frequently, but it was distinct enough to be easily followed. Morl Klun, who was leading the way, pounced upon it eagerly and broke into a trot.

"Not so fast!" I hissed after him. "If we must blunder into something, I insist that we do it with deliberation!"

He paid no attention to me.

The path pointed through thick undergrowth, winding around towering trees that concealed the sky. Wiln Marra and I stumbled along apprehensively, trying to overtake Morl Klun without sounding like stampeding wild beasts. Not until the path took a sudden, sharp turning did he turn and wait for us.

He grinned as though he'd belatedly sensed my apprehension. "You know, of course, that we're violating all the rules for first contacts," he whispered.

"I didn't know," I whispered back. "But I guessed. Why are we violating all of the rules for first contacts?"

"I never did care much for rules," he said. "I have no faith in them. They have the sterilized odor of something contrived in a laboratory, and that's where they should be used."

"What are the rules for first contacts?" Wiln Marra asked. "And why are you suddenly mentioning them now?"

"Mostly they consist of a long list of don'ts. If you take them seriously, you'll never contact anyone."

"One or two don'ts would seem to be in order," I said. "This protective clothing probably makes us look like specters, or monsters, or whatever Earth's primitives have nightmares about. If they see us galloping toward them at the pace you're setting, they'll disappear into the forest and never be seen again."

"Primitive people lead an existence that's surrounded by unknown horrors," Morl Klun said. "What are three more among so many?"

But he agreed when I insisted that we remove our outer clothing and cache it along the path. We knew, by now, that there was no radiation residual to worry about. And when we moved on, he slowed his pace and went cautiously.

The path took another sharp turning, looping around an enormous tree. Just beyond, a clearing opened.

The natives were assembled there.

At worship.

They sat in a semicircle, their backs toward us, their bowed heads directed toward a black box. It contained their totem, I supposed, and I reflected apprehensively that we'd chosen the worst possible moment to intrude. Probably it was sacrilege for a stranger to glimpse either the sacred item or the ceremony. I was about to draw the others back into the forest when Wiln Marra, peering around us, stumbled and stepped on a dead branch.

The crack of sound, followed by the racket he made floundering to regain his balance, sounded thunderous in that silent glade. I hissed, "You clumsy clod!"

The congregation altered in a twinkling. Before we could react, it had rearranged itself into a semicircle facing us, and the members again sank into a worshipful posture with heads bowed.

I was astonished. I turned blankly to Morl Klun.

He was grinning sardonically. "They were praying to the gods," he whispered, "and now the gods have arrived."

"We don't want to be gods, dammit!" I muttered.

My impulse was to turn and run, but flight was not the proper posture for either gods or honest visitors. I could only stare stupidly at the ranks of worshipful natives.

Everything I'd been taught about primitive people had been wrong. I had envisioned them as wearing hand-woven robes brilliantly dyed in ingenious abstract patterns. I expected them to craft masterful pottery, fashion flawless baskets from grass or twigs, live in shelters that were masterpieces of architectural ingenuity, and in all things utilize the material wealth of their environment, whatever it was, totally and with profound understanding. Primitive peoples gleaned where no outsider suspected the existence of food. They were experts in herb lore and knew the medicinal properties of every plant in the tribal territory. They were masters of their surroundings and of all of the creatures who lived there.

But those primitives of my imagination had uncounted generations of tradition to guide them. Survival as a primitive requires a quantity of knowledge and skill much greater than that contained in a university education. My ideal primitives would have benefited from trials and errors and triumphs and tragedies of a long line of ingenious primitive ancestors.

These primitives had no such tradition. They were the pathetic debris of a high-technology civilization that had destroyed itself. Their recent ancestors had been plunged into barbarism with no warning and no preparation. They had survived; perhaps survival was as much as could be expected of them. In the context of a post-holocaust Earth, even survival was a miracle.

Their scant clothing looked like a foul patchwork of items salvaged from an impoverished rubbish heap. It was pieced out from pelts of small animals, from scraps that looked like a child's clumsy essay at weaving, from clumps of grass. My idealized primitives would have accentuated their nudity with artistic garnishments; these primitives had made a pathetic, shame-ridden attempt to conceal theirs, and their garnishments were clumsy affectations. Both males and females wore what we later discovered were seed cones from trees in their hair and strung about their bodies. Their hair was short, and the mature males had plucked their faces. All were emaciated and sickly-looking. All looked elderly, though perhaps a fourth were adolescents and most of the remainder should have been robust young to middle-aged adults. There were no children or babies.

All of them were dark-skinned. The Earth of my great-grandparents' time would have called them blacks or Negroes. This, at least, did not surprise us. Regez Anlf records detailed the racial conflicts among Earth's population, and we had speculated as to whether survivors of the holocaust would segregate themselves by race.

I turned again to Morl Klun. Our supposed expert in primitives seemed as baffled as I was. Wiln Marra's face expressed consternation. He was responsible for the health of this obviously moribund tribe, and he was wondering whether any of its members would survive long enough for him to commence treatments.

The natives seemed to be waiting. Probably our next move would be crucial, and none of us knew what to do.

One of the males, looking elderly even among this congregation of the prematurely aged, with his face a graven mass of wrinkles and his hair a bristling halo of gray, slowly got to his feet and shuffled toward us, keeping his eyes downcast. He sank to his knees before me and spoke.

"We welcome your return, Lee Lukkari."

Our intense study of Earth languages saved us—barely. Strange as his dialect sounded, I managed to understand what he said, but I didn't believe it.

I blurted, "You remember?"

But he could not possibly have remembered. Memory would have required him to add two hundred years to an age of awareness attained at the time of Lee Lukkari's visits to Earth, and we knew that was impossible. There had to be some kind of tradition concerning her that had survived the holocaust.

"I am Lee Lukkari's great-granddaughter," I told him.

His soft, aged eyes studied me gravely. There was a noble dignity about his black face despite its pathetic emaciation. "You look very like her," he said. He seemed to have far less difficulty in understanding me than I did with his strange dialect.

"Why do you think that?" I asked.

He gestured bewilderedly. "But we have seen her!"

He turned to one of the adolescent males, who hesitated, looked at me, looked at him again, and then bounded away. On the far side of the clearing were long, low, crudely constructed, sagging shelters fashioned of haphazard frameworks of branches carelessly thatched with leaves. They were open on one side. I turned to Morl Klun and found him scowling perplexedly. His textbook chapters concerning primitive crafts had shown him nothing like this.

The young male entered one of the shelters on his hands and knees. He backed out pulling on something that was broad and flat and—when he stood up with it—taller than he was. He brought it to the gray-haired elder, who gravely presented it to me.

It was a more than life-sized Lee Lukkari, a full-length portrait painted with astonishing skill. The colors, despite their two hundred years in native huts—or worse places—were surprisingly vivid. The portrait showed Lee Lukkari as she once had dazzled Earth's United Nations: platinum-blond hair, silver blouse, and short, short silver skirt. It was an excellent likeness—somewhat idealized but vividly recognizable.

Except that she was black.

The elder spoke again. "You look very like her. Why did you not speak to us on the rado?"

The rig I wore to carry my equipment probably could have passed as a silver blouse and a very short skirt, and, by coincidence, my work wrap was a dusky color similar to the flesh of the black Lee Lukkari. No doubt that superficial resemblance had dazzled the natives; fortunately they were disposed to overlook the fact that my hair was brown and my white face was nothing like that of their Lee Lukkari. It was my other great-grandmother, Dana Iverson, whom I resembled.

But "rado" made no sense whatsoever.

"Why did you not speak to us on the rado?" the elder repeated. He sounded resentful.

"Rado?" I repeated blankly.

Morl Klun nudged me and pointed to the box the natives had been worshipping. It was a radio, of course—a totally useless artifact in a culture where the only energy source was human muscle.

"Lee Lukkari promised to speak to us on the rado before her Second Coming," the elder said gravely. He still sounded resentful.

He stepped back and resumed his worshipful attitude, leaving me face to face with the portrait of my great-grandmother and pondering what conduct I should display as her stand-in on her Second Coming.

I said quietly to Wiln Marra, "What's the first thing they need?"

"Food," Wiln Marra said promptly. "They're all suffering from malnutrition."

"How do I convince them that I'm myself?" I asked Morl Klun.

"Try telling them," he suggested. "If they'll believe you're not Lee Lukkari, maybe they'll forgive you for not speaking to them on the rado."

I performed introductions with appropriate ceremony. "I'm Kera Jael," I said. "I'm a student. I study worlds. I've come to study Earth. These are my cousins—Lee Lukkari was also their great-grandmother. Morl Klun and Wiln Marra."

The gray-haired man bowed deeply. "I am John's son."

"Johnson?" I echoed doubtfully.

"No," he said firmly. "John's son." He made the pause between words emphatic.

There was another awkward pause while I tried to decide what to do next. Wiln Marra and Morl Klun were waiting for some kind of cue from me. The natives were simply waiting.

"We have come," I said finally, "because we want to become acquainted with all of you. So I ask you, John's son, to introduce the members of your tribe to us. We want to know each of you well so we can invite you to a feast."

It was the right thing to say, and they reacted enthusiastically. John's son solemnly presented each and every member of his tribe to each of us. We shook hands and pronounced names, some of which sounded exceedingly strange. Wiln Marra asked an occasional medical question: "Why do you limp, Megatha?" Or "How long have you had that swelling on your arm, Stayly?"

We formally extended an invitation to our feast to each member of the tribe and had it just as formally accepted. We set the time—the following midday—and the place—the clearing the tribe was occupying. Then, with expressions of goodwill and anticipations of the morrow's pleasure, we left them.

I half expected them to follow us back to the river, but they did not. We moved swiftly along the forest path, pausing only to pick up our protective clothing along the way, and none of us spoke until we had pulled the boat from its hiding place and pushed off.

Then Morl Klun announced ecstatically, "We did it! We're here, and we've made contact with the natives, and all's well. It should have been complicated, but it wasn't—thanks to their portrait of Lee Lukkari."

"Save your impressions," I said, working an oar. "We won't have accomplished much if we drown ourselves on the way back."

The trip over had enhanced my respect for primitive skills. Earth peoples, right up to the holocaust, had effectively used boats such as this one, and we three brilliant RT members, with two years of specialized training behind us, had trouble crossing a river in it without being swept away. Only later did we figure out that we had been trying to use oars as paddles, and Morl Klun should have known better.

We slowly made our way upstream, keeping close to shore, before we pushed out into the current, but we overshot the base by a wide margin and had to flounder back again. When we finally regained the boat tunnel, I took measurements of the boats there, and then I went to the landing craft and sent two messages. The first was to Ilia Sonal, asking her to send down motors for small boats, dimensions specified, with technicians to install them. The second was to the *Hadda* for forwarding to Naslur Rayl, since we had not yet unpacked communications equipment with trans-space capabilities. It read: "First contact successful. Work commences."

I sat back wearily. We were here, and we had done it, and we could go to work. But I felt no elation—I was much too tired. Our first meeting with Earth's natives had been more of a strain than I realized, and the struggle with the boat had exhausted me. I also had a sinking certitude that I was going to be much tireder before we finished. The planet Earth, and its people, would require a lot of rebuilding.

We held a long evaluation conference. "First impressions," I announced. "Let's have the one observation that stands out or the one question that hit you first."

"Where are the men?" Morl Klun asked.

I blinked at him. "But there were—"

But there weren't, as I now realized after searching my memory.

"There were females of all ages from adolescent to elderly," Morl Klun went on, "but the only males were either adolescent or elderly. There were none in between." He added as an afterthought, "They could be off hunting, of course. On the other hand, their absence could be connected with the fact that there are no babies or young children."

We discussed it. We also discussed the ridiculously ragged dress and the slovenly built shelters and wondered why, in two hundred years, these natives hadn't been able to teach themselves better techniques. This was a tribe that was barely surviving.

We discussed their speech, and we wondered how much of the blurred change from Regez Anlf recordings of Earth speech two hundred years before represented a natural linguistic evolution and how much might be due to a regional dialect peculiar to these particular natives. We pondered the paradox of the tribe's manners, which were eloquently civilized, and we speculated as to how they could have survived through generations of harsh and degrading conditions. Hopefully many of our puzzles would be resolved for us by the natives themselves when we got to know them better.

"You didn't give us your first impression," Morl Klun said suddenly.

"I had so many—" I protested.

"The one thing that intrigued you most," he persisted.

"There were two things," I said. "The rado and the portrait. That portrait is no work of a primitive, either in materials or in execution. The rado doesn't fit, either."

"They have to date from before the holocaust," Morl Klun said. "But why not? Lee Lukkari appeared before Earth's world assembly more than once, and there was global television coverage. She made an impression. Probably she inspired a lot of artists. As for the rado—were you expecting it to resemble Regez Anlf equipment? The only thing the Regez Anlf sent to Earth was precious metals to pay for what it bought. Earth built its own radios in an astonishing variety of types and functions. I'd be much more interested to know the origin of the tradition that Lee Lukkari would return and announce her Second Coming on the rado."

Wiln Marra was impatient to begin his medical testing. He wanted to know how he could obtain specimens without frightening or offending the natives. "They *look* as though they're starving," he said, "but that emaciated appearance can be caused by illness."

"We'll start fattening them up tomorrow," I promised.

"No." He shook his head firmly. "The wrong food, or too much food, might kill them. We'll have to go about this cautiously. Maybe they're getting food, but the food doesn't contain vital nutrients. Or maybe their bodies can't effectively utilize nutrients because of illness. It could be highly complicated."

"Let's not make it more complicated than it is," I said. "You saw the reactions when I invited them to a feast. Concentrate on planning a menu that'll nourish starving people without harming them. And don't you dare go around trying to snatch medical specimens at the feast. Our success depends on our keeping the natives' friendship and goodwill and confidence."

Morl Klun nodded approvingly. "We'll need all of that if we're going to teach them. We'll also have to be willing to learn from them. I'm wondering whether they have written records. What a fascinating thing a diary would be if one of the holocaust survivors thought to keep one! The travail endured by the ancestors of these natives is beyond our imaginations."

"They'll certainly have some kind of oral tradition," I said.

"But would it go back two hundred years?" Wiln Marra wanted to know.

"Oral tradition can go back enormous distances," Morl Klun said. "The grandfather who remembers what his grandfather told him and tells his grandson is transmitting a tradition that will span seven generations by the time the grandson tells *his* grandson." He strode to a window and looked out across the water to the distant shore—hazy through the turquoise dome but still alluring. "Detroit," he said. "A great urban and cultural and industrial area with a racially mixed population of millions. Two hundred years later, there are fifty-two survivors—I counted them—and no young children. I'd like to know whether the tribe is indigenous to this territory or whether it drifted here from somewhere else. What are the chances for survival at the center of a nuclear explosion?"

"Virtually none except in well-designed shelters," Wiln Marra said. "Those who did survive would be subject to all manner of afflictions from radiation exposure, most of them fatal. There also would be critical shortages of food and water and shelter and clothing, not to mention the medical care that the survivors would require. Without massive help from the outside, it'd be miraculous if any of Detroit's millions survived for long."

"In that war, there was no 'outside' that could help," I said.

"Exactly," Wiln Marra said. "I've thought about this. The population centers were wiped out. All of them. The people not killed in the first blasts died slowly from disease and starvation or quickly from radiation exposure. The entire planet was subjected to dangerously high levels of radiation, probably spread by the wind patterns. But there would be places of refuge —a plain would be swept clear of life; those in a sheltered valley might survive."

"It's a lot more complicated than that," Morl Klun said. He abandoned the window and returned to his chair. We had scrounged the three most comfortable chairs we could find in the residence hall and arranged them in a room on the top floor of the office building that Ken Jordan had built to house the Regez Anlf headquarters. It was the highest point on the base, with the best view, and all three of us enjoyed that. We had made it our own headquarters and conference center. There was no logic behind our climbing to the third floor to confer when we could have talked anywhere, but the view gave us a sensation of closeness to this world of our ancestors, whereas the lower levels merely gave us a comfortable feeling of the security of the Regez Anlf base.

"Humans are mobile," Morl Klun said. "They wander. Those that were able to get off that devastated plain took refuge in the sheltered valley. They learned to kill strangers who might be carrying diseases and who were trying to poach in the valley. Tribes developed, each zealously protecting its chosen territory. The former cities would be avoided because of the lingering radiation hazard."

"But that's only the first stage," Wiln Marra protested.

"True," Morl Klun agreed. "In the second stage, radiation would diminish, and the tribes would be attracted back to the cities. They'd come scavenging. The rubble would conceal fantastic treasures. Metal buried on the site of an urban area like Detroit would supply the needs of a number of tribes for uncounted years. Finished woods, masonry, crockery, petroleum products, possibly even stocks of food would be scattered in small or large caches over many square kilometers. Once the city attracted them back, the tribes should have remained here. The river has enormous potential as a source of food—did you see those huge fish breaking water? This area should be heavily populated. Instead, we have an impoverished tribe of fifty-two. So where is everyone? And where are the males?"

"Maybe the natives learned to fear this area while its radiation was still deadly," I suggested. "They would develop taboos and superstitions because of what happened to ancestors who were incautious enough to visit it."

Morl Klun shook his head. "No. These are people with an urban tradition. Cities are repositories of wealth, and even if radiation kept them away for several generations, oral tradition would keep the memory of that wealth alive. They'd return when they could, and when they did, they'd mine the wealth and prosper. Remember—this was a high-technology world. That means that there were no natural resources remaining for the easily acquired metals that primitive peoples normally learn to work. All of those sources were exhausted in the remote beginnings of Earth's civilization. The junk heaps that once were cities represent the only convenient store of metals for today's primitives, and the tribe that controls one, or even part of one, is going to prosper and dominate its neighbors. I insist—if there are any people at all in this vicinity, there should be a large population. Since there isn't, I have to make another deduction."

We waited. Morl Klun had leaped from his chair. He was pacing the floor with the tense excitement of one who had just made a momentous discovery.

"The nuclear holocaust wasn't Earth's only catastrophe," he said.

"There's been another since then. There must have been. Perhaps it was simply a time-delayed aftermath of the first—disease, or perhaps starvation due to some unusually severe climatic change that hit before the population could adjust to primitive conditions. But there was *something*. There must have been. Otherwise, we wouldn't find an impoverished tribe of fifty-two starving in an area that has ample food and an enormous potential of buried wealth."

4

During the night, a landing craft dropped in from the *Hadda* with technicians and enough equipment to outfit a small navy. They installed motors and Regez Anlf protective devices in the large boat and in three of the small ones. They also obligingly unloaded the platform for us, stacking the supplies in rooms we'd picked out for storage and sending the platform back to the *Hadda*. At first light, we took the boats for trial runs on the river, with the technicians coaching us. They gave their work a final check and departed with nonchalant satisfaction.

Wiln Marra planned a nutritious menu, calculated quantities, and began assembling a moderate feast for the natives. The accent was on moderation. "If they stuff themselves, they'll get sick," he said. "The more food we place in front of them, the more they'll try to eat. It's psychological. So we'll only feed them a little, to test their capacities, but we'll let them know that there'll be other meals."

His moderate feast, even for fifty-two people, could be loaded into one of the smaller boats without crowding. With the engine purring softly, we shot out of the boat tunnel and turned toward the north shore, where a group of natives already stood waiting where the path met the water. It was John's son, escorted by several of the younger males. They helped us beach the boat, and they seemed bewildered when we refused their offer to pull it into the forest and conceal it. No one could steal a Regez Anlf protected boat, but I preferred not to try to explain that to them.

They were much more bewildered when we loaded them with food containers. Not until we reached the clearing did we understand why.

The casual invitation that I had extended to the natives almost precipitated a catastrophe. After we had left them, they pondered and debated it, and their initial delight changed to despair. The fact that I had invited them to a feast to be held in their own village seemed ominous. It made them the hosts, and that could only mean that we expected them to provide the food.

They had so little, but they did their noblest best. A feast for three, as lavish as their pathetic resources permitted, was arranged in a bower constructed of woven branches and leaves and festooned with flowers. There was meat from two small animals, with a pulpy bread probably made with flour from pulverized tubers, a small serving of that same tuber, and a meager mixture of small fruits, many of them unripe.

We presented our own offering of food and got the natives started on it. Wiln Marra's notion of a moderate feast seemed awesomely lavish to them. The self-heating containers first frightened and then fascinated them. When we saw the entire tribe eating contentedly, we returned to the bower and inspected the feast intended for us.

"We've simply got to eat it," Morl Klun announced regretfully.

I gingerly examined the animal carcasses, which had been prepared in the simplest manner possible—dressed and roasted, probably over an open fire. I said, "What do you suppose they are?"

"It's better not to suppose," Morl Klun said firmly. "Tear off a piece and start eating."

But the meat was quite good even though tough. The bread was inedible, but we managed to swallow some anyway so as not to offend our hosts. The fruits that were ripe enough to eat were delicious. The tubers, small and elongated, had been baked in fire coals, and we found them both delectable and filling.

My first reaction was puzzlement. The meal was decidedly uneven, but there was substance to it and a balance of food values. I would not have called it a starvation diet.

Then I remembered that the portions consumed by the three of us had been destined for fifty-two people and that several days' gleanings may have gone into the assembly of even this much food. I thought about the list of delicacies that the Regez Anlf had, for a brief period, imported from Earth —coffee, tea, candy, marmalade, cheese, bacon, whiskey, beer, wines, and so on—and sighed.

The natives devoured everything set in front of them as fast as they could eat, and—as Wiln Marra had predicted—they would have gone on eating as long as the food lasted. When we rejoined them, they were virtually comatose.

John's son rolled his eyes appreciatively and tendered the tribe's thanks with as much dignity as his condition of satiation permitted. I expressed our thanks in return and asked him about the meat.

"Skirl," he said. "Tree animal. Good. Hard to catch."

"And the tubers?"

"Tatos," he said.

I suggested a walk. He agreed reluctantly. He would have much preferred a nap, but I wanted to encourage him to talk while the mellow afterglow of the feast was still upon him. Morl Klun and Wiln Marra likewise attached themselves to a pair of the tribe's elders and drew them aside for what they hoped would be long talks. This was the artful strategy that Morl Klun had devised—he thought we could make more progress in probing ancestral memories if we interviewed the natives separately.

John's son and I strolled back along the path to the river. Close to the water's edge, we seated ourselves on the trunk of a fallen tree.

"There once was a bridge," I remarked, "that soared high over this river."

John's son nodded complacently. "I have seen its bones."

And he had, of course. Two hundred years of rust wouldn't obliterate all of a bridge's massive steel girders. So I could not count the bridge as an ancestral memory, but I noted the fact that he had recognized the word immediately and knew what the bones had belonged to. Before I could try again, he delivered an appreciative belch and remarked, "One says that there was once a path under the river, but this can't be true."

"But it is true," I said. "One of my great-grandmothers used that path often. It was called a tunnel."

He did not know the word.

"Did your father tell you of this path?" I asked.

He was uncertain as to where he'd heard about it.

"Does your tribe have contacts with other tribes?" I asked.

He scowled. "Bad peoples. They take our hunting."

I remembered the Regez Anlf records concerning Earth's racial conflicts. "Are the bad peoples white or black?" I asked.

He turned and gave me a puzzled glance. "No whites," he said. "Everyone black."

"No white tribes at all?" I persisted.

He shook his head. "Whites die."

"All of them?"

"All," he said. He spoke with the quiet confidence of one expounding universal knowledge. Then he added, "As you know."

"Why did all the whites die?" I asked.

"The Beesee," he said.

Piece by piece I got the ancestral history as he remembered it.

The holocaust was a curtain of indescribable horror. Probably the survivors had not cared to recount the more gruesome details to their descendants. John's son knew only that a frightful punishment had been visited upon the entire world—a concept clearly beyond his grasp except that it meant everywhere. Cities and their populations had been destroyed by fire from heaven. Death had stalked the countryside.

"The people of Earth were wicked," he said simply. "They had sinned. Lee Lukkari punished them."

"Lee Lukkari!" I exclaimed.

"She is just," he said simply. "As you know. Her wrath is terrible. Those who sinned, died."

I was too astonished to protest.

After the holocaust had come a time of wandering and suffering—a time of disease and privation and unending search for food and shelter. Starvation loomed everywhere, day after day. Those fortunate enough—or unfortunate enough—to live gravitated to villages and small settlements that had escaped the worst of the holocaust.

But people continued to sin, and whites were cruel to blacks. "As they always had been," John's son said with poignant sadness. The weight of that cruelty was his heritage. "Always, whites had been cruel to blacks. So Lee Lukkari sent the Beesee."

It was a plague, a ravaging sickness marked by tremors, by the red flush of fever, by legs swollen too painfully to walk on, by a throat so inflamed that one could not swallow even when there was food, by labored breathing that made each gasp of life-giving air a torment. Many black sinners died, but all of the whites died. All. John's son was emphatic about that. There were no whites left on Earth. He *knew*. Their multitudinous sins against the blacks had been revisited upon them by Lee Lukkari.

"All," he said simply. "All died."

He spread his hands, palms downward, in silent lament for a white population whose unspeakable sins against blacks were beyond atonement.

The survivors of this new affliction fled the villages that harbored it, and they suffered renewed horrors of deprivation. They became wanderers. They hunted; they gathered food where they found it. John's son's people had a comfortable territory somewhere to the north, with actual houses to shelter them and lots of skirls and rich places to harvest food. Then a bad tribe had driven them out, killing many. They fled through the forest, fearing that the bad peoples were pursuing them. Skirls were few and hard to find, and in unfamiliar territory they did not know where the food plants grew.

Tradition told them of a temple to Lee Lukkari on an island in the wide river far to the south. They wandered until they found it, shimmering and inviolable on an Earth where all the temples to false gods had been destroyed. One of the more daring youths had swum out to it, but its magic had stung him, and he could not enter.

Fortunately they had preserved the two essential relics of their tribal shrine, and their faith in them was absolute. They established themselves in the nearby forest, and they prayed daily to the image of Lee Lukkari and waited for the rado to speak and tell them that she was returning to save them from starvation and heal all of their woes, as she had promised.

And now the promise had been fulfilled. His smile, as his old voice droned on, was beatific.

That was as much as I could assimilate on a lazy afternoon with the warm sun pouring down and the broad river flowing sleepily at my feet. The work on the boats had kept us up much of the night, to be followed immediately by preparations for the feast, and I needed rest. I also wanted to meditate. I thanked John's son for sharing his memories with me, and the two of us returned to the clearing.

Morl Klun and Wiln Marra were still deep in conversation with the elders they had selected. Both of them scowled resentfully when I interrupted, but I said sternly, "Let's not overdo it. They'll be here tomorrow."

We made our final presentation—a Regez Anlf portable communicator. Even in the Regez Anlf it was considered an amazing little contrivance. It was small enough to fit into a large pocket, it was simple to operate, and it could be reached by a master communicator located anywhere on Earth or in surrounding space. I was still feeling curious about the rado, and I ignored Morl Klun's disapproving scowl and slyly manipulated the presentation into a trade—the old rado for one with a vastly superior magic that enabled the tribe to speak as well as to be spoken to.

The new communicator was received with enthusiasm and installed in the shrine hut beside the portrait of Lee Lukkari. I considered that portrait a priceless potential family heirloom, and I would have manipulated a trade for it if I could have thought of one. I had to content myself with the rado. I suggested that we continue our feast on the morrow, and the natives, their enthusiasm tempered by their innate good manners, agreed with restrained politeness.

John's son and his coterie of young males accompanied us back to the boat. At the water's edge, Morl Klun held a hurried whispered conference with the youths. Then the natives helped us launch the boat, and they stood looking after us with arms extended in a farewell salute.

"What was that about?" I asked Morl Klun as we set course for the island.

"I invited them to go fishing with me early tomorrow morning. We want to make these natives self-sufficient as quickly as possible, and it'd be an enormous boost to their self-esteem if they could provide the meat for tomorrow's feast themselves."

I turned and stared at him. "I never thought to ask. Why do they have to be taught to fish?"

"I don't know. They simply don't know how. Once in a great while they've been able to spear a fish from shore, but since they have no boats—"

"This is unbelievable!" I exclaimed.

"It is," he agreed. "Apparently they were able to gather food easily in their previous location and skirls were plentiful. They never learned to fish with line and hook. Now I'll teach them."

When we reached our headquarters room on the third floor of the office building, I placed my prize rado on a shelf, and we settled in our favorite chairs to exchange information. The others seemed to have acquired more than I did—perhaps their elders had been more garrulous than John's son, or perhaps they had been more aggressive with their questions.

Each had concentrated on his own special interest. Wiln Marra had been fascinated by the enigmatic "Beesee" that had destroyed the white race. He had attempted to trace Earth's medical history. What he got was a tale of diseased and delirious wanderings, from cities to towns to villages to farms, in which first the radiation victims dropped by the wayside, and then, just when things seemed stabilized, the Beesee attacked everyone. And everything.

"Animals?" Morl Klun asked sharply.

Wiln Marra nodded. "It was harder on the animals than it was on humans. Some black humans survived. Some skirls survived. But most birds died, all the large animals died, and some insects died."

"I was wondering what had happened to the meat animals," Morl Klun said. "Cattle were so domesticated in this part of the world that they probably couldn't have survived in a wild state, and this wasn't horse country. But it was deer country, and the land supported enormous numbers before the war. I tried to ask where they went, but I couldn't make myself understood."

"Beesee," Wiln Marra said. "It hit the blacks severely. It wiped out the whites. The blacker the skin, the better the chance for survival—or so their tradition tells it. It also afflicted animals, birds, reptiles, some fish. Those who ate the diseased animals were doomed."

"Perhaps that would explain how John's son's people forgot how to fish," Morl Klun said. "Anything that's poisonous, even temporarily, can become a forbidden food. But certainly some fish survived. Why?"

Wiln Marra shook his head. "The Beesee is ancient history. It didn't happen during these elders' lifetimes, and I doubt that it happened during the lifetimes of their fathers. It's much too late to be putting together a scientific study of its effects or even to figure out what it was."

"What are the chances that it's still endemic in remote tribes?" I asked.

"Very slight. I give it none at all. My hunch is that some common disease mutated, perhaps because of the intense radioactivity. It became so devastatingly potent that it reduced Earth's population below the point where it could sustain itself. After one pass, its potential victims were either dead, or immune, or so few and scattered that it simply could not perpetuate itself. Mutations tend to be unstable anyway. I would be astonished to encounter a new case of Beesee."

"But what was it?" I persisted.

"It sounds like some kind of degenerative blood disorder, and no doubt its impact was intensified by the weakened condition of the population and by the fact that medical care and public health administration had been shattered by the war."

"If it did flare up again, would you be able to handle it?" I asked.

"Show me a case in its early stages, and I'll cure it," Wiln Marra said. "I'd have to know more about the disease to say whether I could cure an advanced case."

"I'm not worried," Morl Klun said cheerfully. He bared his arm and displayed his dusky, green-tinted complexion. "Obviously a dark skin is the best protection. Neither of you would have a chance."

Wiln Marra said dryly, "It isn't the dark skin that's protective. It's the genetic factors that accompany it."

"Were your subjects truthful?" I asked.

"Absolutely," they chorused, and Morl Klun added, "One doesn't lie to the gods—especially when the gods come bearing gifts."

They *knew*, of course—and I knew that John's son had been truthful—because of the Regez Anlf truth capsule. This is implanted in Regez Anlf children at birth. It compels truthfulness in Regez Anlf society because everyone knows instantly when anyone lies. Outworlders with whom the Regez Anlf has business dealings are freely given capsules as a guarantee of Regez Anlf truthfulness and good faith. We had not yet resolved the question of whether this gift should be extended to Earth's primitives. The value of the capsule depended on a people's conception of "truth," because philosophical and ethical and religious prejudices sometimes conflict with the factual. In addition, Morl Klun had raised the question of whether it might become necessary, in the complicated process of rebuilding a world, to tell lies simply because the truth might so contradict primitive knowledge and superstition that it would seem false to Earth's natives even when a truth capsule verified it.

For a beginning, it was enough to know that our three elders had been truthful.

We talked out our impressions, and then we recorded them for the base files. When we'd finished, I gave my cousins the task of preparing summaries for transmission to Naslur Rayl. I had my own long-term plans to meditate, and I started by taking a machete and making a complete tour of the base, inspecting it and all of the buildings much more critically than I'd had time for during our previous rounds. It had been immediately evident that even in the base's present condition it would serve us well as a secure supply depot and as our headquarters and sleeping quarters whenever we worked this territory—but only because we weren't particular and because we planned to spend more time in the field than at the base.

Now I was considering its suitability for other uses.

The dome had protected the buildings against weathering, and the masonry was in fair condition. Inside, there were serious problems with rotting organics and oxidized metals that showed quick glints of color before I touched them and then cracked apart or turned to smelly dust. In the bars, glass bottles had shattered when the shelves that held them collapsed. Others had long since rotted their stoppers and sublimated. Some still contained liquid. I made a mental note to search for Irish whiskey and beer and—if they were still potable—to toast the spirit of my great-grandfather, Ken Jordan.

Electrical fittings had disintegrated. Even though the Regez Anlf power supply still functioned, service to the buildings was uncertain and probably hazardous. The island's water and sewage services had come from one of the mainland cities, and those utilities had ceased to function the moment the holocaust struck. The power supply itself was long overdue for renewal.

Outside again, I traced the outline of an irregular, curved depression in the ground—the swimming pool, packed with the dust and vegetable debris of centuries. Cutting yet another path through the prickly vegetation, I stumbled over an old Regez Anlf dome-building mechanism—the one that had constructed the turquoise protective shield that arched high overhead. I wondered why it had been left there. Perhaps Ken Jordan had planned the construction of other bases. The hoses needed replacing, but the Regez Anlf metals, under a thick covering of dust and dirt, were bright.

I went to the landing craft and called the *Hadda*. I wanted an ecological crew to rework the entire island, following the original planning in as much detail as the old records permitted. The power unit, now in its dying stage, would have to be replaced. Buildings should be restored as closely to their original condition as possible.

There was an inflection of raised eyebrows in Ilia Sonal's response. She said, "Really? What are you going to use it for?"

It was none of her business, and she knew it. I asked politely, "Are your technicians so preoccupied with Stimulation and Tranquillity that they have no time for landside duties?"

She answered, just as politely, "I merely wondered whether you intended to rebuild Earth by settling into a comfortable base."

"Civilization," I told her, "is represented on this planet by piles of rubble. I want at least one place in the world that can stand as a model, and this is the only one where restoration is possible. I'm going to use it as a school."

"I'll send a team down tonight to do the preliminary plans and estimates," she said.

I called Burluf Nori for a progress report. The topologist was patiently compiling a location schematic of the world's surviving life-forms, and his slow spirals had finally reached the east coast of the continent. It was an indescribably tedious task. The heavy forestation made it necessary for his instruments to scrutinize the landscape meter by meter. He described his findings, and we puzzled over them together. Not until that moment did I realize how incredibly lucky we had been.

Earth was a planet almost empty of people. Morl Klun had been right in his deduction that another catastrophe had followed the holocaust, but his conclusion had been a ridiculous understatement. Actually, the Detroit area was sparsely populated because there were no people left on Earth to populate it. Burluf Nori had found a population cluster far to the north. No doubt this represented the "bad" tribe that had taken the hunting grounds of John's son's people. Otherwise—nothing. He had not detected any herds of large animals.

He estimated the "bad" tribe's cultural and technological level as Class Nine. "Probably it's the same as the tribe you just contacted," he said.

I told him that John's son's people rated no higher than Class Ten.

"Do they fire their pottery?" Burluf Nori asked.

"I haven't seen any pottery," I said. "I doubt that they have any. They do weave baskets, but they do it badly."

"It's a confused situation," he mused. "Perhaps they're still able to salvage things they need. It would account for their failure to learn."

"I don't even think they're doing that," I said. "Call me at once if you find anything remarkable."

When I returned to our headquarters, I found Wiln Marra still at work on the report summaries. Morl Klun had gone fishing. He'd had a sudden apprehension that he needed practice before he could instruct the native youths; but he was back almost before I missed him with a prize catch more than a meter long. He and Wiln Marra dissected it and subjected the carcass to every test Wiln Marra had the means to perform before they pronounced it edible. Then Morl Klun proved the point by serving fish steaks to us for our evening meal. The meat was deliciously flaky and tender.

The *Hadda* technicians were energetically at work on their survey of the base when we left for the mainland early the next morning. We took the large boat, which the boat tunnel inventory called a launch. Morl Klun assembled all nine of the tribe's young males on the shore and began to teach them the use of fishing equipment. Wiln Marra found a small, private glade for himself a short distance from the main settlement and set up a medical clinic. I had advised John's son, by way of the communicator, that Wiln Marra would be dispensing health magic, and those who were sick or otherwise had painful spirits wracking their bodies could have their difficulties eased by him. The entire tribe—except for John's son and the youths who had gone fishing—was eagerly awaiting these ministrations.

John's son joined me regretfully. He would have liked to sample Wiln Marra's health magic himself, but I had asked him to show me how he hunted skirls. It turned out that he didn't hunt them; he trapped them, and I marveled that his clumsy, rickety trap ever caught anything. We spent the morning together, and he imparted to me all of the skirl lore that he could remember.

While I listened patiently, I began to formulate the slow steps we would have to follow in order to bring this tribe to a level of healthy sustenance.

I didn't foolishly minimize the task; I knew that there would be staggering difficulties even if the natives cooperated fully, but I also knew that we were capable of coping with both difficulties and natives. The pathetic superstition and ignorance with which John's son described his small universe could not temper my elation.

We had arrived, we had made contact, and we were constructively at work. At that point our job seemed—as my great-grandfather would have remarked in a figure of speech I'd never been able to understand—a lead-pipe cinch.

5

The *Hadda* possessed the equipment, supplies, and personnel to raise Earth's population to a level of moderate technology in a few giant leaps. A single machine could have transformed the economy of John's son's people from the impoverishment of uncertain hunting and gathering to intensive agriculture in one growing season.

Ilia Sonal expected us to present John's son's people with the machine. Immediately. She could not grasp the fact that intensive agriculture is a highly specialized occupation requiring vast knowledge and extensive training. Machines make that job easier, but they are no substitute for the knowledge and training. Further, using machines and keeping them running requires knowledge and training of a different kind. When days drifted past with nothing more significant in our log than fishing expeditions or medical clinics or extensive probing of ancestral memories, she decided to intervene. She would have denied that she was either exceeding her authority or improperly intruding on mine. She was merely trying to be helpful by calling our attention to something we obviously had overlooked.

What she did was send us the machine she thought John's son's people should have. It would have made them farmers in short order, clearing the forest and performing every conceivable agricultural function for them. Her note said, "You may find this useful." I sent the machine back without comment.

Then she requested permission to visit Earth base. I granted the request immediately—it would have been silly not to—but I insisted on a night arrival. The activity of the technicians renovating the base already had attracted the attention of the natives, and I did not want to put an unnecessary strain on their imaginations or confuse them by introducing a plethora of wholly inexplicable gods. I forbade direct contact with the natives by anyone except the Reclamation Team.

Ilia Sonal wandered about the base for two days, poking into everything but asking no questions and making no comment. It was difficult to tell what she thought except that it was certain to be something unpleasant. The health of John's son's people suffered from her visit, because Wiln Marra followed her about like a forsaken house pet and had difficulty in concentrating on his work for days afterward.

Something had to be done about her.

"Now," Morl Klun said. "Or she'll be on our backs permanently so as to better look over our shoulders, and her suggestions will gradually become orders."

I invited her up to our headquarters before she left, gave her a choice of our three comfortable chairs, and informed her, "I'm recording this conversation for the record."

She arched her eyebrows, but she said nothing.

"The members of the Reclamation Team are doing a job they were trained for," I told her. "It's a technical, highly complicated job, and it's one for which you have no competence whatsoever. There's no reason why you should. What is inexcusable is the fact that you still have no comprehension of what we are doing despite all of the reports you've read and all of the briefing you've received. Listen now, and try and understand."

Her eyebrows had lost their arch; her eyes narrowed, but she still said nothing.

"The guidelines we have laid down for ourselves have been reviewed by Naslur Rayl and the most competent and experienced authorities available. They are based upon an intensive review of many centuries of work with primitives. That experience shows that the sudden introduction of technology inevitably leads to disaster. In our program, we will not introduce machines until Earth's people have learned to make and to use hand tools efficiently—but we will teach them to do that. We will feed them while helping them to find sources for food but only until they are able to feed themselves. We will keep them healthy while teaching them sound habits of communal and personal health and laying the foundations for the evolution of their own medical technology, but we won't give them lessons in brain surgery before they can competently incise a simple pustule. Our mission is not to rebuild this world but to guide and assist the natives while they rebuild it themselves. The decisions concerning the execution of that mission will be made here—not on the *Hadda.* Is that clear?"

It was clear. I expected no explanation or apology and got none. She returned to the *Hadda,* making a night departure, and we resumed our plodding efforts to teach the natives to take their first steps.

Morl Klun started his fishers with Regez Anlf lines and hooks, but as soon as they caught their first monstrous fish, he taught them to fashion their own hooks of bone. Unfortunately, there seemed to be nothing at all in the natives' environment from which they could make their own fishing lines.

His next problem was to teach them to preserve the meat, since they were able to catch many times the quantity of fish that the tribe could consume. They responded eagerly to his instructions for drying the fish, but he ran into problems when he suggested smoking it. Oddly enough, smoked meat was a part of their heritage. The tribe's elders were dimly aware of the process, though they had no notion of how to proceed or what woods might produce the best curing smoke. Morl Klun's own experiments were failures; if he did not watch the natives continuously, they let the fires go out.

He finally deduced that they were afraid. They cooked their food cautiously over small fires of dead wood that made as little smoke as possible. The perpetual smudge that would be required to smoke fish could be seen for many kilometers, and the bad tribe in the north might be on the prowl. So they refused to smoke fish.

His second failure came when he attempted to include some of the young females in his fishing expeditions. Fishing was really hunting, the natives thought, and hunting was a job for the males. The males protested; the females refused. Morl Klun accepted the inevitable and began to teach them to shape a large tree trunk into a boat.

I continued my long conversations with John's son, and I gradually perceived a remarkable residue of shrewd common sense in the concoction of superstition and ignorance that he spouted. I took a metal detector with me on our forest wanderings, and one morning I discovered a treasure trove—the buried shop of a vendor in tools.

This accomplished two things in a stroke. John's son had been indifferent to my descriptions of the probable treasure buried in the endless ruins from which the forest grew. Now he had to be restrained from rushing all of his tribe into a perpetual treasure hunt.

And Morl Klun, whose fishing crew had been bewilderedly hacking away at the tree trunk with stone axes, suddenly had an entire portfolio of tools to work with. Many of them had rusted into oblivion, but he was able to salvage a serviceable kit for his boatbuilders. Those youths could not understand the urgency to learn boatbuilding when we already had several that paddled themselves and when fish could be caught just as easily from the shore with the remarkable hooks Morl Klun had taught them to make and with the lines that he furnished, but the boatbuilding went much faster with tools.

We were becoming well acquainted with all fifty-two members of the tribe. The one who intrigued me the most, even more than John's son, was an elderly female called Tild. Each morning she led the tribe's females on a food search. This strange ritual was no longer necessary—the tribe had more fish than it could eat and Regez Anlf supplements to balance its diet —but the practice had sustained the tribe, after a fashion, in a time of starvation, and the females continued it. Each morning's search began with a sortie along a path followed on a previous search. When they reached its end, they began to extend it. Finally they turned back and widened the area of their search as they returned.

A few roots, a few dried or decaying fruits might be the total reward for a morning's search. A newly discovered nut tree was a bonanza, and all of the females gathered there to search the ground for fallen nuts of the previous season. No doubt they memorized its location for future harvesting.

Each female carried a small basket of woven branches lined with dried clay. When they had found little else, and only as a last resort on the return search, they gathered insects and worms, carefully dispatching each by squeezing its head between the fingers. Everything they found went into the soup pot, a crude clay vessel, and a small, almost smokeless fire tended by a crippled elderly male kept the pot simmering. A good harvest meant a rich soup; on poor days, it was thin and watery.

When the younger women were doubtful as to the value of a find, they brought it to Tild. Most specimens she accepted or rejected at a glance. Rarely one puzzled her; when it did, she pondered it fretfully, lips pursed, a scowl accentuating the maze of deep wrinkles that wreathed her dusky face. As with John's son, her manner habitually was one of intense seriousness, and she rarely smiled. Her responsibilities equaled or exceeded his.

The soup—before we introduced fish into the natives' diet—had been their staple. It was a method of evenly distributing the available nourishment. All of the tribe's food had gone into the pot: tubers, fruit, nuts, insects, and—cut into small pieces—the rarely caught skirl. Even entrails went into the pot. The tribe's sources of nourishment had been so limited that they could afford to waste nothing. We sampled this brew day after day and found that its flavor varied startlingly according to the day's harvest. A good catch of certain preferred insects produced a richly flavored, nourishing broth. Sometimes the flavor was thin and the scent disgusting. The natives continued to consume this soup, unnourishing as it was most of the time, even after they had become accustomed to the food we introduced from other sources.

Morl Klun agonized over the mystery of their impoverishment. He reasoned that two hundred years should have been a sufficient time for these natives to learn survival. They should have been able to produce their own tools and use them effectively. They should have known the forest better—known the food potential of every tree and shrub and plant there. He was especially intrigued that they had not discovered how to make cloth with vegetable fibers or from the bark of trees. The fact that all members of the tribe wore their hair short was easily explained: they wove their hair into thread and used it to sew together the pelts of the few skirls they caught; or they braided it into rope.

"It's a tribe that can't cope," he said despairingly. "If we hadn't arrived, they would have starved or died of exposure in the first prolonged period of bad weather. How did they manage to survive so long?"

The obvious explanation for their impoverished condition was their recent expulsion from a rich territory by the bad tribe. We gathered that their former home had been only partially forested and that they had harvested valuable plants of many types that could not be found in the forest. There had been more nut trees and a flourishing population of skirls. When the bad tribe drove them away, they were no longer able to find the foods they were accustomed to. Promising roots and berries that they were not familiar with had been rejected, and they had not been able to teach themselves to fish efficiently.

This did not satisfy Morl Klun. "They should be much more adaptable," he said peevishly. "Surely they had some staple other than skirls in their former home. I want to know what it was."

The *Hadda*'s technicians were transforming our base. The buildings were renovated and repaired; trees and shrubbery were trimmed or thinned out; the tangled weeds were peeled away. Seeds of the tall, prickly weed evidently had found their way into the dome along with other warm-weather flora that Ken Jordan had imported. This weed unfortunately had choked out the original grass, and there would be a problem in replacing that. The technicians labored with great skill and patience though with little enthusiasm. It was tedious work, but they had nothing else to do.

Wiln Marra was watching over the natives' health with concern and no little anticipation. He was awaiting the one event that would signal his success in correcting the accumulated deficiencies the natives had racked up through years of bad nutrition: the first evidence of pregnancy in one of the females. For—he assured us—the young males already had attained a maturity that made it possible for them to sire children, and the older males would probably be potent again when restored to health.

Morl Klun had his own list of mysteries to ponder. One of them concerned the natives' names. "John's son" was unique—apparently this was a title for the tribe's leader. Most of the other names were obvious derivations from long-established Earth names. Morl Klun was trying to figure out whether John's son's successor would be called John's son, or Johnson's son, and what John's son would be called if he surrendered his leadership before death.

I had a considerable puzzle of my own in the continuing survey reports from Burluf Nori. He had wound up his North American search and had almost finished South America, and each new report added to my perplexity.

For one thing, John's son had been tragically correct. There were no white survivors.

None.

For another, the locations of these scattered remnants of Earth's humanity made no sense whatsoever. There was one settlement on the St. Lawrence River near what had once been Montreal. There was one in Louisiana, one in Missouri, and one on the Pacific coast. In all of Mexico, Burluf Nori had found only a few scattered indications that registered so lightly that he had not bothered to confirm them. They may have been wandering individuals or small families; or they could have been flukish survivors from Earth's once enormous populations of large animals.

Central America was blank. The Amazon jungle concealed two tribes, one near the river's headwaters and another at its mouth. There was one confirmed settlement in central Argentina. On the Pacific coast and in Tierra del Fuego, Burluf Nori had found more faint indications that he did not bother to confirm. He intended to run a zigzag search on the entire range of the Andes, on the off chance that a surviving tribe might have found a fertile valley to shelter it. Then he would check the Pacific islands en route to his Asian survey.

There seemed to be no correlation between population and geography

Apparently favorable locations often had the smallest tribes; or they had no human population at all. "What we're facing," Morl Klun said slowly, "is the horrendous impact the loss of Earth's large animals has had on its human population."

He studied the map uncomprehendingly, shook his head, and returned to his own puzzle of John's son's people's past. We decided to postpone contacting other groups until we had solved the major riddles of what we were calling the Detroit Tribe and made it self-supporting. It now seemed clear enough that the adult males—those aged between youth and the premature old age represented by John's son and his contemporaries—had been murdered by the bad tribe to the north or had fallen in battle. The fate of the younger children was not so easily determined. The older males were evasive; the females simply refused to answer. Morl Klun tried to avoid direct questions. He preferred to encourage the natives to talk while he subtly guided their conversation with an occasional observation or comment. Sometimes he related an experience of a primitive tribe he had studied; the natives would listen attentively and then match the story with tales of their own. His techniques usually were successful; concerning the recent past of this Detroit Tribe, they did not work at all.

Our first breakthrough came on the night that Morl Klun launched his fish-smoking project. He finally succeeded in convincing the natives that our magic would prevent the bad tribe to the north from seeing the smoke. This was obliquely true. Every few nights we ran a quick biofilter survey with the landing craft, spiraling out to two hundred kilometers, and we would have been able to detect any invading humans long before they came close enough to see smoke.

Morl Klun taught the natives to build a smoke hut following a design he was familiar with. The tall structure was stacked with racks so that—as Morl Klun put it—each puff of smoke did a maximum amount of work. He located it on the riverbank, where both fish and wood could be brought to it easily. When it was ready to use, he announced a feast to commemorate the lighting of the first fire. It was an enormous success. While young females tended the fire, the tribe reposed along the shore in the moonlight, talking and enjoying the food.

Morl Klun and I chatted with John's son. Nearby, Wiln Marra was listening to Tild expound medical lore.

"You had much meat in your previous home," Morl Klun suggested.

"Much," John's son agreed and licked his lips.

"More than you could eat," Morl Klun suggested.

"Sometimes much more," John's son agreed.

"How did you keep it from spoiling?" Morl Klun asked.

"In the winter, with snow," John's son said. "In the summer, with salt."

Morl Klun and I exclaimed together, "Salt!" We knew that this had been an area of salt mines, but the mines were so deep as to be inaccessible without machinery, and even if some memory of their existence had survived, their locations certainly would be unknown to the natives.

"Where did you get salt?" Morl Klun asked.

"We had much salt," John's son said evasively.

"How much?"

"Piles."

Morl Klun pondered this mystery with a frown and set it aside for later investigation. "So you had many meat feasts," he went on.

"Many," John's son agreed.

"Why did you stop?" Morl Klun asked.

Both of us expected a retelling of the treachery by which the bad tribe had surprised John's son's people and driven them from their hunting grounds. Instead, John's son said simply, "Carl's people ran away."

"What tribe was that?" Morl Klun asked casually. He had the rare quality of being able to act indifferent when he was most excited.

John's son seemed confused. "Tribe of skirls," he said. "Ran away. Meat hard to find."

Morl Klun deftly changed the subject and began to quiz John's son on the tribe's method of salting meat. John's son prated on happily; Morl Klun and I listened in stunned silence. For the first time, he had deliberately lied to us.

Later, on our return to base, it was a sober Morl Klun who invited us to a conference.

"I've been adding up a lot of things," he said. "Until now, nothing made sense."

"You mean it does now?" Wiln Marra demanded.

"About this tribe that ran away," Morl Klun said. "Did you hear the lie?" All three of us had heard it.

"Carl's tribe—or maybe Carl's son's tribe to its members—must have been a smaller and weaker neighbor. John's son's people preyed on it until it fled or its surviving members scattered. That was years ago. Then a stronger tribe moved down from the north and inflicted the same fate on John's son's people."

"According to John's son's descriptions, those were highly desirable hunting grounds," I said. "So that makes sense."

"They *were* highly desirable," Morl Klun said grimly. "But not because of the skirls. I went into great detail with John's son about the technique of salting meat. Those weren't skirl carcasses that his people were salting. They were preserving choice cuts from much larger animals."

Wiln Marra and I couldn't comment. We were stupefied.

"Since there were no larger animals, there's only one explanation," Morl Klun went on. "Cannibalism. Carl's tribe ran away because John's son's people had been killing the members for meat, one or two or several at a time, probably over a period of years, and the survivors became too few to defend themselves and no longer able to retaliate by occasionally capturing one of John's son's people for a hearty meal. Then the bad tribe came down from the north and began to treat John's son's people the same way. These natives are right to be apprehensive. The bad tribe may be after them again as soon as its supply of meat gets low. This is why, everywhere on Earth, there are only isolated groups of humans. The stronger tribes have survived by eating their neighbors. One might say that they ate themselves into isolation."

I said slowly, "But the missing members of John's son's people are the mature males and the young children. How does that fit?"

"The mature males would be captured or killed first, since they'd try to make a defense while the others escaped. After the males fell, the children would be the easiest to capture."

"But wouldn't the mothers carry the young children with them?" Wiln Marra asked.

"We don't know how long it's been since there were young children. This tribe's nutrition has been failing for years—ever since Carl's people ran away. If that continued long enough, the women would stop conceiving."

"That's possible," Wiln Marra agreed.

"But there's another possibility to consider," Morl Klun said. "We don't know how long ago that happened. There may have been younger children when the bad tribe ran John's son's people out of their territory. They certainly had tough going on the flight south and while they were trying to establish themselves here. They may have been close to starvation all along the way, and they were starving when we found them."

"You mean—they ate each other?" Wiln Marra blurted.

"They may have eaten the younger children. That could be why they refuse to talk about some of their experiences. Cannibalism also may be why they welcomed us so enthusiastically. If we weren't gods sent by Lee Lukkari to save them, at least we were a potential source of food. That 'feast' they prepared for us could have been designed to put us off our guard. They presented us with all the food they had in the expectation that their own feast would come later. I'm convinced that nuclear catastrophe and subsequent epidemics converted Earth's humans to cannibals. It was a direct result of the loss of Earth's animal populations."

Morl Klun gestured at my map. Burluf Nori's latest report showed three widely scattered communities of humans in Southeast Asia—plus a few scattered indications. The remainder of the continent was blank.

"These 'indications' he picks up from time to time," Morl Klun said. "If he'd drop a level or two and move more slowly, he might find more. I think they're the scattered remnants of smaller tribes that are fleeing to keep the larger tribes from eating them."

I said slowly, "But you can't postulate global conditions on the basis of sheer speculation concerning one tribe."

"Of course I can," Morl Klun said cheerfully. "I just did. It's something to be confirmed or disproved through investigation. Let's start tonight."

I yawned and shook my head. "No. If Earth's people are eating each other, we won't be able to stop it with anything less than a reclamation job on each tribe like the one we're doing on John's son's people. Let's finish here, and then we can take on another one."

"In the meantime, you should let Naslur Rayl know that this project is going to take a lot longer than any of us suspected," Morl Klun said.

The technicians finished their renovation of the base and departed. They resodded Ken Jordan's sweeping lawns with a grass they found somewhere in the west; probably it was a poor substitute, but it looked wonderful after the tangled weeds it replaced. With it they brought in other seeds—or perhaps the removal of the weeds gave other plants a chance to grow—and our new lawns soon were dotted with bright yellow flowers. Morl Klun researched the subject and pronounced them dandelions—considered a weed in Lee Lukkari's time.

But we liked them.

I'd asked the technicians to leave one corner of the island in its over-grown condition, and now I recruited six of the native youths—three males and three females—to work for us. I intended to teach them gardening and then graduate them to more complicated chores like maintaining the base, operating boats, and handling communications. I wanted the sort of staff that Ken Jordan had recruited from the bright young people of his day.

The project floundered immediately. The young Earth natives had no concept of work. Further, the simplest tasks got entangled in their tribal taboos. The males couldn't crop weeds and plant lawns and gardens—those were female chores, and the males objected. The males didn't seem to care whether the females piloted the boats, but the females did. That was a male chore. My carefully reasoned explanation that a new day was dawning went for naught, so I appealed to John's son. His face puckered with disbelief—first because my young charges were not doing what I asked them to do, and then, when he fully understood what it was that I wanted, because I presumed to challenge such sacrosanct taboos.

I described Ken Jordan's staff of young people, giving Lee Lukkari credit for the project, and finally he relented. He spoke to my six recruits, and I began to get grudging cooperation.

But very little work. I finally canceled the project and sent the six young people back to the tribe.

"A mere two hundred years has transformed Earth's people into a race of indolents," I complained to Morl Klun.

"Not indolents," he said. "Primitives. Their view of everything is circum-scribed. Digging up weeds and trimming shrubs makes no sense at all to them. Neither does planting a garden in order to get food at some uncertain time in the future. Intelligent primitives don't work at things like that."

He was having similar problems in persuading the natives to build a permanent settlement, with weather-tight dwellings, a community building, and a surrounding stockade. The stockade was unnecessary, but he had added it for its psychological value. The males, whose strength was needed for handling the logs, rebelled against building shelters, which was women's work. Morl Klun's village took shape with excruciating slowness.

We nevertheless were proceeding so well with this Detroit Tribe that we began to consider our next move. Morl Klun wanted to investigate the bad tribe to the north and test his prognosis of cannibalism. Wiln Marra wanted to jump to South America. I was undecided, and I insisted that no decision could be made until Burluf Nori finished his survey. I still anticipated the survival of a substantial population in Africa, where the preholocaust population had been predominantly black, and I was curious to know whether these descendants of low-technology societies had done better than those descended from high-tek societies in North America.

When his report finally came, it confirmed my expectations. Africa was dotted with surviving human communities. I counted eleven major settlement areas. All the inhabitants were black; all the communities rated at Class Nine or even a shade higher.

I skimmed the remainder of the report. There were no survivors in Australia. Europe had a few indications but no settlements. Burluf Nori had even nosed down into Antarctica, which he found blank.

At the bottom of the report came the list of islands: Philippines, nothing; East Indies, nothing; Crete, nothing; Sicily, Sardinia, Corsica, nothing; Malta, Minorca, Majorca, British Isles, nothing. Greenland, nothing. Iceland—

My exclamation brought the others at a run.

Iceland was populated.

The Culture was at Class Six or perhaps even Class Five.

Borluf Nori hadn't believed it. He'd been almost at the end of his survey when he finished Europe and headed west for a perfunctory glance at the northern islands. And over Iceland, almost at the Arctic Circle on the old Earth maps, he found himself looking down at a totally unexpected network of human settlements, all well constructed, with signs of organized agriculture and animal culture, with functional seagoing boats in a well-maintained harbor, even with night lights in the buildings.

He could not obtain the photographic evidence he wanted from the level he was restricted to, so he'd sent in a drone camera and at the same time short-circuited a delta. The natives had dashed outside to see what caused the noise, and he got a sensational series of low-level photos. I could count the paving stones, admire the masonry in the stone houses, puzzle over the probable sources of illumination, study the odd nighttime costumes of the natives, and even admire the tense poses they'd struck.

In the terse, three-dimensional clarity of the pictures, there was no doubt at all about the natives' race. All of them, male and female, were white.

6

We searched the Regez Anlf files and gingerly leafed through moldy reference books from Ken Jordan's library in pursuit of clues as to how a high civilization had managed to endure in Iceland and why members of the white race survived there and nowhere else on Earth. We found none. Iceland had had little industry, few natural resources, and a climate that was arduous if not inimical. Even with high-technology support, the island had been more than two-thirds uninhabitable.

Morl Klun and I pushed the problem onto our medical expert. We asked Wiln Marra how it could happen that the Beesee could decimate Earth's white population and somehow miss this picture-healthy group of whites in Iceland. Had they somehow developed immunity, or had they been protected from exposure by the water barrier? And if their isolation had protected them, why hadn't similarly isolated whites in other parts of the world survived?

While he fretfully gnawed his fingernails over his own research volumes, we pursued an equally critical problem through the file's welter of Earth's racial myths and superstitions and prejudices. If the Iceland whites had kept or regained a high level of culture and technology, why had none of the isolated tribes of blacks kept or regained theirs?

"This takes us nowhere," Morl Klun said finally, slamming the stack of books aside. "There are too many unknowns. All we know for certain is that a community of whites has survived and that it seems to be prospering. It has a fishing fleet. The houses are well built and well maintained, and there may even be electrical power. These natives practice both agricultural and livestock cultivation. All of that is incredible. The books don't have any answers. We'll have to go there and find out for ourselves."

"A surviving animal population is just as remarkable as a surviving white human population," I said.

"Right. We've got to find out why. Let's go now."

I went to the window. Night had fallen, and the forest on the north shore was a dark, shapeless mass except for the fire that flickered where the natives were smoking fish. "Our first contact with this group poses an entirely different problem from the one we faced with John's son's people," I said. "I vote that we wait for daylight."

Morl Klun gestured resignedly. "Yes. I suppose we'd better do that."

"And there's a small matter of language," I went on. "The file doesn't have Icelandic."

"It doesn't?" He leaped to his feet and went to check for himself.

"Icelandic," I said, quoting one of the reference books, "was spoken by fewer than two hundred thousand people, and the Regez Anlf documentarian obviously considered it a minor language." I hesitated. "For contact with humans on that cultural level, we should consider the standard Regez Anlf technique."

"You mean—approach them as traders?"

"I think we should consider that."

"You're going to mind-mate with a primitive?"

"Are these people primitives?" I asked.

He stared at me silently for a moment, and then he retrieved the stack of reference books. "Iceland had no fossil fuels," he said. "The technology was not sufficiently advanced to have developed efficient solar power. But there were important hydroelectric installations. If their technologists survived, techniques for running those plants would have remained viable. But over a span of two hundred years, they would have had to make numerous repairs and replacements. Where would they get the metals? And how would they process them?"

Wiln Marra had been listening. "Their main industry was fishing," he said. "They still have a fishing fleet, so they could be importing supplies by water."

Morl Klun snorted disgustedly. "You think maybe all they have to do is sail a fishing boat over to the mainland and take on a load of copper wire? Where on the mainland would they find it? You'd better stick to medical problems. Have you come up with anything?"

"I've come up with another problem," Wiln Marra said. "Greenland is a next-door neighbor to Iceland. Greenland had a population of several thousand people—whites and Eskimos. Why didn't anyone survive there?"

Morl Klun slammed his books aside a second time. "It's like trying to solve an equation when all of the values are unknown," he said sourly.

"But they aren't all unknown," Wiln Marra protested. "We *have* the Icelandic value—a thriving community."

"Communities," I said. "Burluf Nori said villages and farms are scattered through the inhabitable parts of the island."

It was my turn to retrieve Morl Klun's pile of books. The other two gathered around and watched while I compared Burluf Nori's ranging photo with the ancient maps. Iceland was located in one of Earth's more geologically active areas, and two hundred years, a geological flick of an eyelash, had nevertheless brought changes. The southeastern coastline was drastically altered. A large volcanic island had thrust up offshore, and several smaller islands had disappeared. None of these changes seemed likely to have had significant impact on the island's population.

I returned to the question of race—of why whites would survive on Iceland and nowhere else. "Did Iceland have a black population?" I asked.

We could not find a breakdown of Iceland's pre-holocaust population by race. The humans in Burluf Nori's photos certainly looked white—their features were those of Earth's white race and so was their skin color—but this didn't completely rule out a racial mixture. I wondered whether blacks with white genes had been more susceptible to the Beesee and whether whites with a measure of black genes had been more likely to survive.

I settled myself by the communicator and roused Burluf Nori. He'd been enjoying a welcome session of S&T, Stimulation and Tranquillity, after his arduous survey, and he resented the intrusion.

"We need information," I told him. "You've dumped a racial problem onto us. I want to know why whites survived in Iceland and nowhere else. How certain are you that the remainder of Earth's population is black?"

"Reasonably certain," he said. "Ninety percent certain. There could be isolated individuals—"

"Ninety percent isn't good enough," I said. "There was a South American country called Brazil that prided itself on its racially mixed population. Therefore any surviving community in that area should still have a mixed population. Your schematics label the settlement at the mouth of the Amazon as one hundred percent black. I want that verified."

"*Now?*"

"Tomorrow morning, Brazil time. Shortly after dawn. I'm planning on a noon Icelandic contact, and I'd like the information before I go in."

He sighed heavily. "Very well."

"It's critically important," I persisted. "I'd like the racial makeup of that community analyzed as meticulously as possible without setting any alarms off. Get me the information I need, and then you can go back to sleep."

His parting word was a snort of disgust.

"I should have thought of that before," I mused to Morl Klun and Wiln Marra. "Now tell me why a disease would be racially selective."

"All diseases are selective in the sense that some strains may be more virulent than others or some victims may have more resistance than others," Wiln Marra said. "The Beesee killed blacks as well as whites, according to John's son. But it killed all the whites—except in Iceland—so I have to conclude that some blacks were more resistant. And on the basis of the information we have now, I have to conclude that the Iceland whites escaped because they somehow avoided contracting the disease. A theory of immunity for them makes no sense at all."

"They may have devised an inoculation or a treatment for Beesee," Morl Klun suggested. "But in that case, why didn't they share it with the rest of the world? Another unknown. Maybe we'll find out tomorrow. Where are you going?"

The question was directed at me. "I'm going to take a nighttime ride in the landing craft," I said. "We may be gone for several days, and I want to make certain that the bad tribe isn't trying to sneak up on John's son's people."

I got little sleep that night. First I did the tedious biological survey out to a hundred kilometers. Then I lay awake trying to decide on the best approach to a small, technologically advanced population on a primitive world.

Regez Anlf custom in establishing trading relations with an outworld is to put down a landing craft, open the ramp, and accept the first person to enter voluntarily as the Regez Anlf trading representative—provided that the person is willing. Regez Anlf captains are trained for this contact, which involves mind-mating with the outworld subject. Mind-mating—literally a sharing of the total mental makeup of another person—is a protracted and painful experience for both parties. In some circumstances, it can be destructive, which is why we preferred not to risk it with a primitive mentality.

But the Icelanders were not primitive, and mind-mating was a possibility that I had to consider. It would enable me to quickly assimilate the ancestral memories and present attitudes of the Icelanders. It would spare us the tedious sparring and questioning that we had to employ with John's son's people. The opportunity seemed so glittering that I mistrusted it.

A standard Regez Anlf contact was made only after long, intensive study of the outworld people concerned. We knew nothing at all of the circumstances, character, and moral outlook of the Icelanders. Mind-trading would bring us all of that, instantly, and perhaps take us years closer to our goal. I hesitated because I did not know what else it might bring us. Glittering opportunities too often concealed traps.

At dawn I went to see John's son. His tribe was still far short of becoming a successfully functioning economic unit—balanced nutrition was possible only with the supplemental food that we furnished, and we had not yet solved the clothing problem—but the tribe was adapting well to its fish diet, everyone had plenty to eat, stocks of smoked and dried fish for winter were growing daily, and the future looked bright. John's son received my news that we would be absent for several days with an indifference that made me think he was glad to be rid of us. I made a mental note that Morl Klun's regimen of work and education was becoming oppressive, and the natives needed an occasional vacation.

We waited until Burluf Nori's report arrived. He informed me that there were no whites in the Brazil colony. Visual examination had detected no humans of noticeably mixed breed. All of the inhabitants were black. "The blackest kind of black," he added.

"Report noted," I said, "with thanks."

But he had already cut off huffily to return to his S&T.

As we boarded our landing craft, Morl Klun turned to me and asked, "Are you impersonating Lee Lukkari again?"

I thought for a moment. "Wait," I said.

I dashed over to the dormitory building, where clothing salvaged from the possessions of Ken Jordan's employees had been stored. His fondness for short skirts had made them virtually a uniform for his female employees; I couldn't find an outfit in the glittering silver that Lee Lukkari had worn, but there was a choice of skirts and blouses in a very passable white. I donned them over my work wrap and hurried back to the landing craft.

Morl Klun grinned and said, "If they don't know Lee Lukkari, they'll certainly want to. Let's go."

All three of us were tensely expectant. The paradoxical riddle of the Icelandic community had overshadowed our other unanswered questions. We felt that if we could solve this one, perhaps the others would succumb. I angled the craft toward the northeast, plotting a tight parabola of ascent and descent that would bring us down over Iceland. Morl Klun and Wiln Marra impatiently took stances in front of the viewing screens.

As our descent passed the ten-kilometer mark, the magnification units began to pick out a wealth of detail. We had a fleeting glimpse of a ruined city's rubble, for there was no forest to conceal it in that bleak, windswept landscape. We could not decide whether it was the war's imprint or that of some natural catastrophe. We glimpsed an irregular scattering of out-communities, small alignments of buildings that Icelandic references called *boers*, with their distinctive patterns of agriculture and husbandry.

At the one-kilometer mark we hovered, and I shifted the magnification to show us an overhead view of what we'd already seen in Burluf Nori's long-angled photos: a small but obviously prosperous community. It lay where the ocean fingered the land deeply. A few small, weatherworn but meticulously kept boats were tied up at a long wharf in the natural harbor. There was no industrial clutter, and the houses were comfortably spaced along wide streets that converged on a square where a few taller buildings stood. All the structures were of stone, and many were roofed with a green that was indistinguishable from the surrounding vegetation.

"Sod!" Morl Klun exclaimed. "Sod roofs. That means—"

"It means that sod is good insulation," I said. "This is a cold climate. What are the red roofs? Tile?"

Morl Klun wasn't certain about that. We dropped lower, and I targeted the open square in the center of the town, called out, "Here we go," and took aim at it. We plummeted and then settled slowly the final hundred meters to give any chance pedestrian or vehicular traffic an opportunity to get out of the way. As the craft came to rest, I caught indications that Iceland's prosperity had its limitations. Many of the windows on the buildings were covered with a translucent material, certain sign of a shortage of glass or plastics.

Slowly a crowd gathered. We watched incredulously as the people drifted toward us. They were quiet, patient, and—to us—incomprehensibly incurious. Only the children displayed wide-eyed amazement, but they were either subdued or well behaved and clung closely to the parents without prompting. The mature males were bearded, but their facial hair had been trimmed simply and neatly with no concern at all for style. Most of the women wore long braids. There was nothing at all festive about the clothing the people wore. They had come from work, whatever their work was, and all of the garments were sternly practical, even those of the children.

Two hundred years before, Dana Iverson had thought that a Regez Anlf landing craft looked like a slightly flattened, enormous beer keg lying on its side. What it looked like to these Icelanders I could not imagine, but its descent from the sky, and the opening of the ramp, should have been awe-inspiring if not terrifying. Obviously they were neither. I had the silly feeling of having lighted a fuse that turned out not to be attached to anything.

"What do we do now?" Morl Klun asked.

I hadn't the faintest idea.

Then the crowd drew back to open a gap, and a young man strode confidently forward. He was bearded, like the others, but he wore the ornate clothing of a holiday. He did not hesitate. He walked directly to the ramp, and, with exaggerated care, he undressed himself. When he finished, he laid his clothing in a neat pile.

Inside the landing craft, we exchanged wondering glances. "A gesture, maybe," Morl Klun muttered. "He's showing us that he's unarmed."

The man rotated twice on his heels with his arms extended, and then, without any hesitation, he strode naked up the slope of the ramp.

As he entered the landing craft, I flipped the switch that closed the ramp behind him. The crowd faces showed no surprise. Neither did they react with any noticeable surprise as the ship lifted slowly. They simply watched.

I surrendered the controls to Morl Klun and said to Wiln Marra, "Ready?"

He smiled. "He's a fine specimen of masculinity. Standard Regez Anlf contact?"

"No," I said firmly. "There are too many unknowns here. I'll take what he volunteers, and I'll trade a language with him if he's willing. Perhaps that will suffice."

Wiln Marra's smile broadened. "He *is* a fine specimen. Perhaps—"

I said sternly, "Don't involve me in your perhapses. A mind mate is not necessarily a mate." Wiln Marra had been attempting to select my sweethearts for me since I was ten, always with deplorable results. He had ruined some fine friendships.

Morl Klun said sourly, "Don't confuse administrative decisions with personal preferences. Let's get on with it."

Since the Icelander was nude, I decided to remove my own clothing to avoid embarrassing him. As soon as I was ready, Wiln Marra dropped a doorway, and I stepped forward.

The Icelander's eyes widened when he saw me. For the first time a flicker of emotion crossed his face. He blushed. He had assumed his own nudity so nonchalantly that I had not expected mine to startle him.

I seated myself and signaled him to sit beside me. He complied so hesitantly that I regretted my decision to remove my clothing. I studied him for a moment; he was indeed a fine physical specimen. His build was sturdy, with moderate body hair. His flesh had the ruddy color of prime health. His hair was brown, and his brown eyes watched me alertly.

He regained his composure when I handed him a headband. He puzzled over it for a moment. Then he watched me arrange mine, and he awkwardly imitated me and positioned his own.

I thought a question at him; he brightened and spoke an answer—in what I assumed was Icelandic—and it required several minutes of adaptation for him to familiarize himself with mental speech. Since the computer did not have the Icelandic language, we would not know whether it could sort out his mental patterns until he responded mentally.

But he understood my first question, and eventually he thought an answer. "My name is Rek. Rek Steamler."

"I am Kera Jael," I thought.

"Kera Jael," his mind repeated.

Again I regretted removing my costume. It would have been interesting to find out whether there was a Lee Lukkari cult in Iceland. I decided to ask him.

"Do you know who Lee Lukkari was?"

"Lee Lukkari," his mind echoed. "Yes. Yes—she was the alien emissary who came from another world to trade with Earth. For a long time my people have prayed that the aliens would send another emissary."

"She was my great-grandmother," I thought.

"Is this mind-trading?" he asked.

I was startled. I was more than startled—I was confounded. My mental exclamation brought him to his feet. "What do you know about mind-trading?" I asked him.

He sat down again. "Mind-trading is what I am—" The computer sputtered over the translation, offered "am dedicated to," and immediately amended that to "trained for." He repeated the thought. "That is what I am trained for."

I took a deep breath. "You trained for a Regez Anlf contact?"

His smile was beatific. "All of my life," he thought proudly. "As did my father and his father before him."

"Why?" I asked. "For what purpose?"

"The books speak clearly. Aliens sent an emissary to buy the products of Earth and to enrich Earth's peoples. The emissary traded minds with an Earthman and made him her agent. She said it was the aliens' custom. One of my ancestors met and talked with her in New York, when she met with the United Nations. My people have always known that someday the aliens would return and resume their trading, and because my ancestor had met Lee Lukkari, he prepared himself to become her agent on her return."

"And it became a hereditary position?" I asked, still incredulous.

"Yes," he said. "You do come to trade, don't you? One of the things Lee Lukkari bought was fish, and we have plenty of fish to trade. And there is much that we need."

"I come to trade," I told him. "And I have a favor to ask of you. Will you exchange languages with me? We'll be able to trade more effectively if we can communicate directly."

His people had experienced generations of isolation, and he had difficulty in comprehending the existence of languages other than his own. Then he insisted that no exchange was necessary, and I had to explain that Regez Anlf ethics were based on fair trading, on repayment in kind even for something freely given. I also had to explain that an exchange of languages was not mind-trading and that I was not yet prepared to appoint a Regez Anlf agent—which disappointed him. Finally he consented to the language trade. I decided to give him English—the language of our Detroit Tribe—in exchange for Icelandic. Eventually it would be important for Earth's people to be able to communicate with each other. Wiln Marra brought the probes and focused them on our speech centers. We lay side by side and allowed the machine to hum us into unconsciousness.

I awoke first. Rek, on his initial experience of the probe, was certain to have a groggy time of it, so I did not wait for him. I went to dress, and I asked Wiln Marra to find clothing for Rek.

"Why don't you mind-mate with him?" Wiln Marra asked. "He's willing; his people want to trade. We easily could adapt Regez Anlf procedures to these special circumstances, and it would give us a solid link with the world's one surviving nonprimitive culture."

I shook my head. "No. My decision not to trade minds was a lucky one for us. A language probe sometimes picks up unsorted information, as you well know, and there was just enough seepage to reveal Rek's real status in his tribe. He's an outcast, the worst kind of pariah. Making him an official Regez Anlf representative would have been fatal. Merely taking him aboard the landing craft means that we'll have serious difficulties in forming any kind of a productive relationship with his people."

7

The gift of clothing—even badly fitting Regez Anlf work togs—and the ability to speak to me directly transformed Rek. He relaxed and beamed like a delighted child. We had a long talk while the landing craft hovered fifty kilometers above Iceland and Wiln Marra and Morl Klun made themselves inconspicuous in the background.

I was still intrigued by the fact that Lee Lukkari had become a goddess for one Earth community and was merely a name out of history for another. Had Rek ever seen a picture—or a portrait—of her? He could not remember. He supposed there might be one in the archives, but the books and newspapers that survived there were sadly deteriorated, and the government archivist did not like to have them handled.

His own information came from journals his ancestors had kept, and pasted in one of them was a picture that was his prize possession. It was a photo—not of Lee Lukkari—but of Ken Jordan! The same ancestor who had seen Lee Lukkari in New York had also seen Ken Jordan, and met and talked with him, and photographed him.

The Earthman who had become the aliens' agent and who had faced down all of Earth's leaders at the United Nations and run the Regez Anlf trading business as he saw fit had assumed a heroic stature in Rek's family tradition. Rek did not worship him, but he very much hoped to emulate him.

I asked Rek whether he had heard of a tradition that Lee Lukkari—or Ken Jordan—would return to Earth and announce his Second Coming on the rado or radio. Rek knew nothing about that and could only dimly recall what a radio was. The fishing boats once had devices like that, long before his time, to talk with each other, but they had long since ceased to function. No one on the island would have had time to listen to such a thing; there was too much work to do. The Icelanders did have telephones, though— there was a telephone link to each community and to some of the outlying boers.

The telephone startled us more than a radio would have until questioning established that there was only one per community, kept in repair by cannibalizing a rapidly diminishing salvage stock and used only in severe emergencies.

Finally I told Rek I wanted to meet his people and determine for myself what their trading needs were and what they could offer in return. He leaped with delight—literally. He was unaccustomed to low gravity, and he almost fractured his skull.

Three hours after we had taken off, Morl Klun set the ship down with an expert touch on the precise spot where we had landed previously. We did not have to wait for an audience on this second arrival; the one we'd had earlier was still there. No one seemed to have moved.

From the top of the ramp, Rek made a speech. His voice glowed with pride, and in his excitement he spoke so rapidly that my newly acquired Icelandic did not—quite—enable me to follow all of his allusions.

From the top of the ramp, I made a speech. I spoke slowly, preferring precision to speed with a new language, and my audience listened with an attentiveness that was frustrating because it was wholly undemonstrative. It gave me no clue at all as to how my speech was being received.

Then I chanced to mention that we had reactivated the old Regez Anlf base and that we'd already made contact with a tribe in that vicinity. I was halfway through my next sentence when I noticed that I was losing my audience. It simply began to melt away, and suddenly everyone was running. Parents with small children were carrying them or hurrying them out of sight. The square was empty before I could do anything but stare in dismay.

I turned bewilderedly to Rek and found his face a distorted, stunned mask.

"What did I say that was wrong?" I demanded. I had an apprehension that I'd somehow mispronounced words and inadvertently converted all of my compliments to insults.

Rek's voice quivered with emotion. "You landed another place—you contacted another people—before you came here?"

"Of course," I said. "We had to have a base to operate from, and since the old Regez Anlf base was still functional—"

"We thought that you would know," he said bitterly. "You have scientists. You have doctors. You should know better than we."

"Know what?" I demanded. "What is there to know? What are you talking about?"

He turned away. His body was slumped with despair. "I see that you don't know. If you did, certainly you would not have come. I cannot believe that you would intentionally bring us death."

"Death?" I echoed perplexedly.

"You have doomed my people."

I exchanged startled glances with Wiln Marra and Morl Klun. "The Beesee!" we exclaimed together. I asked Rek, "Do you mean the Beesee?"

The name meant nothing to him. I tried to describe the disease John's son had told me about. My description probably was inexact, but Rek recognized it at once; to his people, it was a disaster with a legacy of terror.

"The Mainland Fever," he agreed sadly. "And now you have brought it back to us."

"Is that why everyone went home? Because they fear contagion?"

"They left, but they know that it is already too late. Merely to stand in the shadow of one who bears the disease is to die." He paced wearily down the ramp and settled to the ground, a pathetic, disconsolate figure. This was to have been his moment of triumph, when his fellow citizens would have to make atonement for his long years of ostracism—the moment when his family's generations of lonely dedication had finally brought prosperity to Iceland. Instead, he had doomed this community—he thought—and perhaps all of Iceland, and he felt so completely a traitor that he refused to risk human contact by going home. He intended to die where he lay.

I walked halfway down the ramp. "Listen," I called to him. "There is no more Mainland Fever. The people we met near our base are healthy. We do not bear any disease. Even if we did, one of us is a doctor. He is able to cure anyone who sickens. You must tell your people that their fears are groundless."

He spoke without looking up at me. "The Mainland Fever has no cure." He was being enormously, ritually brave. "I will remain here until my death. My body must be completely burned on this spot."

I retreated back up the ramp and went into hurried consultation with

Morl Klun and Wiln Marra, who were still wondering what was going on. As a result, we rigged a primitive vocal amplifier, and I boomed a message and sent it echoing about the town. "There is no more Mainland Fever," I proclaimed. "We do not bear any disease. We have a doctor with us who can cure any sickness you have."

Wiln Marra protested—he felt that this description of his medical talents was unnecessarily exaggerated. "No doctor can cure *every* sickness," he said. I told him to shut up—I was coping with an emergency.

Nothing happened. Rek remained huddled at the foot of the ramp. The vanished townspeople remained in hiding, waiting for death.

"This may be a long night," I sighed.

Morl Klun asked impatiently, "What, precisely, are we waiting for?"

"The plague," I told him. "These people may have electric lights, but their outlook is still primitive. Susceptibility to suggestion, or mass hysteria, or some related psychological bias may produce a run of patients before morning. The Mainland Fever warped their ancestral memory beyond our feeble powers of reasoning."

"And no wonder," Wiln Marra said. "It almost exterminated the white race on this planet. It almost exterminated all of the large animals, too. I can understand that the descendants of survivors would be apprehensive about it."

I went back to the ramp and looked down at Rek. He still lay on the ground, huddled and weeping and totally alone, and he did not look up when I spoke to him.

"You were right," Wiln Marra said. "He's a genuine pariah. Everyone else went home to die with family and loved ones. He'll be an outcast even in death."

"Worse than an outcast," I said. "His people are thinking that he betrayed them."

Again I called down to Rek. For a long time he did not respond. Finally he raised his tear-stained face.

"If you insist on dying, die with friends," I told him. "Come in here. It's going to be a chill night, and you need food. There's no sense in lying uncomfortably on the ground when hospitality is freely offered."

We finally coaxed him inside and fed him, and then he gloomily sought a cushion near the entrance and went to sleep.

I sent my proclamation echoing about the town twice more before we set watches and I snatched some sleep for myself. About midnight, Morl Klun shook me awake. A father and mother stood at the foot of our ramp, each carrying a squawling infant. I spoke reassuringly to the parents, handed one child to Wiln Marra, and took the other myself. The parents refused to enter the landing craft. They settled to the ground where Rek had lain, perhaps to await the touch of death themselves, and we retired with their children.

Wiln Marra, a bachelor, handled the small boy as though he were a particularly repulsive laboratory specimen. The child sensed this and squawled louder. Half an hour and a battery of tests later, plus desperate consultation with our entire file of Earth medical references, Wiln Marra produced a diagnosis. "I think," he said slowly, "that Earth doctors would have called it diaper rash."

The second—and elder—child had nothing at all wrong with her. The parents' behavior had frightened her, and she cried because her brother was crying. Wiln Marra sprayed the diaper rash with a soothing ointment. I gave both children sweets to suck. By the time we returned them to their parents, they were sleeping peacefully.

"They're in good health," I told the parents. "Take them home and put them to bed. Put yourselves to bed. No one is going to die."

Perhaps they did that, but first they gave relatives, friends, and neighbors their own version of the medical miracle we had wrought. Within an hour, spreading news of our curative powers brought a long line of waiting patients to the landing craft. It was quickly evident that we would make slow progress if we attempted to deal with one patient at a time, so we awakened Rek and hooked Morl Klun and Wiln Marra to him for a linguistic transfer. With all three of us possessing a fumbling skill with Icelandic, we began to deal with the patients systematically. Morl Klun and I acted as medical references, recording names and symptoms and then passing the patients along to Wiln Marra.

The oddity was that those symptoms bore a startling resemblance to the characteristics of Beesee that John's son had described: the fevers, the tremors, the sinister red flush, the aching limbs, the difficulties in breathing and swallowing, the blurred vision. Wiln Marra worriedly performed his tests, found each subject to be in robust good health, and finally had the inspiration to rig a "cure" chamber in which patterns of laser flashes bathed his patients with blinding but innocuous colored lights. By midmorning, he had put most of the town's population through this chamber. Some citizens, overly obsessed with dying, returned for second and third exposures. The only holdouts were two classes of skeptics—those few villagers who refused to believe that the disease had returned, and a few more who were convinced that we aliens couldn't cure it if it had. Eventually the waiting line dwindled to zero, and even Rek, whose unpopularity diminished noticeably as confidence in Wiln Marra's cure increased, took himself off to his solitary living quarters.

We closed the ramp to protect ourselves from interruptions and wearily bedded down in what had been the consultation room. I was dozing off when Morl Klun said suddenly, "If their ancestors never had the plague— and I feel certain that they couldn't have had it—how does it happen that they remember enough about it to produce psychosomatic symptoms?"

"That sounds like a very good question," I told him sleepily. "After we've had some sleep, why don't you try to find out?"

We slept until late afternoon. When we awoke, a few pessimists were waiting for one more treatment, but the remainder of the population seemed to be going about its normal business. Sails on the horizon marked the position of the small fishing fleet. Children played. Older children tended herds of animals on the lower slopes of the surrounding hills, and adults tended their gardens.

We served ourselves a quick meal, and while we ate it, we talked about the Beesee, the Mainland Fever. Wiln Marra thought his earlier speculation about it had been correct. It had been a mutated pathogen. "Either it was an unstable mutation, or it suffered the inevitable penalty for being too successful and multiplying too rapidly. It committed suicide by killing off the available hosts faster than they could reproduce. I'm certain that it struck after the war, when the population was already weakened by radioactivity and other diseases, not to mention bad nutrition and shortages of clothing and shelter, and when Earth's medical centers had been destroyed. Otherwise, Earth's scientists would have found a way to cope with it."

I asked whether there could have been more than one mutated bacteria or virus.

"There could have been many," Wiln Marra said. "But I'm certain that the Beesee and the Mainland Fever were the same one. Virtually identical descriptions from two widely separated populations make this disease remarkable even in extraordinary circumstances. It must have had its own unique vector to so completely decimate a world population. Virulence alone wouldn't do that—it had to have an incredibly efficient means of spreading."

"Which brings us back to the question I've been asking myself," Morl Klun said. "How does it happen that the Icelanders have such exact knowledge about an ancient disease that their ancestors never experienced? Their ancestors couldn't have experienced it, or they would have been wiped out along with the rest of Earth's white population."

"Why don't we find an elderly Icelander and ask?" I suggested.

"Good thought," Morl Klun said. "Is Rek waiting in attendance?"

He was seated where he had waited to die the night before, but it was a vastly different Rek who sprang up alertly as we descended the ramp. Our "cure" of the plague had conferred a new status on him. He greeted us with poise and composure, though he was bursting to fulfill his destiny as our trading agent in Iceland. He began to talk quietly about the island's urgent needs and what it had to offer.

"The herring catch is very good this year," he said. "We have a surplus of many tons for trading."

"We'd like to appraise your needs ourselves," I said.

"Certainly," he said. He squared his shoulders importantly. "I will introduce you to our Althing. There will be appropriate ceremonies, and our leaders will tell you whatever you wish to know."

We had difficulty in convincing him that our first interest was in his island's history, but eventually he relented, and we found ourselves paying court to a wizened old blind woman who sat in a cushioned chair in the fading afternoon sun, expertly combing animal fibers.

She had not been one of the previous night's patients. Wiln Marra asked her why.

"Wasn't sick," the old woman said, cackling. "Wasn't any sicker than usual, I mean. No point in bothering doctors about an old body like mine. They haven't got any cure for old age." She cackled again.

"You weren't worried about the Mainland Fever?" Wiln Marra persisted.

She hunched a warm sweater more tightly about her, and her blind eyes looked up, smilingly, at the sun. "Got so many aches now I couldn't tell a new one if it happened. No, I don't worry about any fevers. The young people, they've got lives to lose, and it's right that they should worry. Me, all I have to lose is my aches. So I wasn't getting out of a warm bed to run to any doctor."

We asked her to tell us what she remembered of the recollections handed down to her, and all three of us listened in fascination to the meanderings of her cracked voice. It was no more than a muted echo of a world's agony, but it was the first detailed account that we had heard.

Iceland had stayed out of the war. Her leaders had the practical view that the island's tiny resources couldn't affect the outcome in any case, so why become involved in an insane orgy of mutual destruction?

But one contending power had thought that Iceland was providing support and bases for its enemies. Without warning it unleashed a searing horror on Iceland's coastal cities and towns. It was not a nuclear attack; it was an avalanche of high explosives whose purpose was to destroy the harbors and their facilities. If, in the process, towns and cities were leveled as well, that was a fortune of war and a salutary lesson for the people of Iceland. Casualties were extremely heavy because the attack came without warning and because the citizens, thinking they were at peace, had no shelters.

There had been an effort to rebuild. Then *the* earthquake came. Earthquakes were no novelty to this elderly Icelander, but the memory handed down to her of *the* earthquake was of something horrific. Makeshift buildings had been shaken down on their occupants. Damage had been widespread all over the island. After that, there was no further attempt to rebuild the demolished cities because there were so few people left to occupy them.

While Iceland was contending with a natural catastrophe, the remainder of the world was contending with the unnatural—with the Mainland Fever.

Iceland knew. It was isolated, because ship and air traffic had long since been cut off, but its medical authorities gravely monitored reports, compiled information, talked directly by radio with health authorities elsewhere when any could be contacted, and kept informed about the progress of the plague and what was being done.

They made their own plans. The island's fishing boats became patrol boats, diligently seeking out and turning away boatloads of refugees fleeing the mainland. The Icelanders felt that they had no choice; they were condemning to death only those who were already doomed, and it was the one way that they could save themselves.

And then a boatload of refugees eluded the watchful patrol and made a night landing at a small fishing village. Most of the refugees were already ill. The authorities acted instantly according to plans already formulated. The refugees and all who'd had contact with them were isolated; the village was quarantined, with concentric zones of isolation established around it. The plague struck the village like a greedy flame devouring dry timber. First all of the refugees and then the townspeople sickened and died. The plague spread into the first zone of isolation, and the unfortunates living there and all of their animals were moved into the village to join those already dying. One case in the second zone condemned all of its occupants to death, and the widening vacant ground was repeatedly dosed with antiseptics and purified by burning. In the village, the plague victims burned the bodies of their dead as long as they were able. Ultimately the plague was contained. Long afterward, the government sent machines, with hooded and masked operators in protective clothing, to burn both the dead and the village. The ashes were buried; the site became wasteland. To this day, no one ever went near it.

Wiln Marra's eyes sought mine. He was as moved as I was. Morl Klun remarked quietly that such a disciplined self-sacrifice to ensure the survival of the larger community was very rare.

The old woman's voice droned on. The following year, the plague had struck again—but this time no refugees had reached Iceland.

"Perhaps some slipped ashore unnoticed," Wiln Marra suggested.

"No." The old woman was adamant. There had been no refugees. Winds brought the disease. Winds of Death had circled the globe, searching out humans and large animals wherever they were to be found. One of these Death Winds had brought the plague to an interior village. Again the government's containment plan had worked. The villagers had perished, but the plague had not spread. The village was burned along with its dead, and the ashes were buried by machines.

The plague had not returned, but Death Winds still blew, and the people of Iceland stood ready.

We understood, now, the strange reaction of the townspeople when they learned that we had come from the mainland. Down through the years they had been taught that such a visit meant inevitable death, and they had been taught what they must do about it. Accepting death with resignation so that others might live was the discipline that had enabled the Icelanders to survive.

That same measure of discipline had helped the Icelanders to overcome shortages and maintain a semblance of civilization. One hydroelectric plant had been kept operating by scrounging parts from other plants. The fishing fleet was diminished to a size needed to feed Iceland's reduced population, and surplus boats were conserved. Wood, especially, was salvaged from war-damaged cities and towns and conserved. Metals were salvaged. Radio communication was maintained for a time, but when sets and batteries began to fail, that was abandoned. Only the telephone was zealously maintained, one set to a community, for emergencies—such as the return of the Mainland Fever. The old woman doubted that anyone had kept records or recorded eyewitness reports of those years when Iceland tenuously survived with a world dying around it. Once the island ran out of paper, no more newspapers or books had been printed. She was recounting tales handed down to her, and her accounts were unemotional but appallingly vivid. We thanked her, presented her with a box of sweets, and headed back toward the landing craft through darkened streets with Rek self-importantly leading the way.

"So the plague was spread in two ways," Wiln Marra said suddenly. "By contact and by the Winds of Death."

"Is that possible?" Morl Klun asked.

"I wouldn't have thought so except on a very restricted basis. Certainly not for an entire world. I've never heard of such a thing, but then—I've never heard of anything like this Mainland Fever, either."

"I'm trying to envision the circumstances when the plague struck," I said. "The population had been wracked by a nuclear war. There were wandering refugees everywhere who were already sick and starving, and large areas of Earth had little or no medical care. Those are ideal conditions for a plague to take root. Iceland demonstrated what might have been done elsewhere with a functioning government and imaginative leadership."

"And a remarkably courageous populace," Wiln Marra suggested.

"But Iceland also had the good fortune to be isolated," Morl Klun pointed out. "So it had only two minor outbreaks of plague to contend with."

Wiln Marra shook his head. "Other communities were just as isolated— or more so. There were populated islands that were even more remote than Iceland. Now they're depopulated."

"Could it be that global wind patterns turned the Winds of Death away from Iceland?" I asked.

"That must have been it," Wiln Marra said. "Either that, or this island is so windswept that the Mainland Fever was simply blown away from it. Have you noticed that trees don't grow here? But probably it took a combination of things, plus luck and an uncommon discipline and dedication, to let these Icelanders survive."

"Since they did survive, what are we going to do about them?" Morl Klun asked. "They're an anomaly that isn't going to fit in with any plan for rebuilding Earth. They don't need rebuilding, and they won't want any. What they will want is an opportunity to trade for materials that are in short supply. After two hundred years of scarcities and scrimping to make what they have last, their shortages must be devastating. Can we rebuild Earth on two different levels simultaneously?"

"We'll have to," I said. "The isolated tribes that are scattered about this planet desperately need the things Iceland has to offer—animals for food and clothing and transportation and such technological competence as still survives here. Iceland desperately needs metals and wood. It's a natural trade situation—but will Iceland accept any kind of products from the mainland?"

"Not knowingly," Morl Klun said. "They accepted us only because they thought we came directly from outer space. They're not going to trade with other Earth peoples as long as they think that the slightest contact with the mainland means death, and it'll take more than Wiln Marra's sleight of hand with colored lights to convince them that the danger of plague is past."

8

We slept exhaustedly until noon the following day, when we awoke marveling at how much had happened during the two days since I first set the landing craft down in the town square. After we had eaten, we lowered the ramp and found Rek waiting faithfully. A young male his own age was keeping him company.

"If you please," Rek blurted, "we have arranged a display of things we have to trade."

"Good thought," Morl Klun said. "Let's go see it."

I expected another enjoyable stroll along streets paved with stone and lined with the neat stone buildings we already had admired; but our destination was a large, two-story building across the square. As we moved toward it, I looked back and saw a group of adults and children gathered at the rear of our landing craft. I told Wiln Marra that he had overlooked some patients; but these people were not interested in medical treatments. In the turmoil of the previous day's events, they hadn't satisfied their curiosity about the strange object from outer space.

Rek hurried back to chase them away, and I hurried after him to prevent it. "Let them look," I said. "Let them go inside and look, if they like. Nothing there will harm them, and there's nothing that they can harm."

The sudden elevation from outcast to someone of genuine importance had a heady effect on Rek, and he resented my interference. He wheeled and strode haughtily away.

In the building across the square, we were led to a large room on the lower level, where a trades fair had been hastily assembled. Several young people of Rek's age, both male and female, were waiting eagerly to guide us through this display of Iceland's wealth and crafts. They were wearing their holiday costumes. They were gay, smiling, robustly healthy young people, and their masterfully crafted, colorful clothing gave them an aura of wealth. I thought ruefully of the shoddily clad Detroit Tribe.

I said quietly to Morl Klun, "We should trade for that bale of fibers so John's son and his people can have winter clothing."

He laughed scornfully. "What would they do with it? They wouldn't know how to begin to process it. We should trade for complete outfits of clothing for the entire tribe."

"No." I shook my head emphatically. "Gifts will make them totally dependent on us. Eventually they'll have to learn to make their own clothing. Why not now?"

"Because they can't keep themselves warm with eventualities. Their first problem is to survive the coming winter. Handcrafting clothing from fiber to garment requires considerable knowledge and skill." He spoke to Rek. "Would you have any problem in providing clothing for fifty-two people?"

"None at all," Rek said with bland confidence.

One of the young women interposed a more practical answer. "There would be no problem if we knew the sizes of those who were to wear the clothing."

"They're easily obtained," Morl Klun said. "We'll arrange a trade for you —fifty-two outfits of clothing for something you need."

He was fishing for a reaction, but he got none at all except nods of satisfaction. It didn't occur to the Icelanders to ask who or where those fifty-two people were, and the import of this proposed trade with the mainland escaped them. We followed our guides past the displays of Iceland's wealth: dried herring; animal products that included hides, dried meat, fibers, cloth, finished clothing, and an assortment of milk products—powdered milk, butter, cheese. There were artworks—carvings in stone and bone—and paintings, but the paucity of color was a reminder of the shortages Iceland had to contend with. Nothing was offered of metal or wood.

It was an impressive display from a people who had survived two worldwide devastations. We were urged to touch, to handle, to taste. We had circled the room and were asking questions about the last objects, the art display, when a voice boomed out coldly, "What is this?"

Three men in rough work clothing stood in the doorway. One of them, a sturdy, robust elder with white hair and beard, took a pace forward and spoke again. "Well, Rek Steamler, are you unable to answer a simple question?"

"We are displaying the products of Iceland," Rek said proudly.

"The aliens have brought this island its third taste of plague death. Would you foolishly invite another visit?"

The angry and embarrassed Rek was not an outcast on this encounter; his young confederates, both male and female, boldly gathered around him in support. The elder faced them, his own face reddening with a suppressed anger that threatened to become rage. The other two men, middle-aged but looking oddly youthful because they were clean-shaven, merely watched thoughtfully.

The white-bearded elder turned abruptly and directed his venom at me. "You have done enough damage here, Kera Jael," he said. "Your great-grandmother destroyed this world. Now you are attempting to finish off its survivors. As Prime Minister, I ask you to leave. Now."

"We are peaceful traders," I told him. "You have products that we can find a use for. We will pay for them in materials that Iceland needs. This is not an act of destruction. My great-grandmother did the same. She destroyed nothing."

One of the middle-aged men spoke. "Let's not be hasty, Ira. We can't claim that the aliens have brought death when no one has died. It will cost us nothing to listen."

Ira dismissed Rek and his confederates with a contemptuous gesture. "These ignoramuses presume to exercise authority that belongs to the Althing by law. I shall prefer charges against all of them. The aliens have landed here unlawfully. I shall likewise prefer charges against them."

The middle-aged man stepped forward; Ira wheeled and faced him while the other Icelanders watched tensely.

"Our forefathers had the wisdom to save Iceland despite the calamities that surrounded them," the middle-aged man said. "Take care that you don't void in anger the fruits of their careful planning. The hereditary position of factor survives because they wanted the memory of the alien traders kept alive and so that Iceland would be prepared to profit if they returned. They considered the matter of utmost importance. Rek is merely fulfilling the function that is his by tradition, by training, and by law. He should be commended."

"Do you challenge my authority?"

"I challenge your authority and your judgment."

"I shall call the Althing into emergency session at once!"

"Please do. If you had been alert to your responsibilities, it would have been done two days ago."

Ira stalked away. The middle-aged man turned to us, smiled, and said pleasantly, "I'm Jorn. Jorn Cloudler, Jorn of the Clouds, and Ira likes to pretend that I usually leave my head there."

"Is the Althing a council of elders?" I asked.

"It is a council of elected representatives. Of course you aren't familiar with Icelandic history. Before the war, our Althing was the oldest parliamentary assembly on Earth. Now I suppose it's the only one. The Prime Minister and his cabinet are responsible to the Althing. Unfortunately, too many of its members are elderly. Our elders have more time for politics than the rest of us, but in normal times there is little for them to do but argue, and by electing them to the Althing, we make it possible for them to argue with each other instead of plaguing their fellow citizens. In our rare times of crisis, we always wish the Althing had more youthful members."

I felt like blushing. I had hurriedly studied Icelandic history, but I'd paid no attention to the history of its government.

Ira came storming back. He handed a disk of metal to Jorn and one to the other man, whose name was Var. These ornate coins were of aluminum, and they were struck from a masterfully engraved die. They showed Iceland's natural beauties in miniature. The disk served as the summons to the emergency meeting.

To my astonishment, Ira stonily presented a disk to Rek before he wheeled and stomped out. "Rek—a member of the Althing?" I exclaimed.

Jorn smiled. "He's a nonvoting member. It's a distinction that accompanies his hereditary office. Since he doesn't have to stand for election, like the rest of us, he can fearlessly ally himself with every unpopular cause. Sometimes I think we need more hereditary members, but there are also times when I think Rek overdoes it." He turned to Rek. "How have you chosen to honor our guests?"

"With a feast," Rek said defiantly.

"Ira will want to know—of whose food?"

"Many have volunteered food out of gratitude."

Jorn nodded. "Well thought. It would be tactful to invite the Althing to this feast."

"Everyone will be invited."

"But the Althing is not 'everyone,' and too many of its members would resent being thought of as 'everyone.' It would be tactful to extend special invitations and provide places of honor."

"Perhaps," Rek muttered. He still sounded rebellious.

"At the beginning of the emergency meeting," Jorn persisted, "offer your special invitation. Then leave the discussion to me."

Rek regarded him sullenly. For a moment he teetered on the brink of eruption. Then he subsided and muttered, "Very well. I will arrange for the places of honor."

He went out. Jorn smiled after him sadly. "Youth," he murmured. "Youth is inclined to recklessness. It flouts danger. It prances on the edge of a cliff and leaps blindly over geysers. It delights in taunting the old. It especially infuriates the old by occasionally being right. Few elders who are also politicians can tolerate the thought of anyone else being right."

"Since you are neither young nor old, I suppose that you are caught in the middle of these clashes between youthful recklessness and venerable intransigence," I said.

"I attempt to leaven both positions with moderation," he confessed. "But it is never easy."

"What is it that Rek wants?"

"He wants to sail a ship to the mainland, as Leif Ericson did many centuries ago, and bring back a cargo of wood. We need wood badly to renew our fishing fleet."

"That sounds like a splendid idea," I said.

"So say the young. The old affirm that the wood is a splendid idea, but they ask, persistently and hostilely, what else he would return with. There was no Mainland Fever for Leif Ericson's crew to contract. The mainland also may harbor other dangers that are beyond our imaginations, even though our imaginations are capable of fabricating far worse dangers than any that could exist. So the elders vote 'no' year after year. Our young people, with justifiable concern about our diminishing fleet, are in a state of near rebellion, and we of the middle years wonder whether there is a middle ground, a method of prudently obtaining the wood that we need while avoiding the dangers. Now I must attend this emergency meeting and strive to exercise prudence in another direction." He turned to Rek's colleagues. "Consider yourselves the temporary hosts of these visitors. Make them welcome. Minister to any need they express. Show them what they would like to see. Tell them anything they want to know. Conduct yourselves so that if the Althing commits the gross foolishness of ordering them to leave, they will still remember Iceland with pleasure."

He gave us a nod and a smile and left.

Morl Klun took a deep breath. "That was educational. Would it be in order to ask when this feast is to take place?"

"At the twilight," a youth answered promptly.

"That's a splendid time for a feast," Morl Klun said with a smile. "It permits an entire day of preparations, and a feast that requires that long to prepare is one to look forward to. I suggest that we return to the landing craft and wait. Jorn's words were generous, but if distrustfulness dominates the Althing, I wouldn't want to leave an increment of suspicion around those who made us welcome."

"Agreed," I said. I told the young Icelanders, "We'll wait at our landing craft. When the Althing has completed its deliberations, let us know the result."

We recrossed the square and found the group of townspeople still curiously gathered about the landing craft. Or perhaps it was another group. None seemed to have taken advantage of our invitation to enter and inspect it. We entered it ourselves and closed the ramp.

"The fact is," Morl Klun said, "I was getting hungry. And it would be questionable etiquette to ask for food when you've just been promised a feast."

We ate, and then we rested, waiting for one of two things to happen: the delivery of an ultimatum to leave or an official invitation to make ourselves welcome. Characteristically, the Althing produced neither. It debated most of the afternoon and finally decided to ignore us, an exercise in ambiguity that could be recognized as typical of the genus "politician" wherever it existed. Rek considered it a slimy feat of cowardice, and he would have said so at great length if Jorn had not told him good-naturedly that he should not vent his personal frustrations in public on festive occasions. The members of the Althing attended the feast—at least, some of them did—but they came as individuals, and the places of honor prepared for them were occupied by younger Icelanders who were eager to ask questions about our home in the stars.

We feasted. The variety of meat and fish dishes seemed astonishing to us after the culinary monotony practiced by the Detroit Tribe. The vegetable dishes were fewer and much more simply prepared. We were offered cold cow milk to drink, an experience totally new to us, and all three of us had our mugs refilled twice. The young people at our table did not allow the holiday atmosphere to be dampened by the fact that Ira seated himself across from us and glowered at Rek through most of the evening—when he wasn't glowering at us. It was slowly dawning on the Icelanders—the young ones, anyway—that our visit had lifted the specter of death that had hung over them for generations in tales vividly retold from father to son and mother to daughter. It was a horrible death that struck suddenly and without mercy and spared neither humans nor beasts, and we had routed it. If we brought the disease, we also cured it, and that meant that death was mortal. The momentous visit from outer space, so portentous for the future, was linked with the extinction of a menace from the past. The young people were *happy*.

I could not understand why the elders persisted in their gloom. After studying Ira's foreboding countenance through most of the evening, I expressed my perplexity to Morl Klun.

"I've been wondering about that, too," he said. "The only possible answer is that the Mainland Fever bugaboo had an underlying purpose that had nothing to do with the threat of plague. In destroying the threat, we've also shattered its usefulness."

"What sort of purpose?" I asked.

"Rek wants to sail to the mainland, like Leif Ericson, and bring back a cargo of wood. That would burst the boundaries of a comfortably circumscribed island world. Mainland Fever has been an excellent excuse for keeping the community's adventurous young people at home. Rek's hereditary position also serves a purpose. All of the speculation about Earth outside Iceland and the universe outside Earth has been made the responsibility of one person—who is ostracized. What a splendid method of keeping the Icelanders' minds on Iceland and honest work! Don't worry about the mainland—it's dangerous. Don't worry about the aliens' return. Both of those are the responsibilities of that wastrel Rek. Watch!"

Morl Klun turned to Ira. He called across the table, "What is your *real* objection to our trading wood for clothing?"

"Anything brought from the mainland is deadly," Ira said.

"But that simply is not true," Morl Klun told him with a smile. "Disease is caused by microbes, and it would be rare indeed for such life-forms to survive an enormous span of time without a host. If they have somehow managed to survive, the medical science of my people will control them and put them permanently to rest the moment they appear. There is no danger." He paused, and then he slowly spoke a deliberate challenge. "There is absolutely no danger."

"There are other dangers," Ira said stubbornly.

"What are they?"

"We do not need to know what they are to know that there are dangers. We Icelanders have survived indescribable hazards that we had no awareness of until they happened, and we did not do it by being careless. We survived because our ancestors exercised extreme caution in all things. They did not go looking for dangers, for that is the sure way to be overwhelmed by them. They wisely held themselves constantly alert for the dangers that came to them." He paused. "Besides, we have no critical need for wood. We already have a source of supply."

Morl Klun arched his eyebrows. "You have a source of supply for wood? I saw no forest during our descent."

Jorn, who was seated nearby, said dryly, "The ocean is our source of supply for many things. Occasionally the Gulf Stream brings us a floating tree."

Rek had been listening attentively. "But when that happens," he said bitterly, "we must beach the tree at an isolated place and leave it to rot for a year before we're allowed to use it."

Jorn said with a twinkle, "Now that the Mainland Fever is no more, and there is a cure for it if it does return, perhaps the Althing will no longer insist that we quarantine our gifts from the sea."

We sat late with the Icelanders, talking with them and freely answering their questions about other worlds and about the Regez Anlf. When finally they began to drift homeward, it was—to our surprise—Ira who remained the longest. He was troubled; he wanted to continue our talk in private.

"This beautiful island supports our people well," he said sadly. "It will do so as long as we continue to restrict our births. But the young people consider it a prison. Instead of looking at the beauty and bounty that surrounds them here, they dream of beauties beyond the horizon. They pretend that ugliness and danger could not exist there. Why does Rek persist in the insane notion of sailing a boat to the mainland?"

Morl Klun answered him with intense seriousness. "In Lee Lukkari's time, there still was memory of a famous mountain climber of this world who said that he climbed the tallest mountain because it was there. Rek wants to visit the mainland because it is there. The unknown is a challenge to intelligent peoples wherever they are. Your ancestor Eric the Red took a colony to Greenland. His son, Leif Ericson, took one to the mainland. Other humans explored this world; still others ventured to other worlds. Sometimes the objective was said to be material wealth, but often that was no more than an excuse. Humans venture into the unknown because, like the mountain climber said, it is there. This is the one human trait that, more than any other, brings progress. Don't condemn Rek because he has it."

"If we let Rek go, he will visit the mainland like Leif Ericson," Ira said. His voice throbbed with a terrible intensity. "He will return and tell of his adventures, and—also like Leif Ericson—he will want to go back again with other young people and establish a colony. Tell me—who owns the mainland?"

"Perhaps no one," Morl Klun said.

"Or perhaps someone—even you don't know! Perhaps many own it!"

I knew that there were only three widely separated tribes in all of the northeastern continent. The nearest, the tribe near Montreal, was more than a thousand kilometers from sections of the coast that an exploring party from Iceland was most likely to touch. Even if the Montreal Tribe had a firm notion of its own territory and a willingness to defend it, it seemed unlikely that its claim extended for such a distance or that it would even be aware of the Icelanders' landing. I tried to explain this to Ira.

"That doesn't matter," Ira said. "If Rek takes a colony to the mainland, sooner or later his people will move inland and clash with the tribe you mentioned. They will attempt to take whatever they want, and the result, always, is war. Leif Ericson had to battle those who came before them and claimed the land, and his people were driven out. Others remained and fought. Human history is a history of wars because of people like Leif Ericson and Rek, who insist on their right to go where they please and take what they want no matter who it belongs to. This is how humans destroy themselves. They take, and they fight and kill over it. This is why there are so few people left on Earth. We have a healthy and prosperous Iceland because my predecessors wisely prevented their people from taking what did not belong to them. I intend to do the same. Iceland is ours, and as long as we limit our births and share our possessions fairly, we will prosper. We may have to fight to defend our island, and we are prepared to do so, but the Althing is determined that we will never become involved in fighting because we are trying to take what belongs to others. Even trade can result in war, so we don't want trade. No debate or negotiation will weaken the Althing's position. We want no exploring. We want no trade. We want no contacts at all with outsiders—including yourselves. If they are forced upon us, we will terminate them as quickly as possible." He paused. "When do you plan to leave?"

"In the morning," I said promptly.

He nodded gravely. "I hope that you will never find cause to return."

He gave us one more grim nod that fluttered his white beard. As he strode away, Morl Klun grinned at me. "Kera Jael, I hope the Regez Anlf won't judge your talent for trading on the basis of your success in Iceland!"

9

Early the next morning, we had a final talk with Rek. I presented him with a Regez Anlf portable communicator. "We'll be speaking from time to time," I said when I had shown him how to use it. "If Iceland has a crisis, of any kind, let us know immediately."

He thanked me effusively, describing the gift as a window in the wall around Iceland that the Althing elders had constructed. He wanted to give us something in return.

"Maybe later," I told him.

I felt certain that the Icelanders had preserved a treasure trove of relics of Earth's perished technology. They knew that there would be no replacements of anything that they could not make themselves, so they had hoarded everything. I had in mind a dim, unshaped plan for a technological museum dedicated to the vanished past, but it could wait until we had ensured that Earth would have a future. The rado that John's son had given to me in exchange for his tribe's communicator still stood on a shelf in our headquarters room, untouched because of the crush of more urgent matters.

"About the clothing for fifty-two people—" Rek began.

"Ira is opposed to any kind of trade," I said. "So we'll leave the trading for later, too. Time changes all things. We may think of a different approach, or your needs may change, or even Ira may change."

"We would like to make you a gift of this clothing," Rek said. "We have a surplus of silver—"

"Silver!" I exclaimed. I was still fumbling with the Icelandic language, and I had to be reminded that "silver," in Icelandic, also meant wool—because that article had been the symbol of wealth in Iceland down through the centuries.

"We can easily spare this clothing," Rek said. "If you will tell us the sizes of the fifty-two people, we can quickly find what you need. Every family has extra garments."

I accepted gratefully, and I handed Wiln Marra the task of attempting to match the sizes of the Detroit Tribe with those of the sturdy Icelanders. Soon Rek and his colleagues were carrying bundles of clothing to our landing craft.

We took leave of Iceland with warm farewells, and most of the town's population turned out to watch our departure. Ira and his Althing contemporaries were conspicuous by their absence, but Jorn was on hand to add his farewell salute to those of the young people.

As soon as we left the ground, I turned the controls over to Morl Klun and got busy with a plan of my own. I called the *Hadda* and had a brief talk with Ilia Sonal. She paraded her objections as glibly as usual, but in the end she could not logically forbid a brief landing by some of the *Hadda*'s technicians on a deserted stretch of coast. I stated for the record that they were needed on a project that had enormous potential importance for our mission.

I selected that coast myself, a heavily wooded shore in what had once been Labrador, and two landing craft loaded with technicians met us there. I selected twenty-one enormous oak trees—oak being a preferred wood for primitive boatbuilding—and felling them and trimming them into logs was the work of less than an hour. Bundling the logs into packages that the landing craft could handle took longer, but by late afternoon the job was done. The three craft flew into the dusk with their bundles, traveling low over the sea. It was night when we approached Iceland, and we left the logs on a remote beach on the island's northwest peninsula.

Then we dismissed the technicians and returned to our own base in the Detroit River. The next morning, I called Rek. "We have left a gift for you," I told him and described the location. "Tell Ira that this is a token of our appreciation for the warm hospitality we received in Iceland, and we'll be offended if it is not accepted."

"And that," I told Morl Klun and Wiln Marra, "might even convince a few Icelanders that trade is a worthwhile activity. Now let's take the clothing to John's son and see what his reaction is to the idea of trade."

Fall was already touching the Detroit region. Leaves had begun to turn color; fog lay on the river in the morning and delayed the start of the fishers. If the tribe had given any thought to facing the rigors of winter in its scant clothing, it showed no sign of it. Neither had there been any visible effort to devise new clothing. All fifty-two members were well fed, and there was an impressive quantity of smoked and dried fish stored for the coming winter. Apparently that was considered preparation enough.

We were welcomed with a feast of fish and fish stew. Afterward, we invited the entire tribe to the river bank, and we unloaded the bundles of clothing from the launch.

The natives were overwhelmed. They abandoned their usual modesty in an orgy of dressing and undressing. With peals of laughter they exchanged garments, paraded, pawed through the bundles, examined, rejected, tried on different sizes. The males had to model the female dresses; the females coquettishly flung themselves about in male trousers. There was one male worksuit of leather that almost sparked a riot until John's son peremptorily appropriated it for himself. It fit him badly. Rek had furnished us with three complete outfits per person, two sets of drab but eminently practical work clothing and one of holiday attire in colors, and the shuffle continued until the entire tribe had assumed holiday clothing.

John's son approached me, beaming his delight. It was a warm day, and he was perspiring under two oversized sweaters, trousers, and a long skirt gathered about his chest.

"Please send our gratitude to those who make this gift to us," he said earnestly. He fingered the cloth of the skirt. "Where did they learn to do such things?"

"They've always known," I said. "They live on a large island in the ocean, and the war did not totally destroy things there as it did here. The Beesee touched them only lightly. They still have their herds of animals that supply them with fibers and leather and other materials, including food, and their ancestors learned the effective use of these things over many generations and passed the skills to their children."

John's son was immensely curious about the animals and the method of making clothing. He listened raptly while I described Iceland and the lives of its people. Then I chanced to mention that the Icelanders were probably Earth's last surviving community of whites.

He leaped to his feet. "There are no more whites," he said angrily. "The Beesee killed them all."

"The Beesee destroyed only two communities in Iceland," I said. "The others survived."

"Whites made this clothing?"

"They did. They sent it to you as a gift."

He towered over me. His solemn black face had assumed an expression that I first interpreted as astonishment, but I was wrong. It was rage. He began to remove the garments, and his fury grew as he struggled to extricate his limbs from binding sleeves or legs. As each item fell free, he wiped his feet on it. When he was totally nude, he kicked the clothing into a pile and went to seek his discarded rags. He spoke to the others. They abandoned the clothing where they stood, and the entire tribe faded back into the forest.

"If you had some wild vision of setting John's son's people to cutting down trees for trade with Iceland, you can forget it," Morl Klun said ruefully. "We'll have to restudy Earth's racial problems. What could have happened to make the hatred persist through all those years of noncontact?"

Wiln Marra was incredulous. "They simply refuse to think about winter before it arrives. It's amazing that we persuaded them to lay in a stock of food."

"I'm wondering about the Icelanders," I said. "We didn't tell them that the clothing was intended for a tribe of blacks. Would they have donated it if they'd known that?"

I feared that we had alienated our Detroit Tribe by offering them clothing made by whites, but on our visit the next day we were received with the usual grave hospitality. John's son didn't mention the clothing again, and neither did we.

We agreed that there was little more we could do for John's son's people before winter. I wanted to begin our contacts with the other North American tribes, but first I wanted to renew my work experiment with the three young males and three young females. The problem was to devise a reward for them. This had been the fatal flaw in my first experiment. Ken Jordan's young people had the incentive of jobs with excellent pay and a promising future. But money had no meaning to the youth of the Detroit Tribe even if we were to contrive some, and a tribe that would refuse to accept desperately needed winter clothing in the fall, for whatever reason, was not about to work hard for a future harvest of anything. I learned that when we tried to encourage them to clear some ground for spring planting.

I wanted to solve the problem. I also wanted to know whether all of the black tribes were equally intransigent. While I worked on a long report about the Icelanders for Naslur Rayl, Wiln Marra and Morl Klun paid the Detroit Tribe a visit for the specific purpose of finding out what kind of wage might inspire the young people to work.

Morl Klun was back in little more than an hour. He strode into our headquarters room with a broad grin on his face, seated himself nonchalantly, and announced, "We're in serious trouble."

"That's nice," I said. "Tell me about it so we can laugh together. A funny crisis is just what I need."

"You've got one," he said. "It's absurdly funny, but it's no laughing matter at all. One of the native girls is pregnant."

"But that's wonderful!" I exclaimed. "Isn't everyone delighted?"

"It's a catastrophe, and everyone is furious. The girl, Sulette, is one of the young people you were trying to teach to work. You took them away from the control of their tribe, which gave them the freedom to find other ways to pass the time when they weren't working. As you know, they did very little work. The problem is that the boy is considered too young to have a mate, and the girl had already been claimed by one of the elders. All kinds of customs and regulations and taboos and laws have been violated."

"Customs and regulations and taboos and laws—phooey," I said. "Don't they want the tribe to survive? Stop that—you said it was no laughing matter."

He clapped a hand to his mouth, though his body continued to shake. "Don't you remember?" he asked when he could speak.

Suddenly I did, and we both dissolved in laughter. My great-grandmother, Dana Iverson, had been in charge of Ken Jordan's young people, and she'd also had to cope with pregnancies that the society of that time frowned upon. But she had coped, and so, I thought, would we.

"Where's Wiln Marra?" I asked.

"He's examining all the females to see whether any more might be pregnant. He's elated, and he's trying to convince John's son that times have changed, and tribal taboos must change, too. The future belongs to the new generation, and the young people should be permitted to marry."

"Of course."

"He wasn't making any noticeable progress, but he was trying. John's son's attitude seemed to be that in spite of all of our good works, and the food and the fishing and the medicine and tools and shelters, his tribe would have been better off if they'd never seen us."

"It may be that we've been using the wrong approach," I said slowly. I thought for a moment. Then I jumped to my feet. "A drastic change is in order. Come on."

I went to our communications center and called John's son on his portable communicator. Eventually its beep summoned him. I told him sternly that I would be arriving in two hours with an important message, and I wanted to present it to all of the tribe. He stammered objections. I said, "I know some may be fishing and some gathering, but I want everyone there. *Everyone.* Understand?"

He understood.

I turned to Morl Klun. "This requires some preparations. Let's get to work."

When we strode into the forest clearing slightly more than two hours later, the entire tribe was assembled and waiting. Wiln Marra, as curious as any of the natives, was making himself inconspicuous in the background. All of the attention centered on me; I was attired in a long cloak that completely enveloped me from neck to ankles, and that astonished the natives. They watched me with mouths agape.

I stood motionless for a full two minutes, just for effect. Then I tossed the cloak to a scowling Morl Klun, who stood behind me like a dutiful attendant. He disapproved vehemently of what I was doing, but I had been adamant. It was too obvious that his approach hadn't worked.

The natives took one panicky glance at me and sank to the ground, eyes averted.

I was wearing the Lee Lukkari clothing I had displayed for the Icelanders, who had not recognized it. These natives did. I probably looked more like the portrait in their shrine than the real Lee Lukkari would have.

"Lee Lukkari is angry with you," I told them sternly. "She has sent her personal representatives, her great-granddaughter and two great-grandsons, to help you pay the debt you owe to the future for your survival in a time of trouble. You have defied their teachings. Tell me now whether there is any reason why Lee Lukkari shouldn't punish you as she punished Earth's white population."

John's son looked up as though he wanted to speak. Then he thought better of it and lowered his eyes again.

"You were shown how to build yourselves a safe village," I went on. "But the only buildings completed are those you did with Lee Lukkari's representatives helping you. You were shown how to make clearings for the planting of crops next spring, but not one of them is half finished. You have refused the winter clothing that Lee Lukkari's wisdom provided. Now you defy Lee Lukkari's wishes concerning the mating of your young people. Listen to me! Sulette—come here!"

Sulette was terrified, but she managed to stumble forward. She sank to her knees in front of me.

"Who is the father of your child?" I demanded.

Her whisper was inaudible, but I already knew the name. "Car!" I called. "Come here!"

The youth came as though he'd already been sentenced to be executed and sank down beside her.

"Do you want to marry Car?" I asked Sulette.

She whispered, "Yes."

"Do you want to marry Sulette?" I asked Car. His lips moved, but no sound came out. I asked the question again, and he nodded.

"It is Lee Lukkari's command that young people be permitted to marry when both parties are willing," I said. "Therefore it is my intention to perform the solemn ceremony that will unite Sulette and Car. Is there anyone here who dares to object?"

John's son thought that he did and then changed his mind. I performed a marriage ceremony, improvising as I went along, and I made a show of it. The natives were awed, and even Morl Klun was sufficiently impressed to lose his scowl. When I had given the newlyweds Lee Lukkari's blessing, I called for Tild, the tribe's eldest female.

"Take Sulette in charge," I told her. "Car is not to be permitted to claim his bride until he has a home to take her to." I strode to the edge of the clearing where we had laid out ground plans for dwellings. "He is to build a house here, with his own hands and with such help as his friends give him." I marked the place with a stomp of my foot. "The house must be as large and as well constructed as those already built. It must be furnished so as to provide comfort. When Car has done that, then Sulette shall be free to join him. Until then, guard her well. Other youths wishing to marry, and having a girl who is willing, will have Lee Lukkari's consent, but only after they have prepared homes for their brides. Now, then. On your feet, all of you."

I led the entire tribe to the river bank, where Morl Klun and Wiln Marra loaded them with the wool clothing the Icelanders had donated. They carried it back to the village under close supervision and assembled the various outfits and hung them in one of the completed buildings.

"You will claim the outfits that most closely fit you," I said. "When the weather turns colder, you will wear them. Lee Lukkari arranged this to ensure the tribe's good health during the coming cold weather. She also arranged that you would be taught to build good houses for yourselves. When I return, I want to see them completed. Remember—Lee Lukkari is watching!"

Morl Klun released a cloud of smoke. When the natives had stopped rubbing their eyes and coughing, I had vanished. It was crude but effective, as Wiln Marra told me afterward. Morl Klun didn't think so, but he was still sulking because he disapproved of my exploiting the natives' superstitions. Even he had to admit that when he and Wiln Marra stopped their polite counseling and issued stern instructions, the natives listened and obeyed. John's son had been told precisely what we expected to find when we returned, and he had not argued.

"You shook them up," Wiln Marra said jubilantly. "Also, I gave them a stern farewell sermon about the debt they owe to the future. It'll change their whole outlook for maybe as long as ten minutes. But you were right—we were using the wrong approach."

"They'll need some reinforcement," I said. "I'll ask the *Hadda* for a modulator to disguise my voice so I can send them an occasional message by communicator in the guise of Lee Lukkari."

"Good idea," Wiln Marra said. "Now what are you going to do about Rek's people?"

"I don't know," I said. "We can't treat them like primitives. But it's obvious that we're going to have to treat the primitives like primitives if we're to achieve any measurable progress. And if we want continuing Regez Anlf support, our progress had better be measurable."

10

That ended the first phase of our attempt to rebuild human civilization on Earth. We had a comfortable base, we were working well together as a team, we knew what our problems were, and we had solved some of them. In our contacts with communities of natives, we could list one success and one failure. Fifty percent seemed like a very good ratio, and I was confident that we could ultimately convert that failure to success.

With the vision of a vengeful Lee Lukkari hovering over it, the Detroit Tribe was energetically pushing the construction of its permanent village, and I was able to stop worrying about the problem of motivating the natives to do some work. Morl Klun continued to mutter complaints about my violation of all of the time-tested principles of dealing with primitives, and I continued to tell him to shut up.

"Your principles don't work," I told him, "and I know why. They were devised for the study of natives by scholars who were scrupulously following dicta that forbade them to change the natives in any way. But we want to change them. We've got to change them if only to teach them to survive, and to do that, we've got to do more than study them. From now on, we're using a different approach."

"It won't work," he said gloomily. "This particular tribe worships Lee

Lukkari. When you flaunt your short skirt for tribes that have never heard of her, it'll take years to undo the damage."

"Until I find out otherwise, I'm going to assume that everyone has heard of Lee Lukkari," I said. "The Detroit Tribe had. The Icelanders had. Also, I happen to like that short skirt."

I had one chore to take care of. I asked Ilia Sonal to install a three-stage communications center in our office. I wanted the best equipment the *Hadda* could provide for handling global communications. These would become complicated when we had supplied all of the Earth tribes with communicators. I wanted the best trans-space equipment so I could send my reports directly to Naslur Rayl. I suspected Ilia Sonal of editing material sent by way of the *Hadda*. Finally, I asked for an audiovisual sweep that would cover the solar system. When Ilia Sonal wanted to know what possible use that would be to us, I told her I wanted to see her face to face when she was trying to evade my requests. She told me I was impertinent and cut off in a huff, but it happened to be true.

The *Hadda*'s technicians went to work, and we embarked on Stage Two of rebuilding Earth's civilization: an inventory of human resources on the planet. We set out to systematically contact all of the Earth tribes.

We dropped our landing craft through a thick cloud cover that overhung the St. Lawrence River valley. Like Detroit's ruins, those of Montreal were overgrown with a forest that stretched to the water's edge. The river lay like a shimmering, untraveled highway dotted with a multitude of gems. In summer, the scattered islands would have been emeralds, but now, since the fall change of deciduous foliage was further advanced than around Detroit, they looked dullish red or yellow from the air.

And the river was not completely untraveled. The Montreal Tribe had crude fishing boats. There were ten of them visible off the point of land where the village stood, and a scattering of others could be seen both upstream and down. The houses were of logs, sturdily built and arranged in a well-ordered pattern. This was no tribe of impoverished refugees.

Over Morl Klun's vehement objections, I landed in the center of the village, dropped the ramp, and sat back to wait. The natives did not flee in terror as he had predicted. Cautiously, but curiously, they gathered about the landing craft. They seemed expectant, rather than frightened. When a sizable audience had collected, I made my entrance, prancing down the ramp in my short skirt. It was a chilly day, and the wind off the river had a cutting edge to it. I stood there looking out over the natives and cursing my great-grandfather's taste in feminine apparel.

Then a tribe elder came forward to meet me. We were uncertain as to the language we might encounter here; before the war, the dominant language had been French, but there had been a large English-speaking minority.

The dignified old black man spoke a recognizable English. He said, "Are you Lee Lukkari?" And then: "Why did you not speak to us on the rado?"

They were a sturdy, even robust, tribe of blacks. The Detroit Tribe had fattened up considerably since our arrival, but those people would have looked frail beside these healthy specimens. The Montreal Tribe differed from John's son's people in another way: They wore an air of quiet confidence. They had faced up to the problems of their environment and solved them. John's son's people had a furtive attitude and an air of always listening for pursuers.

The Montreal people called themselves Habs, though they had no notion of where the term came from or what it meant. Like the Detroit Tribe, they'd had the problem of fashioning clothing with limited means, and they'd contrived ingenious interweavings of vegetable fibers and bark cloth with strategic reinforcements of leather made from skirl skins—though they called the skirls nussets, and we were a long time in tracking the derivation of that term back to the French language. Their shoes were nusset-skin moccasins.

They had the look of a people who ate well and enjoyed their food, and the feast they invited us to share with them featured lavish servings of fish, legumes, bread, nut cakes, and a potent beer. The following day we returned their hospitality, and they politely feasted on Regez Anlf food. Obviously they preferred their own.

Their ancestors had struggled heroically against the same horrors the ancestors of the Detroit Tribe had faced, and even the young adults had memories of starvation winters, but now they had triumphed. They were as healthy as they looked. Wiln Marra's offer of a free medical clinic brought him only a few elderly patients who were suffering from rheumatism or arthritis, one female with advanced breast cancer, a wasted young male with a heart condition, and an assortment of children with mild ailments. The miracles he performed were received gratefully, but no rush of patients followed. No one else felt sick.

There were more than three hundred in this prosperous and growing community. When I told these people that we had come to help them, they seemed bewildered. They had no awareness of needing help.

They were happy. They sang songs around the night fire—songs with a cadence and inflection and words that seemed unrelated to the musical heritage that Regez Anlf files had recorded. Their English speech was sprinkled with strange words possibly derived from the region's French language, though we could establish no direct connection.

Their religious shrine contained a portrait of Lee Lukkari and a rado, both bewilderingly identical to those of the Detroit Tribe. I traded them a Regez Anlf portable communicator for the rado. We thanked them for their hospitality and told them that we would look in on them from time to time and exchange feasts with them. "If there is sickness, or hunger, or you lack something essential," I said, "tell us and we'll try to help. If one of your tribe is severely injured, the doctor will come as quickly as he can when you ask for him. If there is danger—"

But they could think of nothing that could possibly threaten them, and neither could I. They promised to use the communicator in a time of need, and we departed.

I told Morl Klun, "Those people don't want help any more than the people of Iceland wanted it."

"They can't imagine resources they've never experienced," he said. "We'll have to buy, trade for, or steal some of the Icelanders' animals. The living conditions of the black tribes would be transformed if they had the clothing materials and additional food sources that animals could supply. The loss of Earth's large animals was devastating to humans trying to survive in primitive conditions. And," he went on meditatively, "I still don't understand it."

From Montreal, we went directly to the bad tribe, the tribe that had displaced John's son and his people. It was located in the center of the Michigan peninsula in an area distinctive for its lack of significant features. There were no lakes nearby and only a small river.

The people of this tribe were city dwellers. A rural town had somehow survived the holocaust and the years of decay with fully half of its buildings still habitable, and the tribe lived in them. They posed a new problem for Morl Klun: They were primitives living in high-tek houses, lounging on high-tek furniture, even sleeping in high-tek beds. They used high-tek cooking utensils, though they cooked over open fires. It was no wonder that their predecessors, the people of the Detroit Tribe, had not learned to build primitive shelters.

We landed in the center of the town's principal street. As the excited natives gathered around the landing craft, we experienced a second revelation. Enormous stocks of cloth or clothing also had survived the centuries in usable condition. The tribe was outfitted in dazzling colors and patterns, even though the clothing was clumsily fashioned.

The tribe's elder greeted me with a ceremonial bow as I descended the ramp. "Lee Lukkari!" he exclaimed ecstatically. "Why did you not speak to us on the rado?"

We called these people the Town Tribe, and afterward we wondered whether they had taught us more about John's son and his people than about themselves.

The town was surrounded by a splendid growth of nut trees, but there were few skirls in evidence. Morl Klun muttered that if he were the only source of meat to a large community of humans, he also would keep out of sight. But it must have been the Detroit Tribe that decimated the skirl population; the Town Tribe fished the small river and even sent occasional expeditions to a large lake that was all of fifty kilometers away. The tribe's women practiced crude but efficient agriculture in the open land nearby—it was too late in the season for us to watch them at work, but they'd had a good harvest and stocked tubers and other plant foods for winter.

We looked for distinctions between these blacks and the other two tribes. The males' hair was kinkier. They were less robust than the blacks of the Montreal Tribe but taller. They ate more vegetables than either of the other tribes, and they consumed enormous amounts of nuts. Every dish they served at the feast they provided for us tasted strongly of nuts.

Morl Klun examined their meat dishes suspiciously for signs of cannibalism. He found none. "But that may mean either that they've already eaten their victims or that they keep the most prized delicacies for themselves," he muttered.

Our most interesting discovery was an enormous building with rusting steel walls in a small complex of storage buildings some distance from the town. The storage buildings contained the rusted remains of machines intended for road work. The large building contained salt piled more than a meter deep throughout. This was the source of John's son's lore of salt preserving.

The Town Tribe's rado was identical to the two I already possessed. This seemed odd. Its portrait of Lee Lukkari also looked identical to those owned by the Detroit and Montreal Tribes, and that was perplexing.

"But we know that Lee Lukkari made an impression," Morl Klun said. "We also know that mass-produced art was commonplace in Earth's high-tek culture. Probably portraits such as these were circulating within days of her United Nations appearance."

Wiln Marra conducted a successful medical clinic. I traded a Regez Anlf communicator for the tribe's rado, and we parted with mutual pledges of friendship and our promise of assistance whenever they needed it.

We returned to our base for a day of rest, and I placed my two new rados on the shelf in my headquarters room.

"Still planning to save them for the museums of future Earth?" Wiln Marra asked.

"Of course," I said.

"But will anyone be interested?"

"The people of the future will be avidly interested in the misguided civilization of their remote ancestors. Archaeologists will dig on the sites of all of the great cities for clues to mysteries of the past. They'll be delighted to have an item or two that's intact."

"Or they may be avidly disinterested," Morl Klun said. "They'll still have unpleasant ancestral memories of what the past's high-tek civilization did to itself, and they may not want a museum of reminders."

"In that case," I said, "we can put them in our own museums. The Regez Anlf needs reminders of its responsibility for what happened."

We headed south, and in the former state of Louisiana we found an extensive agricultural community of blacks whose ancestors had been farmers. Agricultural traditions had been handed down to them, and they had been spared a blundering learning period. The community contained more than five hundred persons in three villages under a single leadership, and each village was the center of its own communal farm.

We set our landing craft down beside the largest village, which was situated in rich bottom land beside a broad river, and I walked down the ramp toward a cluster of awed natives and was greeted with two questions: "Are you Lee Lukkari?" and "Why didn't you speak to us on the rado?"

The three villages were stable communities with viable economies. Despite the proximity of the river, they were inept fishers, but they caught enough to supplement their vegetarian diet. They had devised wheeled tools to assist them in cultivation, and their agriculture was richly productive. Wiln Marra considered their nutrition more than adequate. They had learned to fire pottery and even to make a serviceable cloth from the fibers of a native plant, though their milder climate made the clothing problem much less urgent than it was for the northern tribes.

Their only immediate needs were medical. Wiln Marra cured a few serious illnesses and successfully treated a number of minor afflictions, and they were properly grateful. Before our arrival, the seriously ill had died, and the minor afflictions produced long periods of suffering and only too frequently became major.

There was little more that we could do for these people, but there was much that they could do for us. We described the plight of the Detroit Tribe—a tribe of unfortunate blacks.

The chief nodded wisely. "All whites are dead. They sinned against the blacks, and Lee Lukkari punished them."

Our request for teachers was politely declined, but they willingly showed us whatever we wanted to see of their techniques of building and farming and cloth making. Morl Klun thought that eventually we would be able to arrange for trade with the Detroit Tribe—fiber for fish; but we would need more than a fast inspection tour before we could teach the Detroit Tribe to make cloth.

I admired the Louisiana Tribe's portrait of Lee Lukkari—identical to the others we had seen—and traded a Regez Anlf communicator for an identical rado. We moved on to our next planned stop, the tribe in the former state of Missouri.

Its village was located near an enormous river, and the members fished skillfully with nets woven of vines. They also had subsistence agriculture, and they lived in moundlike dwellings with walls and roofs of sod. They greeted me as Lee Lukkari and asked why I hadn't spoken to them on the rado. We shared feasts, we pledged friendship, and Wiln Marra conducted his medical clinic. In parting, we admired another identical portrait of Lee Lukkari, and I traded a Regez Anlf communicator for their rado.

On the Pacific coast, the pattern was repeated with a tribe that lived similarly to that of Montreal—except that it fished the ocean bays and the people lived communally in several enormous log buildings. Again I was Lee Lukkari, I admired a portrait of myself, and I traded a Regez Anlf communicator for a rado.

We returned to Detroit Base for two days of rest and report writing, and we briefly visited John's son and admired the progress with the village before we moved on to South America. We first visited the tribe at the mouth of the Amazon, which we called the Amazon East Tribe, and we spent several frustrating hours in attempting to communicate with the natives in Spanish before Morl Klun suddenly remembered that the base language in this part of the world had been Portuguese. Both Amazonian tribes recognized me as Lee Lukkari, but only the tribe at the mouth of the river had a portrait and a rado. The Amazon West Tribe had lost these irreplaceable relics. Both tribes were forest people, living on the bounty of the river and the fertility of the tropical jungle, and they suffered the severe health problems that environment produced. The Argentine Tribe also had settled near a large river. These natives fished effectively and supplemented their diet with small rodents, but they had a severe clothing problem. Again Wiln Marra conducted his medical clinic, and I admired the portrait of Lee Lukkari and traded a communicator for the tribe's rado.

We spent five days with each of the three South American tribes, and then we returned to Detroit Base to rest, to write reports, and to try to determine whether we had learned anything.

One thing was obvious. The rebuilding of Earth was going to be a larger —and much longer—project than anyone in the Regez Anlf had anticipated. Our lifetimes would not be long enough. The small tribes, the poverty of resources, linguistic problems that would intensify as we moved into Africa and Asia—these were matters that no one had anticipated. We had to consider the long-term implications of Earth's shortage of metals and the difficulties primitives would have in processing what metal they could salvage. We had to consider the possible importation of alien plants and animals and their inevitable impact on Earth's ecology. We had to consider ways and means of assisting Earth tribes that did not want assistance.

Most of all, we had to consider the impact of an enormously long project on the Regez Anlf. After a year or so, pangs of conscience would fade, and the Earth project would come to be regarded first as a nuisance and then as an intolerable expense.

"What do we do if we're suddenly ordered home?" Morl Klun asked.

"I won't go," I said. "I was ordered here to do a job, and I intend to do it."

"None of *us* would go," Morl Klun said confidently. "But the *Hadda* would. And how long can we function without support?"

"The question is how long we could function effectively on a global basis without support," I suggested. "We could work in a limited area indefinitely."

"I meant what I said. Once the supplies are exhausted—"

"You have a point," I agreed. "We'll have to do something about that."

"How will Ilia Sonal react?"

"Negatively," I said. "She always reacts negatively."

Wiln Marra started to protest, and we hushed him. "There are more than supplies involved," I said. "The *Hadda* has a wealth of technical talent sitting up there doing nothing. We should make every possible use of it while it's still here."

The plan we contrived required more persuasion than could be exercised through a face-to-face confrontation on our new communications installation. I didn't want to leave Ilia Sonal in a position where she could simply cut off when she became angry. I hopped up to the *Hadda* to confer with her. I presented the plan to her, and she listened with grave courtesy and then began to recite all of the objections we anticipated.

I nailed her quickly on the first two. The money for the supplies the *Hadda* held for us had already been appropriated, and the supplies had been selected by the Reclamation Team for its own use. The *Hadda*'s personnel had absolutely nothing to do when they weren't working for me, and Ilia Sonal's fiction about training programs was as silly as it sounded—which I didn't hesitate to point out to her. The *Hadda* was on station indefinitely. It would have ample time for training when we got our Earth program fully established and functioning.

Her lovely, cool, poised face took on a flush of anger. "Do you guarantee the safety of my personnel?" she demanded.

"The only dangerous life-forms on Earth are people, in a few widely scattered small tribes, and the *Hadda* personnel won't be working anywhere near them. I expressly forbid contacts between *Hadda* personnel and Earth natives. Your technicians will have no reason to leave the safety of their work sites."

"You're proceeding on the basis of a fallacious assumption," she said belligerently. "The rebuilding of Earth is your task—not the *Hadda*'s."

"The *Hadda*'s officially assigned function is to support the efforts of the Reclamation Team," I said coldly. "I'm presuming to draw upon that support. Isn't it available?"

"And you feel that one Regez Anlf base is not sufficient for a team consisting of three people?"

"It would be splendid for three people working in one place—if that happened to be the place. Unfortunately, we have a world to cover. We need bases strategically located on all the continents—even the unpopulated continents. I'm speaking for the record. Bases are needed for the convenience and efficiency of the Reclamation Team—both now and in the future—and also for their psychological impact on primitive mentalities. A base on the other side of the world has no meaning to the natives. One in distant mountains that can be pointed to assumes a supernatural stature. It's a reality they can visualize and turn to in time of need. This is highly important."

"And it's important even on unpopulated continents?" she inquired sweetly.

"Now—when technicians are available—we are making long-range plans that anticipate the future needs of Earth's population."

She abandoned her fictions. "Very well. Select your locations and submit the list. Subject to my approval of each one, my technicians will proceed."

"I'd prefer to do it this way," I said. "I'll indicate the general areas. Your technicians can select the sites they consider the most desirable, subject to my approval."

She agreed, and I returned to Detroit Base. *Hadda* technicians arrived on my heels to pick up the base-building machine that had been left there from Ken Jordan's day. They pronounced it operable; it would speed their work, since the *Hadda* had only one other such machine on board.

"You were wrong," Wiln Marra said triumphantly. "She's willing to cooperate."

"She cooperates in the most negative way possible," I told him.

"I think you're unfair to her."

"Perhaps so. As long as we get what we ask for, we needn't concern ourselves about her mental attitude. Now we can get on with our work."

We made the jump to Africa, and while we occupied ourselves with the tribes there, the *Hadda*'s technicians began to build new bases for us. A single Regez Anlf base had been inconvenient even in Ken Jordan's time when Earth still had a lavishly developed communications network to serve it. To conveniently serve the needs of a future Earth population, we wanted a network of bases—a minimum two to a continent. I asked Ilia Sonal for a protective dome for each base roughly enclosing the area of Detroit Base, with one all-purpose building that eventually could function as a hospital—because medical services were a universal need and a means by which we could gain and keep the natives' confidence—and a volume of underground storage capacity that made her blink in astonishment. She couldn't reasonably object—underground storage capacity cost very little except in terms of work and machine increments, and neither her machines nor her technicians had anything better to do.

It was only when I followed my request for bases with a requisition for a landing craft at each base that she exploded. Her diatribe made the communicator sputter.

"Listen," I said when I could make myself heard. "Thus far, the three members of the Reclamation Team have been working together. But after our first round of contacts, we'll be able to cover three times as much territory by working alone, and we'll be three times as effective. We also need spares in case of breakdowns."

"I have never, in all of my experience, heard of a landing craft failure, for any reason," she said caustically. "It's the most reliable machine ever built."

"Your experience doesn't include situations where a failure could isolate you on a primitive planet," I answered just as caustically. "We have no technicians to call on in emergencies. We need spares rigged for remote control. We also have to provide for future personnel."

"Future personnel can bring their own," she snapped. "I'm not stripping the *Hadda* of landing craft to meet your needs for the next hundred years."

She finally agreed to let us have six in addition to the one we already had, and that was better than I'd expected. I didn't tell her that eventually we hoped to train our own native pilots.

The *Hadda* technicians selected sites near water and on an island if possible. The water was important. The base-building machine fabricated the dome out of air and water. One at a time I approved the sites, and they began their preliminary surveys. And Morl Klun, Wiln Marra, and I continued our work with the African tribes.

We were in Africa for more than a hundred days.

I had expected the black tribes there to make the easiest adaptation to a primitive Earth. Their living conditions would have changed the least; they were still primitives when the holocaust struck, and I reasoned that they could continue a way of life they were already accustomed to.

This reasoning ignored the roles that animals had played in their primitive existence. The more primitive the tribes, the more directly dependent they were on their animals, and they had enormous problems in adapting to the loss. They were unclothed, suffering severe malnutrition, and wracked by diseases.

But all of them had rados and portraits of Lee Lukkari.

The linguistic problem was severe, but we managed. Oddly enough, though the Regez Anlf files had not contained Icelandic, they did have several African native languages. I deduced that some student of exotic tongues had found them interesting.

We went to work treating the sick, giving the tribes adequate food, and trying to teach them to make use of the wealth that lay untouched about them. We showed them how to fish more efficiently. We tried to dispel their suspicions of plant foods they were unaccustomed to eating—sometimes we had monstrous superstitions to contend with. We worked ourselves to the point of exhaustion. Then we took brief vacations during which we replenished our supplies and paid courtesy visits to tribes we already had contacted.

And we returned to Africa to work harder.

Winter closed in on the northern tribes. John's son's people were now enjoying their permanent dwellings. Car had claimed his bride, Sulette, and I performed three more marriages during one of my visits. The Detroit area was snow-covered, and there were deep drifts where the Town Tribe and the Montreal Tribe lived. Morl Klun taught the youths of the Detroit Tribe to fish through the ice of the frozen lake near their home. Inside our Detroit Base, the warm, humid environment brought us a tall crop of hay where I had hoped for green lawns. *Hadda* technicians rigged a robot mowing machine for me—and when the grass was cropped short, the dandelions attempted to take over the base. They grew in such profusion, and so enormously, that I wondered whether we were dealing with a strain that had mutated during the holocaust. I meant to ask the *Hadda* technicians to devise a selective plant spray that would deal with them, but I kept forgetting. They were a very small problem compared with the situation that confronted us in Africa.

Eventually we were able to move on to Asia, and by that time we were recognizing patterns of development, though there were tantalizing exceptions. Tribes having a modicum of success with agriculture were likely to be descended from an agricultural society. Tribes having to learn it on their own rarely progressed beyond the stage of haphazardly gathering wild plants that were easily recognized as food. Tribes with access to fertile streams or lakes or rich ocean waters prospered in direct relationship to their mastery of an effective technique of fishing.

Earth people everywhere were desperately handicapped by the absence of animal life. There were animals other than skirls that were still extant, and these varied from place to place; but all were small rodents, many were tiny, and most were burrowers. All of the African tribes had been barely surviving when we arrived. A perplexing puzzle concerned a Southeast Asian tribe, where the growing of rice should have been a centuries-old tradition. The rice still grew wild in low areas where conditions favored it, but the black humans living there seemed not to recognize it in its native state as an edible grain. As Morl Klun pointed out, the fact that a particular tribe now lived in a former agricultural area didn't necessarily prove that its ancestors had lived there or even that they had been farmers.

We inventoried the planet's human resources. We made friends, we exchanged feasts when the natives had food reserves and made gifts of food when they did not. Wiln Marra healed the sick. I traded Regez Anlf communicators for rados when a tribe had one and made a gift of a communicator when it did not. One Asian tribe had two rados and two portraits of Lee Lukkari. I acquired both rados and, after a protracted trading session, also secured one of the portraits. "It'll make a first-rate family heirloom," I told Wiln Marra and Morl Klun.

Once we had visited all of the tribes and dealt with their most severe problems, we established a schedule so that each tribe would be visited regularly, given such continued assistance as it needed, and have the health of its members monitored. Along the way we inspected our new bases, checking the progress at each one and allocating the supplies to be stored there as soon as facilities were ready. To Naslur Rayl, I reported that Stage Two of our work was almost completed, and we were looking forward to Stage Three.

It was spring in the Detroit area when we returned to Detroit Base for a badly needed vacation. We caught up on our sleep, we visited the Detroit Tribe and admired their new buildings, I conducted two more marriage ceremonies, and we sponsored a special feast in honor of the four brides married previously, all of whom were pregnant.

We enjoyed walks in the spring forest by ourselves. Earth's forests were in several ways more pleasant places than they'd been when my great-grandparents Dana Iverson and Ken Jordan enjoyed them. Various parasitic insects, including the most ubiquitous pest of all, the mosquito, were no longer around. They became extinct when holocaust and Beesee wiped out the life-forms they preyed on. But the forests were also much lonelier, with no animals and few birds.

The Detroit Tribe had been so impressed by the treasure trove of tools we had dug up for them, and so eager to search for more, that I had lent John's son a metal detector. Now they owned a large collection of artifacts, most of them rusted almost beyond recognition, and I spent a day trying to identify these. There were tools, kitchen utensils, and household appliances, many that had once been motor-operated. I wasted an hour pondering the possible uses of half of a waffle maker, a contrivance whose function is not obvious and whose shape lends itself to technological mystification, and I finally took it back to the base to check against references. There even were fragments of radios. Items that were fairly intact and that had no immediate use for the tribe went onto shelves in our headquarters room along with my collection of rados, which now occupied a wall of its own.

We were more than pleased with the progress the Detroit Tribe had made, but here and everywhere else we were confronted with an economic insufficiency directly due to the loss of Earth's animal resources. Finally, in one of my regular conversations with Rek—by communicator; we had carefully avoided Iceland in our travels—I asked him to humbly petition the Althing and find out what payment would be acceptable for breeding stock of the large animals that had survived only in Iceland: cattle, sheep, horses, goats, pigs.

Rek reported back that the Althing was favorably disposed, since it was merely a question of giving up something Iceland had in plentiful supply to people who were in need and since no direct contact with the mainland would be required. Some Althing members felt that the trees we already had supplied were ample payment; others believed that any additional payment offered should be accepted.

However the argument resolved itself, it was certain that we would obtain the animals. We were elatedly in conference, discussing Earth plants and their products as potential items for trade with Iceland and wondering whether we could teach the natives to gather a product like rubber and whether the Icelanders would be able to process and use it if we did, when the blow fell. Suddenly the rados we had obtained from the native tribes in exchange for Regez Anlf communicators spoke.

All of them spoke, simultaneously, in the same voice. It was a sultry female intonation, and it pronounced its message enticingly in English and then repeated it in ten other Earth languages.

It said, "I am Lee Lukkari. I am returning to you as I promised. Push the switch on your rado to let me know where you are, and I'll come to you."

11

We were staring at the rados in total astonishment when our trans-space communicator cut in sharply. The voice was Ilia Sonal's, and her words had the rasp of command.

"Crisis Nine. All Personnel. Crisis Nine. All Personnel."

She was hitting the Regez Anlf panic button. We transferred our astonishment to the communicator and then to each other. Before I could focus my sputtering into words, Ilia Sonal's voice cut in again. "Crisis Nine to Point Two. I'm moving the *Hadda* to Point Two. Crisis Nine to Point Two immediately."

Morl Klun whistled softly. "She's pulling out!" he said incredulously. "She's actually pulling out!"

She was moving the *Hadda* from its Earth orbit opposite the moon to a solar orbit opposite Earth. This meant that the *Hadda* was in great and imminent danger—there was no other justification for such a move. Otherwise, she should have collected her groundside personnel before moving. She was acting for the safety of her ship and ordering the *Hadda* technicians who were at work on our bases to come to her in her new position—if they could.

From the rows of rados, the alleged Lee Lukkari's syrupy voice went on repeating its announcement in a succession of languages.

Ilia Sonal spoke again. "Crisis Nine for Kera Jael. Respond at once."

I moved to the communicator. "Kera Jael at Detroit Base. What's going on?"

"We've screened an Unknown approaching Earth," she rasped. "Report to the *Hadda* at Point Two immediately. The entire Reclamation Team is ordered to report to the *Hadda* at Point Two immediately. Kera Jael, Wiln Marra, Morl Klun, report to the *Hadda* at Point Two immediately. We're departing this system as soon as all personnel are collected."

"Hold everything!" I exclaimed. "I request immediate transmission of all relevant data. I must evaluate it in terms of my assigned mission."

Ilia Sonal's voice dripped liquid nitrogen. "Regez Anlf Regulation One requires instant departure from any system approached by an Unknown. That regulation overrides all others and has binding priority over every Regez Anlf mission. If you and your team do not report to me aboard the

Hadda as quickly as you can get here, I'll cite you for violating regulations and refusing to obey orders."

"Hold everything again," I answered evenly. "I am under direct order of the Council for a unique mission, and Regez Anlf Fleet Regulations don't apply. I've requested immediate transmission of all relevant data so that I can properly assess its probable impact on my mission. If you don't comply immediately, I'll cite you for refusing to obey your orders, which require both support and cooperation with my mission."

The screen flickered to life. Ilia Sonal's face looked out at us grimly. "The data will be transmitted," she announced. "The *Hadda* will depart this system as announced, estimated maximum two hours, regardless of your evaluation." The screen went blank.

Morl Klun went over and began fussing with the controls. We had our own limited space probe, but he picked up nothing at all within its sweep. "If it's coming from this direction," he said, "it hasn't approached Earth very closely."

Wiln Marra said apologetically, "She does have to act for the safety of her ship."

"We're entitled to know just how urgent the danger is," I said. "Precisely where is this Unknown? That electromagnetic transmission of the fake Lee Lukkari's voice could be coming from another galaxy."

"She said the *Hadda* has screened an Unknown approaching this system," Wiln Marra said.

"She did not," I told him. "That's what the regulation says. She said it was approaching Earth, which implies that it's already within the system. Nothing less than that could justify her panic, but I don't believe it. Is the *Hadda*'s entire watch enjoying Stimulation and Tranquillity? As long as her thinking is that muddled—"

I broke off. The screen flickered to life as the *Hadda* began beaming data to us. This time we saw the Unknown—a tiny, utterly insignificant-looking blob against the vast backdrop of space. I cut in our own magnification unit. Distance blurred the image, but it definitely was an Unknown. It was unlike any spaceship anyone in the Regez Anlf had ever seen or imagined, and it was not tiny. It was colossal. The data line indicated a size three times as large as the *Hadda,* and it was approaching Earth at a speed that was nothing short of spectacular.

But it was still far beyond the orbits of the system's most remote outer planets.

I snorted. "The *Hadda* certainly is not threatened—yet."

"It's coming awfully fast," Wiln Marra pointed out.

"If it's coming here," I said, "it's already braking. And it must be coming here. Otherwise, why the Lee Lukkari message? Shall we tell Ilia Sonal it isn't chasing her, it's just headed for Earth, and she can relax?"

"That wouldn't matter," Morl Klun said.

"We have to make a quick decision," I told the two of them. "What do we know?"

"They've been here before," Morl Klun said promptly. "They gave the natives the rados. They must have."

"What else?" I asked.

"They know about us," Wiln Marra said. "Maybe they know all about us. They know that Lee Lukkari commanded a Regez Anlf trading mission to Earth. They must have had the planet under observation at that time."

"Not from space," I objected. "Lee Lukkari's ship would have detected any observation from space. They may have had ground stations, or they may have found out about Lee Lukkari long afterward. In any case, sometime after the holocaust they returned and distributed the rados and portraits to surviving tribes of humans, and they promised that Lee Lukkari would return and that she would announce her return on the rados. I should have paid more attention to the rados and the portraits."

"This is an extremely deep matter," Morl Klun said meditatively. "I'm suddenly wondering whether the Regez Anlf was as responsible for the destruction of Earth as we'd thought. But what could these Unknowns want here? What's their purpose?"

"Certainly they aren't up to any good," Wiln Marra said.

We sat for a time watching the blob on the communicator screen and the data line that flowed beneath it. The strange ship was still approaching at extreme speed, but the *Hadda*'s instruments had detected a strong braking action.

And it was still far beyond the outer planets. Ilia Sonal had, quite properly, taken immediate action to collect the *Hadda*'s personnel when the approaching Unknown had been detected, but there was no necessity for the panicky exit she had ordered.

Her nerve had failed her, and—equally serious—her ship's organization had broken down. I said grimly, "You will have noticed that the Unknown wasn't detected until it started broadcasting the fake Lee Lukkari message. That means that the *Hadda*'s key personnel were caught napping."

"But that isn't our problem," Wiln Marra said.

"It's certainly made the situation more difficult for us," I told him.

"Our unesteemed captain has earned an official reprimand," Morl Klun said. "She's more concerned about the letter of her regulations than about the objectives of her mission and ours. I'd suggest that we file a complaint signed by all three of us."

"But her first responsibility is for her ship," Wiln Marra protested.

"Never mind that now," I said. "We have three responsibilities of our own. First, to find out what's going on. Second, to assess its probable impact on our mission. And third, to decide what we're going to do about it. Thanks to the *Hadda*'s goof and Ilia Sonal's jitters, we have very little time. Let's get on with it."

We watched the *Hadda*'s transmission more calmly than we had any right to, because we were witnessing history in the making. The Regez Anlf had never possessed such overweening conceit as to assume that it alone, among all of the intelligences and potential intelligences of the universe, was capable of developing faster-than-light space travel and exploring the stars. All of its actions were premised on the expectation that sooner or later its far-flung trading activities would encounter another such intelligence.

The regulation for handling this potentially dangerous event had been evolved centuries before, reviewed repeatedly, and never changed. The office of the Third Secretary had to be notified immediately. The ship that inadvertently made such a contact was to withdraw at once, collecting as much data about the Unknown as possible, and proceed to the nearest assigned neutral station. The object of this maneuver was to learn as much as possible about the Unknown while permitting the Unknown to learn as little as possible about the Regez Anlf. If the Unknown somehow managed to follow, the trail to the neutral station led nowhere.

An unknown intelligence posed a potential threat of superior weapons, superior machines, superior intelligence, or—much worse—inferior morals and ethics. Badly handled, such a contact could result in a ruinous war. And though it was considered an indescribably remote contingency, so serious was the potential danger that the Regez Anlf kept a specially constructed ship with a crew trained and alerted for just this situation.

Now that remote contingency had occurred. The *Hadda* would retreat to its assigned neutral station, a defense fleet would be rapidly assembled to form a cordon that would bar the Unknowns from Regez Anlf territory, the special defense ship would take what it hoped would prove to be a strategic position, and interminable meetings would be held to decide what should be done.

In the meantime, the people of Earth, who were the responsibility of our three-member Reclamation Team, would be left at the mercy of the Unknowns. As we stared at the screen and attempted to form our own evaluation of the data, the command decision I was going to have to make momentarily hung over me like a cloud of doom.

"Two points," I said slowly. "First, the people of Earth are likely to need our assistance now much more than they did before. Second, in the face of a probably hostile alien presence, our efforts to help them are certain to be severely restricted if not prevented altogether."

Morl Klun bounced out of his chair and stood over me. "Surely you're not thinking of leaving! We have more than an obligation to the people of Earth. We have an honor to uphold—two honors, that of the Regez Anlf and that of ourselves. Also, I'm convinced that we can render the greatest service to the Regez Anlf by remaining here and learning as much as we can about these Unknowns."

"*I'm* staying," I said. "I never considered leaving. But I'm not going to order either of you to stay. Make up your own minds—but you'll have to decide quickly."

"I'm staying," Morl Klun announced. He returned to his chair and faced Wiln Marra with a grin. "Unfortunately for the natives, the most important member of our team, by far, is our doctor, as has already been demonstrated. But our doctor persists in thinking with his glands, and his glands are about to leave on the *Hadda*."

Wiln Marra said bitterly, "It's nice to know that I'm not the only one who will miss my glands. These Unknowns may or may not complicate Earth's health problems, but those are complicated enough already. Of course I'm staying. But—" He turned appealingly to me. "No complaint about Ilia Sonal. She's merely doing her job."

"Doing it badly," I said. "We have too many critical things to do and too little time to concern ourselves about petty administrative matters like complaints. We're obligated to register our displeasure with the way she's handled this crisis, though. Watch."

I went to the communicator and called Ilia Sonal directly. She had composed herself since our previous conversation, and she looked as coolly poised as ever. She started to speak, and I interrupted her.

"This is for the record," I told her.

"Very well," she agreed. "We're recording."

"First, this Reclamation Team considers that it has an obligation to the people of Earth. Regez Anlf regulations for trading missions in no way negate that obligation. Our unanimous decision is to remain."

"When the Unknowns capture you," Ilia Sonal said icily, "they'll soon know everything you know—about the Regez Anlf and everything else— and the result may be disastrous. That's why Regulation One has overriding priority. When it is invoked, all other Regez Anlf regulations and orders are canceled automatically. Read your regulations!"

"The Unknowns will have to catch us first," I said cheerfully. "A planet is a large place to search for three individuals, and we have our Regez Anlf defenses. There'll never be a better opportunity to test them."

Before her silence could become overwhelming, I decided to retaliate. "Second, we enter a formal protest over the handling of this emergency by the captain of the *Hadda*. There is now indisputable proof that the Unknowns visited Earth previously. They may have been here during the previous Regez Anlf contact. It is overwhelmingly important to the Regez Anlf to learn as much as possible about the previous visits and their purpose. We are broadening the scope of our mission to include that objective. If the captain of the *Hadda* had attended to our reports, she could have made that interpretation for herself. Her panicky decision to depart when the Unknown was still in remote approach has seriously impaired our ability to plan for the ordeal ahead of us. I have reached the reluctant conclusion that Stimulation and Tranquillity were given priority on the *Hadda* over the support that our mission required. Every request that I made, every decision that I confided to her, every supply requisition that I filed was disputed by the *Hadda*'s captain, and the Unknown was allowed to approach so closely without detection that the captain had to declare a crisis where none should have existed."

Now she was glowering at me from the screen.

"These are our final instructions to the *Hadda*," I continued. "Load all

available platforms with our supplies. Balance the selection on each platform as well as possible. Send the platforms to all the bases that are sufficiently operational to receive them. This is our final message. I invite the
captain to record her comments, if any. Neither of us has time for debate.
The Reclamation Team has an enormous amount of work to do immediately. So does the captain—I want those supplies moving at once."

I cut off and turned to the others.

Morl Klun had his mouth puckered into a silent whistle. "That's what I
call knocking out all the props," he said admiringly. "Anything that happens from now on is going to look like her responsibility. She detected the
Unknowns too late; she left too soon; she ran a lax ship; her mission was to
support you, and she paid so little attention to it that she didn't know what
was going on; and if we run out of anything at all during the next twenty
years, it'll be her fault for not getting enough supplies down to us. If you
ever decide to leave Earth, don't go on her ship."

"I'll try not to," I said.

Wiln Marra was glum. "I still think she was right to act for the safety of
her ship."

"Her ship wasn't in danger," I said. "It still isn't. But don't worry—they
won't court-martial her without us there to testify."

I looked again at the screen, which had reverted to our view of the
unknown ship. The data strip showed that it was now braking decisively,
but there was no indication that it had detected either the *Hadda* or the
landing craft leaving Earth.

"We have some time," I said. "It's critically important that we use it
effectively. I'm going to talk with the tribes. They need to be warned at
once. I'll also tell them to expect a visit from one of us. We'll divide the list
into three parts, and one of us will call on each tribe and prepare it as well
as possible. Hiding places should be picked out. Emergency food supplies
should be cached there. All the tribe's stores except what will be used
immediately should be hidden. Each tribe will need a warning alarm—see if
you can rig something. As for us—everything we do from now on will have
to be concealed. Fly low. Secrecy is more important than speed. Each tribe
should prepare a place where a landing craft can be hidden on future visits."

"How much time do you figure we've got?" Wiln Marra asked.

"That depends on how cautious the Unknowns are. If they take time to
survey the situation, as they should, we may have several days. But we'll
have to work fast just in case they don't. Divide the list geographically.
Each of us will check the bases in the area to see which are operational and
what supplies are on hand."

As I settled into my task of talking with each of the scattered tribes, it
seemed to me that the Unknowns' timing had been miraculously in our
favor. We'd been able to make ourselves known to all of the tribes. We had
given them medical care and food and such help as we could contrive, and
we had asked nothing in return. Further, we'd told them we were always
available in time of need. They considered us friends, and they trusted us. It

seemed natural enough to them that I would be warning them that a time of danger was at hand. I went through the complete list, beginning with John's son and ending with a brief conversation with Rek.

The Icelanders worried me. Their conspicuous communities on a windswept island, and their herds of animals, made them terribly vulnerable. On the other hand, they were far more capable than the other natives of understanding the danger and taking measures to cope with it. I told Rek that I hoped to see him within a day, and that whenever I arrived, day or night, I wanted to meet with the Althing at once to describe the approaching danger and make suggestions.

Morl Klun and Wiln Marra left the tribes in the American continents to me because I would be starting last. They also left a box of alarms to distribute—electronic horns that could be heard for kilometers. I began my tour with the Detroit Tribe and set my landing craft down in the center of their village. There was no time to fuss with a boat.

The tribe gathered around the landing craft and watched uneasily as John's son stepped forward to greet me. My message had greatly alarmed them, but they thought only of a possible raid by the bad tribe in the north.

I gave John's son an alarm and demonstrated it; the booming rasp was much admired. "We have little time," I told him. I explained the necessity for establishing hiding places and caches of food in locations remote from the village. "This is a far worse danger than the bad tribe," I said. "These Unknowns can drop on you from the air without warning. You'll have to post sentries day and night, and you'll have to organize yourselves for instant flight. Many small groups will have a better chance to escape than one large group provided that each one knows what to do and where to go."

John's son studied me with the grave courtesy he always displayed. "Kera Jael, what is going to happen?" he asked.

"I don't know," I told him. "And because I don't know, I want you to be prepared for anything."

"But you do think there's a danger?" he persisted.

"I'm certain there's a danger. I'm certain that these Unknowns have an evil purpose. They will come to you pretending to be Lee Lukkari or to have been sent by her. They'll use lies and deliberate deceit. Don't listen to them. Pick your shelters carefully and flee to them the moment the Unknowns appear."

He nodded. "That is clear. We will prepare them now."

I lifted the landing craft again. Several kilometers from the village, I found a small forest clearing. I called John's son on his communicator to tell him where it was, and then I lowered the landing craft, picked a direction where the trees seemed to be growing further apart, and nudged my way forward until I had created a tunnel that would be invisible from the air.

John's son, accompanied by several young males, found me there, and we circled outward, selecting hiding places for the caches of food and for emergency shelters. When I was satisfied that they understood what they must do and how it should be done, I bade them farewell and headed northward to repeat the process with the Town Tribe.

There it took me much longer. The bad tribe, with a proper proportion of healthy, mature males eager for battle and with no recent history of murder, defeat, and harried flight for its life, had to be convinced that the nebulous Unknowns really constituted a danger. As I followed my route, circling around to the west coast and then looping down into South America, each tribe posed a special problem. None doubted my friendship; none disparaged the help that the RT had given them; but most were inclined to question my judgment. Every tribe had a plethora of primitive fears relating to nonexistent dangers, and it seemed astonishing to me that it could be so difficult to convince them of the urgency of a real threat—especially when we ourselves had demonstrated how easily aliens from outer space could descend on them. I proceeded with one tribe at a time, doing the best I could, persisting until they'd selected hiding places and begun to stock the emergency food caches. Then I moved on. I looped back to North America to visit the tribes in Missouri, Louisiana, and, finally, Montreal.

I left Iceland until last, and throughout that tedious journey and through all of the convoluted discussions I held with the black tribes, my mind was furiously churning the problem of Rek's people. Iceland was as invaluable to Earth's future as it was vulnerable. It had to be preserved. I criticized myself angrily for not having had the foresight to ask Ilia Sonal to build a base there. The sturdy homes of rock would be no protection against the Unknowns. They might become death traps.

I had informed Rek that I was on my way, and he was waiting for me in the town square when I landed. He had convoked the Althing, and he escorted me to the meeting room at once.

I had been without sleep for two days. The protracted discussions and arguments with the black tribes had exhausted me. Perhaps my failure was inevitable, but it was nonetheless inexplicable.

Most of the faces were familiar to me. Some members, like Ira and Jorn, I felt that I knew well, and all of them knew me. On this visit I encountered no hostility. My colleagues and I had cured their plague—they thought—and we had made them a gift of wood. They had been about to sell me animals for more wood. They understood that my concern was for them—that I was asking nothing for myself.

But they were skeptical. The concept of aliens from outer space had been with them through all of their remembered history, but they could not grasp the possibility of deliberate evil coming to them from afar. Earth people, they knew, took what they could for themselves and destroyed merely to deprive others of something. But people able to travel through space, they thought, would be so wealthy and so advanced that they could not possibly want anything from that small island.

"What do we have that anyone would travel so far to take from us?" Ira demanded.

I could only point out the inconsistency between their long-standing belief that aliens would come to trade with them and their refusal to believe that aliens might take from them without trading. The longer I talked, the more their skepticism deepened.

Then it occurred to me to suggest that the Unknowns mighty ally themselves with Earth tribes in a general assault on Earth's resources. That was a danger they could understand, and they readily agreed to take every precaution I could suggest.

So we worked out plans for a warning system, for sentries posted in every community, and for food reserves in cave shelters in the mountains. I wasn't enthused about the caves—they sounded too much like holes for the Icelanders to be trapped in—but there was no convenient forest to hide them. Also, their mobility would have been severely restricted by their animals even if they'd had a forest.

It was night in Iceland when the meeting finally ended. The temperature was cold compared with what I had experienced further south, I shivered as Rek and I walked back across the square to the landing craft. We stood for a moment looking up at the clear, star-flecked sky, and Rek grabbed my arm when he saw an unfamiliar star, moving quickly.

"What is it?" he asked.

"That's the Unknown," I said. "It's also a pollutant. An excrescence on the fair sky of a beautiful world, and I won't rest until it's been exorcised."

He watched it doubtfully. Probably it did not look dangerous to him.

"I want to show you something," I said. I led him into the landing craft and displayed the portrait of Lee Lukkari and one of the rados. "Most of the tribes of Earth had these," I said. "Have you seen anything like them?"

He recognized the portrait of Lee Lukkari but only because she was dressed as I had dressed on my first visit to Iceland. Her black skin puzzled him. "It must have been painted by a black artist," he said. "Blacks always tried to take credit for what other races accomplished."

"Where did you hear that?" I asked.

"We know. Ira thinks blacks were responsible for the war and the Mainland Fever. The reason Iceland escaped is because we would not permit blacks to come here."

I was still reluctant to tell him that Icelanders were the only whites who had survived, so I changed the subject and asked him about the rado. It was completely strange to him. There was no Icelandic tradition about either the portrait or the rado. This could have been an indication that the Unknowns had no designs on Iceland, but more likely it meant that they hadn't expected to find any whites alive.

I took my leave of Rek and told him to get started on those shelters.

"A shelter is really no defense, is it?" he asked.

"Not much, I'm afraid. But some. We'll help you as much as we can, but our problem is that we have no offensive weapons. We aren't trained to attack others, just to defend ourselves. Our defensive weapons are very good, but unfortunately I didn't think to place a base here that would have given your people a secure shelter."

"The Althing would not have permitted that," Rek said. "The elders would have thought that such a base would make an attack inevitable."

"Perhaps so. But your existence as a prosperous community also may make an attack inevitable. Better get to work on those shelters."

My own work was far from finished. I had to cover the two continents again to check the condition of the bases the *Hadda* technicians had abandoned. I returned to the Pacific coast, where the western North American base was situated in a lovely valley on a long ocean inlet on the coast of what had been British Columbia. En route I checked with Morl Klun, who was still visiting tribes in Africa, and with Wiln Marra, who had finished with the Asian tribes and was visiting bases there. Neither of them had seen any sign of a landing by the Unknowns. The *Hadda*, of course, had long since departed.

I slipped my craft through the landing slot in the dome of what we were calling Pacific Base and brought it to rest beside a well-loaded platform from the *Hadda*. Only the foundation for the base's building had been completed, and construction materials, along with lumber cut from the surrounding forest, were arranged neatly about the angular ground plan of a structure that perhaps would never be finished.

But the underground storage facilities were complete. I tugged open the massive double doors that led into a downward-sloping tunnel—the automatic openers had not been installed—and I floated the long platform down to the underground room below. The platform was loaded to capacity, but what the various bundles contained was a question I had no time to investigate. I could only hope that the *Hadda* supply chief had used a modicum of judgment in balancing his load.

I parked the platform and left it, closing the doors behind me. They had no lock; they needed none. The *Hadda* technicians hadn't rushed their work, but what they did, they did well. The base's protective screen was operational. It was the foundation of Regez Anlf defenses. No Unknowns could penetrate it—or, if they did, we would quickly lose more than our reserve supplies.

One South American base was located in coastal mountains in what had been Venezuela. We called it Venezuela Base. It looked down on the ruins of cities that had themselves looked down on a steaming coastal plain. This base had two loaded platforms parked beside a building that was almost completed. I floated both of the platforms into the underground storage room, did a superficial check of their contents, and took time for a quick tour of the building.

The second South American base, Andes Base, was located above Lake Ranco in what had once been Chile. Only the dome was finished, but the power supply had been installed and the base was operational. No supplies had been sent there—probably because the underground storage facilities had not been built.

Despite this disappointment, I felt smugly pleased with myself for the inspiration that had prompted me to order the extra bases. We now had ample reserves of supplies in the Americas, along with four functional bases. Two of the domes lacked living facilities, but most of the necessary building materials were on hand, and the bases could be completed as needed. The same would be true of the bases on the other continents. I had no idea what action we might have to take against the Unknowns, or what the Unknowns would try to do about us, but if we failed to protect the people of Earth, it would not be through want of bases and supplies.

I set course for Detroit Base, and at that point my intuition failed me. Or perhaps I was tired. I forgot my instructions to the others about flying low. I forgot it until I caught the indicator passing five kilometers. I arched downward at once, navigating myself because we'd turned off the direction beams. I hit the base dead on, slipped through the slot, and at that instant the roof almost literally fell in.

Almost.

They'd slipped a missile on my tail; fortunately, I hit base just before it caught up with me. Both the landing craft and the base protective fields were on automatic—meaning that they came on only when something triggered them—and that missile had been something special. The landing craft's screen wouldn't have reacted in time. The base's screen did—barely. The blast bent it inward, and the bounce knocked the landing craft to one side. I clipped the roof of the dormitory building and came to a very shaky halt that plowed up a section of my restored lawn.

I climbed out, and Wiln Marra was there to support me as I staggered down the ramp. I looked up into the gray morning light and said furiously, "I blew it. I goofed."

"At least you blew it emphatically," he said. "It was a very impressive blow. What happened?"

"I've got to warn Morl," I told him. I circled around the two loaded platforms that had arrived at Detroit Base during my absence and made an unsteady dash to our communications center. I managed to catch Morl Klun just as he was about to leave Africa.

Tersely I described what had happened. "From now on, all of our fields will have to be full on at all times," I told him. "And you'd better stay where you are until we evaluate this."

"Your only goof was in not monitoring," he said. "And it's my goof for not thinking to mention it to you. The Unknowns have had some kind of cruise missiles in low orbits since last night. I've already evaluated them. They're fast, but they're rather dumb machines. I played games with one. By bouncing a beam off the ground at just the right angle, I managed to turn it in a circle and start it chasing itself. They're nothing to worry about except that they *are* fast. As you say, our fields should be kept full on. I'll be back directly."

"Wait," I said. "Maybe those particular machines are dumb, but we don't know what else they've got."

"They won't trot it all out the first night, especially when some of their missiles seem to be malfunctioning. *You* know you got your tail nipped, but they don't know whether you were real or the same shadow that bollixed the one I played with. I'm on my way."

I sat back with my eyes closed. Wiln Marra served me up a glass of Irish whiskey from one of the few intact bottles we'd discovered in the ruins of Ken Jordan's bars, and I sipped it slowly while thinking a silent toast to my great-grandfather.

I needed it. I no longer felt inclined to criticize Ilia Sonal. As Reclamation Team captain, I hadn't responded any better to my first emergency.

The full significance of the *Hadda*'s departure had just smacked me squarely between the eyes. We were totally alone and totally on our own. Instead of rebuilding the civilizations of Earth, we now would have to concentrate on Naslur Rayl's first principle: How to survive.

12

Another communicator beeped; it was John's son. His people, panicked by the explosion, had already taken to the forest. The rash young males had wanted to rush to the riverbank to see what had happened, but he had restrained them.

"Have they come?" he asked.

"They have," I told him.

He wanted to know whether the tribe should immediately split up and go to the emergency hiding places. I hesitated; then I said, "Yes. That would be a good idea. Hide the tribe until we find out what's going to happen."

Wiln Marra had been making an instrument survey of the base area. "No sign of radioactivity," he said. "So it was an ordinary explosive. What's that about hiding? Are you hitting the panic button?"

"I'm using common sense—I hope," I said. "All of this has the shape of a shrewd and sinister plan. The Unknowns took advantage of the impression Lee Lukkari made. They converted her into a religious symbol. They passed out the rados and the portrait and promised that she would return. When she did, the rado would speak. Then all an Earth tribe had to do was press a button, and Lee Lukkari would come. Obviously the rado emits some kind of a direction beam. If each of the scattered Earth tribes had turned one on, the Unknowns would have been spared the trouble of tracking them down."

"Yes," Wiln Marra mused. "The Unknowns may lack sophisticated biological survey equipment, and even with our equipment, surveying a planet is a chore, as Burluf Nori would testify. Certainly a direction beam from each tribe would simplify matters immensely. But for what purpose? What do they want of a bunch of illiterate primitives?"

"Nothing good for the primitives. We don't have to wait for proof of that. I'm concerned that the Unknowns will investigate their exploded missile. If they do, they won't need a location signal from the Detroit Tribe —they'll see the village. I'd rather they found it deserted."

"Ah—yes," Wiln Marra agreed gravely. "That certainly would be best."

Morl Klun arrived, dashingly enthusiastic about the games he'd played with a couple of missiles along the way. "They've placed their ship in an Earth orbit," he said.

"I saw it from Iceland last night," I told him.

"They have landing craft out—I saw at least three—but there weren't any over eastern North America. I've now made several of their missiles misbehave. Probably they're writing reports about the peculiarities of Earth's magnetic fields."

"Nonsense," I said. "They've visited Earth periodically over a long stretch of time. Certainly they've studied it. They know all about Earth's magnetic fields."

"Have a look at their landing craft," he said.

He had been playing games with their landing craft, too, and he had several photo strips to prove it. He screened them for us, and we watched the blips of light flit past. Then he repeated the strip with magnification. Seen directly overhead, they were virtually circular. Seen from the side, they were exaggeratedly elliptic.

While Wiln Marra and I puzzled over them, Morl Klun sat watching us with a smugly superior smile. "What's the joke?" I demanded finally.

"No joke," he said. "Whatever else these Unks may be—I'm calling them Unks because thus far they've behaved unkishly—whatever else they may be, and certain selected individual Unks may be quite nice or even hilarious, their presence here is no joke. Have you two forgotten your Earth history so soon? Lefkir Bonrin would give both of you failing marks and order you back to class."

"The flying saucers!" I gasped.

"All of that," Morl Klun agreed. "A multitude of sightings extending back long before the Regez Anlf came to Earth, and while many of them certainly were imagined, there were more real sightings than Earth authorities in those days cared to give credence to. Flying saucers or flying cigars— they were the same thing, of course, depending on which profile was seen."

That shot the remainder of our day. It was startling to puzzle over totally unknown aliens from outer space and then to suddenly discover that they were part of the historical record; but Regez Anlf records contained a volume of material about the reports of flying saucer sightings. They also included a psychological analysis of the types of mass phobia that could have produced such illusions. I meditated writing a follow-up paper on the phobias of Regez Anlf psychologists.

The file contained the complete texts of several Earth books on the subject. While Morl Klun and Wiln Marra settled down to read them, I ran another check of the tribes. Apparently everything was peaceful everywhere on Earth. I repeated my warning to each tribe, made certain the hiding places were ready, and described the flying saucers.

"The moment you sight one, leave," I told each tribe. "Don't wait to see what will happen. You won't like it. Split up into small groups, take nothing with you but your communicator, and head for your emergency shelters. When you get there, then take the time to call me and tell me about it."

The information was received with appropriate alarm by everyone except the Detroit Tribe, which was already in its emergency shelters and which had been alarmed ever since that morning. I made no attempt to reassure anyone. Until we found out what was going on, the more frightened the natives were of Unknowns, the better.

"Do we assume that they know we're here?" Wiln Marra asked.

"We have to assume that much," I said. "They should have detected the activity surrounding the *Hadda*'s departure. They probably sighted our landing craft. They certainly know that this base is here and operating, and by now they should have all of the new bases plotted. An intelligence that can master the problems of interstellar travel is able to scan a world competently. Why would they launch cruise missiles if they didn't know there were potential targets?"

"Even so, their behavior seems inexplicable," Wiln Marra said. "They boldly crashed this system, and now they're holding back as though they don't know their next move."

"They're not only Unknowns," Morl Klun said. "Probably they're also unlikely, unapproachable, unbearable, uncouth, unfriendly, unspeakable, unmerciful, unprincipled, unpredictable, unthinkable, and a lot of other things, but 'Unks' covers all of it. If they don't know their next move, neither do we know ours."

"We're waiting on them," I said.

"Maybe they're waiting on us. In which case it'll be a long wait."

"We've warned all of the tribes," I said slowly. "We've given each one an escape plan and instructions as to when and how to use it. Is there anything more that we can do?"

Neither of them could think of a thing.

"Then let's find out how much of the flying saucer file is good metal and how much is slag. If there's anything useful there, we're going to need it."

Morl Klun and I attacked the file. Wiln Marra took on another task. There had to be some kind of communications between the flying saucers, and also between them and the spaceship, and he set about devising a methodical search for it. He was handicapped by two facts: our equipment hadn't been designed for such a task, and there was absolutely no way to predict what kind of signal the Unks would be using, or which of the whole span of frequencies might be carrying it, or whether it was being modulated in such a way that our equipment wouldn't pick it up even if he accidentally found it. But we agreed that a search should be made.

The flying saucer files contained mostly slag. We dismissed without discussion the fanciful reports of humans being kidnapped by flying saucers or even of humans meeting flying saucer crews. The descriptions all sounded biologically improbable. For the rest, the Unks certainly had surveyed Earth repeatedly over a period of years and perhaps over a period of centuries, but the records contained no clue as to why, or what they were looking for, or whether they had found it—except, as Morl Klun suggested, if they had found it, either they wouldn't have left or they would have taken it with them and not returned.

"What it amounts to," I said finally, "is that they came, they saw a high-tek civilization, they looked it over carefully, they probably recorded and studied as much as they could, and they left. Then they returned again. And again. And again. Maybe they're just curious."

"No government," Morl Klun said firmly, "is sufficiently detached in its outlook as to finance that much interstellar travel out of curiosity. I don't see any kind of pattern in all of this activity, but I do see a total, if only in the expense involved. No one is putting out this much money without expecting something in return. All we have to do is figure out what it is."

I yawned. "Tomorrow will be soon enough for that. Do you realize how long it's been since we've had any sleep? Anything we figure out now will have to be refigured tomorrow anyway."

"It'll also have to be refigured the day after that," Morl Klun said cheerfully. "Probably there's no way of knowing what they want until we see them grab it. But I refuse to make a lump of myself while waiting for them to grab. We know they're after something valuable. If we make a list—"

"Tomorrow," I yawned, and Wiln Marra seconded me with a yawn of his own. The two of us staggered toward our rooms, leaving Morl Klun to his own speculations.

The planet Earth seemed unchanged in the morning. The day dawned bright and sunny over Detroit Base. The three of us ate a hearty breakfast together, and then Wiln Marra returned to his communications search and Morl Klun to his study of the flying saucer file, while I did the only other thing I could think of—I talked again with all of the Earth tribes. None of them had anything to report except Rek. His description, which was being relayed to me second or third hand, seemed distorted, but the facts were clear enough. Shortly after dusk the previous day, a late-returning fishing boat had seen a flying saucer low over Iceland. We already had photo strips of flying saucers high over Earth, so it came as no surprise to know that they also were low over Earth. I could only repeat my warning to Rek. Then I called the Detroit Tribe, which I had left until last.

John's son did not answer.

This was not surprising or even unusual. We had no set times for communicating with the tribes, and no tribe had a communicator custodian constantly on duty waiting for us to call. In those tribes where the leader asserted an exclusive right to use the communicator—and the Detroit Tribe was one of them—no one dared to answer during his absence. When he returned, someone would tell him that the magic box had beeped, and he would call me.

John's son did not call.

After an hour had passed, I called him again—with no response.

I must have looked alarmed. Morl Klun had been watching me, and he pushed the file aside and got to his feet.

"What is it?" he asked.

"John's son. No one answers."

"Let's go," he said.

I maneuvered the landing craft into the forest tunnel I'd made for it, and we walked from one emergency hiding place to another. No one was there. There was no sign of panicky arrival or departure, the emergency stores seemed to be untouched, there were no clues at all—but the people were inexplicably missing.

We walked slowly back toward the village, searching for indications of a struggle, of a flight, of anything at all. There were none, but in the center of the village, several three-point depressions suggested that tripodal landing supports had touched down there. Several craft had landed, or one had landed several times. The huts were empty. There was no evidence that anything at all had been taken. The Regez Anlf communicator still reposed in its place of honor beside the portrait of Lee Lukkari.

"They've been abducted," Morl Klun said. "Obviously."

"How?" I demanded. "They agreed to put out sentries. They had an alarm. How could the entire tribe be taken without any struggle or attempt to escape?"

We continued to search, but there were no more clues. All fifty-two members of the tribe, including the pregnant young women, had vanished.

I took the communicator and the portrait of Lee Lukkari, and we walked back to our ship—making another search along the way—and returned to base.

"Let's get things in the right sequence," Morl Klun said when we had despondently settled ourselves in our headquarters. "The explosion happened, and you recommended that they take to the emergency shelters. Right?"

"Right," I said. "And they did. Then I called them again, along with all the other tribes, and described the flying saucers."

Morl Klun nodded. "This is what I think happened. The Unks were expecting to be led directly to the Earth tribes by direction signals from their rados. But you had collected all the rados that survive, so the syrupy message from the fake Lee Lukkari brought no response. At that point they were in a flap, cruising about aimlessly and wondering what had happened to the people of Earth. Then the missile that was on your tail hit the base's protective field and exploded. One of their craft dipped down to investigate and saw the Detroit Tribe's village."

"But the people weren't there!" I objected.

"No, but I think they returned later. Your flying saucer message frightened everyone else, but to them it may have been reassuring. They'd fled from something unknown. Then you described the danger—the flying saucers—in specific terms, and they figured they had nothing to worry about until they saw something shaped like that. Or maybe they just figured it would be all right to return to the village after dark to sleep. In any case, they went, and the reason I know they went is because the portrait and the communicator were back in the village. We know they took the communicator to the emergency shelters with them—you talked with John's son there. They certainly would have taken the portrait, too."

I nodded glumly. "All right. They returned to the village."

"And the Unks, who now knew where at least one tribe of Earth people could be found, floated over the village in the dark, used some kind of chemical to inflict unconsciousness, and collected the whole village. It must have happened that way."

"But what could they want with fifty-two people?"

"There's no way of knowing," Morl Klun said. "But it is interesting that they took nothing else. If I were abducting fifty-two people of an alien race, I'd also want to bring along some of their food, if any were available, to keep them going until I found out what they could digest. The Unks didn't bother. Maybe they were in a hurry. Maybe it worried them that the village was so close to our base. Or maybe they already know everything they need to know about the digestions of Earth people. What do we do now? A planet is a large place to search for fifty-two people, even when it's certain that they're there to be found. They may be on the spaceship."

"I'll warn the other tribes to take to their hiding places immediately and stay there," I said grimly, "but I don't see how we can protect all of the scattered tribes of Earth when we couldn't protect one living next door to us."

I sat down with my list of tribes and began calling them.

It took a long time. I wanted to describe the danger as graphically as possible. They had to know that it was imperative not to leave any sign of their presence visible from the air, and for some tribes this posed almost insurmountable problems. All the time I was talking, I worried about Iceland. There was no way to conceal either communities or hiding places on that treeless island. I finished the list of black tribes, finally, and turned to talk with Morl Klun and Wiln Marra before I called Rek.

"Any suggestions for Iceland?" I asked.

"Unless you want to resettle the entire population in the middle of a safe mainland forest—" Morl Klun began.

"If we did that, even if they consented, they'd lose something very precious to them," I said.

"Is it more precious than life?" Morl Klun demanded.

"I'm afraid it may be."

I called Rek.

He was a long time in answering, and my apprehension intensified while I waited. Finally I heard his voice, and I began to describe the new danger the flying saucers posed.

He interrupted me. "Mainland Fever!" he gasped.

13

Each of us took a landing craft. Into one we slipped a complete medical laboratory packed in cases that unfolded to form instrument-equipped worktables fully supplied to cope with any medical emergency. At least that was the theory, and we could only hope that no one on the Regez Anlf supply circuit had goofed. We quickly rigged the second craft as a medical clinic, and into the third we packed enough general equipment and supplies to outfit a small hospital. We did not even consider the possibility that this second outbreak of Mainland Fever would be psychosomatic—all three of us had heard Rek's gasped message.

We set the three craft down in the town square with the clinic craft resting head to head with the craft containing the laboratory. The hospital supplies were parked nearby. Rek staggered forward as the ramp went down, and we rushed him into the clinic and hooked him to an evaluation unit while Wiln Marra dashed to the laboratory with a blood sample. Morl Klun and I monitored the instruments anxiously, waiting for a restructure, and nothing happened. The computer digested information, requested more information, suggested tests, asked for cycles to be repeated—and had no comment. I turned away twice—once to look at the growing crowd of very sick people gathered about the ramp, and once to glance into the adjoining craft where Wiln Marra was still puzzling over test runs on the blood sample.

Still there was no restructure. Morl Klun looked up at me suddenly. "I never thought about it before," he said bitterly. "Medical computers don't know how to deal with death. They're programmed to tell us how to support life. When they encounter a human for whom death is inevitable, they remain blank. Either there are no answers or the computer knows that anything it suggested would reinforce death rather than avert it."

"Nonsense," I said. "Don't start attributing an emotional involvement to a computer. It diagnoses as soon as its data are complete. The blank screen only means that the disease isn't known to it, and there's no reason why it should be. Wiln will be out shortly with a serum, and we'll start injections."

"A disease this virulent may damage organs irreversibly. What if we arrest it and find ourselves with an entire society of mental or physical invalids?"

"Make up your mind whether you're going to be merely ridiculous or preposterous," I said disgustedly. "Then shut up."

He shrugged and pointed to the screen, which still offered no restructure.

Wiln Marra was having no better success with the lab's computer, which was attempting to analyze while the clinic's computer synthesized. He came in, finally, looked at our screen, and shook his head.

"I need more samples," he said. "Bring in as many as you have stations for."

"Adults?" I asked.

"Anyone."

Morl Klun and I went down the ramp to look for volunteers, and the waiting Icelanders watched our descent with a dull hopefulness.

The symptoms of the deadly fever were running their course much more slowly in reality than they had somatically, but the full dimensions of the disease already were evident: the red flush; the aching limbs that sometimes caused grimaces of agony at the slightest movement; the severe tremors; the wracked and tortured breathing. Most of those waiting consisted of families with young children. Probably it was an indication of the Icelanders' confidence in us that a substantial part of the town's population had been content to wait at home for word that our cure was ready. But the parents of young children whose bodies were writhing with pain found that wait impossible.

I did not like to separate parents and children, so I took a family of four and hooked all of them to evaluation units. This gave the computer five times as much data to work with. It hummed happily, but there still was no restructure.

Wiln Marra came in to pick up blood samples from the new patients. Before he hurried away, he nodded at the three stations that were still unoccupied. "Bring adults," he said. "I'll need more blood."

Morl Klun and I returned to the ramp. At the top, we paused for a moment to look out on a hushed and paralyzed community. There was no sound except for the whimpering of the sick children waiting below us and the murmured attempts of their parents to console them. We had been so preoccupied with medical tests since our arrival that I'd had little opportunity to reflect on the full dimensions of the catastrophe. Now I took the time to ask a few questions of those gathered about the ramp, and their answers staggered me.

Entire families had become ill almost at the same moment.

All of their neighbors had become ill virtually at the same time they had. So had the entire town.

The return of the dreaded fever had been reported immediately to all of the communities of Iceland—even the most remote settlements—by the telephone network maintained for that very purpose. Wherever the warn-

ing went, it arrived too late. The fever was there before it. This time there
would be no heroic self-sacrifice to contain the disease. The disease was
everywhere.

Suddenly the atmosphere of quiet tenseness was shattered. An angry
voice rang out. "These purveyors of iniquity, these treacherous aliens who
once again bring death to our beautiful island . . ."

It was Ira. His voice rolled on and gained in virulence. I anxiously
searched the faces of the crowd around him to see what the reaction was.
But all of those faces were wracked with illness, and it was impossible to tell
whether Ira knew what he was saying. He was flushed with fever and acting
delirious.

He was desperately sick, but he was nonetheless a menace. We had a
grim struggle ahead of us to save an entire stricken population, and he was
behaving like a saboteur. He would have to be dealt with instantly. Morl
Klun and I exchanged glances, and then we determinedly started down the
ramp.

Before we reached the bottom, a woman's voice cut in sharply. "That's
enough, Father. Come home, now."

Ira moved a step closer to us. His fever-flushed face was twisted with
hatred. "These perfidious aliens . . ."

"Father!" The speaker gripped his coat and firmly turned him around.
She handled him like a small child. Hers was the only striking figure in that
huddled crowd. She was noticeably taller than the other waiting females,
and her slender form and graceful posture made her look taller than she
was. Her gleaming blond hair was wrapped into a neat package behind her
head. Everything about her seemed simple and matter-of-fact. Because this
gathering of dying people was taking place in the public square, the other
females had covered their illness with holiday dress, but she wore drably
colored work garments and made them look striking. She, too, carried the
flush of fever on her face, but her attitude was one of calm determination.
She had come prepared to do battle, and the inner force that sustained her
was not the mere resiliency of youth. I guessed her age as thirty-five.

"You're being silly," she told Ira sternly. "You're making a nuisance of
yourself. The aliens are working to save our lives. Anyone who is unable to
help should go home."

Ira allowed himself to be persuaded. A younger man took him in hand
and helped him away.

His daughter stood frowning after him for a moment, and then she
turned with resolution and pushed her way through to the ramp.

She spoke with reprimand in her voice. "If there is anything that we can
do, tell us. Otherwise, we won't know, and it won't be done."

"We're still conducting tests to analyze your disease," I said. "Until that
is done successfully, we can't produce a medicine for you. We need three
more adults for testing."

She turned, looked over the crowd, and called out two names. Another woman and a man came forward, and the three of them followed us into the landing craft.

Wiln Marra was waiting for us. He stepped aside to let the new patients enter, and then he followed after them. He lent us a hand with the hook-ups, but instead of dashing off with the blood samples he'd been in such frenzied haste to obtain, he stood looking down at Ira's daughter with an expression that looked remarkably like rapture.

"She has a regal manner," he murmured. "Queenly! Queenly!"

I could have slugged him. "If she does, she doesn't come by it honestly," I snapped. "Iceland has the oldest parliamentary government on Earth, and there are no queens here. And if you don't get your glands under control and do some work, she's going to die along with the rest of the population."

He started. Then he snatched at the vials of blood and scurried away.

We waited, monitoring the eight stations and pondering with puzzled helplessness the oddly fluctuating body temperatures, the heartbeats that alternately raced and faltered, the tremors, the tortured faces that dripped perspiration and then were shaken by chills. We were watching robust good health under siege by desperate illness. With a weakened population, I thought, a disease of this virulence already would have begun to pile the town's streets with its dead, for there would have been no one with the strength to carry the bodies away. This had happened to Earth once before, decimating the population that had survived the holocaust. The Icelanders were healthy, and that gave us a little time.

But only a little. The oddly fluctuating curves of temperature and heart-beat seemed to be edging minutely higher with each upward leap. We watched tensely and waited, wondering how things were going elsewhere in the town and in other communities. Our help was needed everywhere, but we had to fight the battle here where it was joined, to win or lose.

We waited for two dragging, tension-filled hours, while Wiln Marra burst in intermittently, took more samples, paused for a bewildered glance at our instruments, and hurried away. Once I asked him if he needed help, and he muttered angrily, "Yes—but none that you could give."

Finally he brought a vial of colorless fluid. He snapped it into place and began to program injections for each of the eight patients. He looked indescribably weary, and he had to pause, scowling and clapping his hand to his forehead, while he puzzled over the appropriate doses for the children. He said nothing at all.

"Have you got it?" Morl Klun demanded.

"I think so. I hope so."

He dropped into a chair. "I hope so," he said again. "Do you remember mention of an Earth disease called malaria?"

"Vaguely," I said. I turned to the medical referencer and punched in the word. Morl Klun came over, and we read together. "A microscopic one-celled protozoan parasite," I mused. "Insect vector, numerous species spread among several hundred vertebrate hosts. So it attacks animals as well as humans. The vector—"

I turned to Wiln Marra. "Are you saying that this is malaria?"

"Look at the symptoms," he said.

"It can't be malaria," I told him. "Mosquitoes must be virtually extinct on Earth. They depended on the blood of warm-blooded animals for breeding, and unless they could adapt, they certainly died out when Earth's population dropped drastically. The malaria protozoa must be virtually extinct. Without blood and the mosquito, it couldn't have survived."

"Look at the symptoms," Wiln Marra said again.

I did. "Yes," I said slowly. "I suppose this could be malaria if it were much more virulent and if its cycles were accelerated enormously and if everything about it were exaggerated. The more common strains of malaria produced a debilitating disease of low mortality. It was as old as human history, and, over the centuries, it killed millions and brought down civilizations by sapping their energy, but it never struck like a killing plague. Are you saying that it mutated and found new hosts and a new vector?"

Wiln Marra shook his head. "No. Not a mutation. I don't believe it could be a mutation."

"Then what is it?"

He did not answer.

"Do you know?" I persisted.

"I know," he said, "and I don't believe it. It's a synthetic organism. It's totally unrelated to any kind of life on Earth. It's silicon-based. It shouldn't be able to survive here as a parasitic life, but it does, just long enough to function, because it's genetically engineered to do that."

"How can you know?" I asked.

"It's the only answer that fits all of the questions."

"I still don't see how you can tell positively—"

Wiln Marra waved a hand irritably. "Watch them," he said, pointing to our eight patients. "They're the ultimate question. If they recover, you can take the answer as given. A genetically engineered disease."

He already had the medical lab on full production. Even while we waited suspensefully to see whether the serum worked, the lab was producing it in quantity. After an hour, we administered second injections. We worried fretfully about the size of the doses, especially for the children, but all eight patients were sleeping peacefully.

I went to the ramp and looked down at a huddled, miserably ill population—a dying population that was slowly filling the square in a last, desperate appeal for help. I returned to Wiln Marra, who sat gazing tenderly at Ira's daughter.

"Her name is Heldi," he said suddenly.

"How the devil did you find that out?" I demanded.

"Someone must have mentioned it when we were here before. 'Ira has a daughter named Heldi.' I just remembered. The name suits her, doesn't it?"

"Perfectly. And if you don't start mass injections at once, I'm going to give *you* a suitable name that you won't like."

"If I'm wrong, it might kill people," he protested.

"At times like this, rules and regulations and procedures don't count. If you wait long enough to make certain you're right, they'll die regardless. They'll also die if you're wrong and have to start over. How do we proceed?"

He sighed and got to his feet. "For the entire population of Iceland, this is going to take some organizing."

We put large numbers of seriously ill people to work—there was no other way. We converted all of the buildings around the square into hospitals, improvised beds as best we could, invited those who could walk to occupy them, and instituted a house-by-house search for those already too weak to respond to the landing craft's amplifier. The serum had to be administered in a hospital situation, however crude, because the patients promptly lapsed into unconsciousness the moment they received it. A second and occasionally a third dose was necessary before the disease was completely arrested. Eventually the patient awoke—cured, comfortable, but terribly weak. By the following day we would have had a town full of invalids to care for had it not been for the fact that we had moved on to Iceland's other communities as soon as we finished treating the first town's population. The invalids had to care for each other as best they could. I made a quick trip to Detroit Base for a landing craft full of emergency rations—since the Icelanders couldn't prepare food and were barely able to feed themselves—and at first many of them were too weak to pull the tab that opened the package and activated the heating unit. Those who were able helped those who were weaker, and Morl Klun and Wiln Marra and I made our separate ways back and forth across the island, first treating the entire human population, and then—with help as some of the Icelanders began to regain their strength—administering to the island's animal population, an enormously exacting task that frequently had Wiln Marra talking to himself as he tried to calculate doses.

He didn't have to do *much* talking to himself, for he had acquired an assistant in the person of the queenly Heldi, the first Icelander to recover, who followed him about so devotedly in repayment for the care he had lavished on her that he failed to realize that any man Heldi followed was being led.

But I tactfully made no comment. Rek followed me about just as devotedly. Morl Klun, who had to settle for the far more capable assistance of the Althing member Jorn, made savage remarks whenever we met, but in our hectic struggle to save life on the island, that was seldom.

I had little time to worry about anything. When I did, I worried about what malice the Unks were likely to wreak upon us next. I also worried about John's son and his people, but for the moment we were helpless to do anything about them. I talked daily with the other tribes, and I told them about the new outbreak of fever. The Town Tribe recognized the term "Beesee." All of the others had their own names for it, but every tribe recognized the symptoms. They were following the precautions I had suggested, or they said that they were, but I knew that with the passage of time some of them would become careless. There was little that we could do about that. I told them to let us know immediately if anyone became sick, and we would come and cure the disease. And I promised to visit all of them as soon as I could.

Iceland had taken on the aspect of a massive convalescent estate. The entire population, human and animal, was tottering about in various stages of recovery. We did not lose a patient, either human or animal, though Wiln Marra had some anxious moments over baby lambs.

When we of the RT were finally able to meet and talk, we slumped exhaustedly onto cots in one of the landing craft and kept ourselves awake through perverse stubbornness. We had much to talk about.

"The Unks," Morl Klun said, "must have done it deliberately. Not only this epidemic, but the previous one. Would either of you care to guess why?"

"They want the world," I said. "Why else would they be trying to exterminate its population?"

"The situation can't be that simple," Morl Klun said. "What use would they have for a world that required the elimination of all the indigenous life? Life-forms are a major component of any world's wealth."

"What do we know?" Wiln Marra asked.

He was lying there quietly with his eyes closed. He had carried a heavy burden of responsibility, and he looked more tired than I had ever seen him. None of us felt triumphant; we were totally drained of energy and emotion. We should have been furious over this attempt to wipe out the planet's one surviving civilization, but we were too tired even to feel angry.

"What do we know?" Wiln Marra asked again. He added, "Know—*positively.*"

"The Unks visited Earth before," I said. "Earth records of flying saucer sightings prove that they returned periodically over many years. They may have been here during the Regez Anlf's first visit. They certainly were here after the holocaust. They made an intermittent but intensive study of Earth that may have lasted for centuries."

"Correction," Morl Klun said. "We know positively that they were here. We don't know that they were studying Earth. The motives of alien intelligences—"

"Bosh!" I said. "We have to make *some* working assumptions. They came, they observed, but as far as we know they took no action. It wasn't until they found Earth in a state of devastation following the holocaust that they engineered a synthetic disease and tried to wipe out Earth's population."

Wiln Marra nodded his agreement. "They took no action until the moment when Earth's population would be most susceptible. Now they've returned again, and they're trying to exterminate the little life that's left here."

"Naslur Rayl said our first problem was to survive," Morl Klun said. "Our overwhelming second problem is to ensure that life on Earth survives. They can try again and keep trying. Since we're completely without offensive weapons, we're reduced to trailing after them and frantically trying to counter their moves after they make them."

"There are a few things we can do," I said. "Much as I'd like to sleep, I don't think we dare waste the time. A delay of hours could be fatal. Let's go."

Both Rek and Heldi were keeping a vigil at the foot of the landing ramp. I'd been unable to persuade them to go home. I told Rek that I wanted to meet immediately with a representative segment of Iceland's population.

"The Althing—" he began.

"Not the Althing," I said. "It may be parliamentary, but it's not representative. I want old and young, male and female, fishers and farmers. I want all of Iceland's settlements represented, and I want those people just as quickly as you can collect them. Move!"

He dashed away.

Heldi was watching me with frosty disapproval. By this time I knew a few things about her. She was thirty-seven years old. She had never been married, preferring to devote herself to the care of her father, a widower.

"She knew that her father was easier to manage than a husband would have been," I'd told Morl Klun.

"She's a career woman, just like you," he said and moved before I could retaliate.

But there was no doubt that she was capable. In our work on the plague, Wiln Marra had performed far more efficiently than either Morl Klun or I and not merely because he had medical training. Once the lab had developed the serum, our actions became routine if not mechanical. Wiln Marra was more efficient because he'd had Heldi helping him.

"I have a job for you," I told her.

The disapproval shifted instantly to suspicion. "What kind of job?"

"Important. No one ever devised one that was more important." And I told her what it was.

Rek gathered four hundred Icelanders. They came from all inhabited parts of the island, and, because no building would hold them all, they filled the square, and I spoke to them through the landing craft's amplifier.

I kept my presentation simple. The evil aliens, whom we were calling Unks, were attempting to kill everyone and everything. The Mainland Fever was not a real disease—it was something the Unks had designed and made, the way an Icelandic cobbler designed and made shoes or a boatbuilder designed and made a fishing boat. The Unks had spread the Mainland Fever over almost all of Earth after the holocaust. Then they left, confident that they would have the world for themselves when they returned. They had miscalculated. There were a few scattered tribes left, and there was a remnant of civilization on Iceland. They already had abducted all of the members of one of the remaining tribes, and they had spread the fever a second time in Iceland.

"Fortunately, we were able to thwart them," I said. "But they'll certainly try again. As soon as they realize that we have a medicine for Mainland Fever, they'll manufacture a new disease. Or they will attempt to kill you in some other way. We are dedicated to helping you as much as we can, but there are many of them and only three of us, and we have the entire world to protect. Sooner or later they will succeed. You will die. Your animals will die. The other human tribes that survive will die. Then the Unks will have achieved their goal—there will be no life left on Earth."

I would have elaborated, but Heldi moved forcefully into the role I had assigned to her. "We understand all that," she said. "All of us have had the fever. Tell us what you want us to do."

I wanted a small colony of Icelanders, complete with a breeding stock of each of their animals, placed in the security of each of the Regez Anlf bases. I preferred young married couples with children.

Heldi interrupted again. "The only thing to decide is who is to go," she said firmly.

From that point, the show belonged to her. The elders of the Althing showered her with objections, and she fended them off until she lost her patience. Then she demolished them. The Althing, she said sarcastically, was preeminent in debate; would the elders perhaps inform her as to how they intended to debate the Mainland Fever or any of its possible successors? She returned unerringly to the question, and she posed it over and over. "Who is to go?"

Finally they yielded, the only proviso being that the colonies must be made up of volunteers. That posed no problems for us. Heldi was capable of drafting as many volunteers as we needed, but no persuasion was necessary. As I had anticipated, every young couple in Iceland wanted to save its children. They had no desire to watch them dying from another fever.

Heldi clashed with me only over my insistence that the colonists be married couples. That, she told me icily, was nonsense. Why shouldn't anyone go who wanted to?

After she had bested the Althing elders in debate and got my program accepted, she wasn't going to let me exclude her. But I wasn't about to set myself up for another run of the child-out-of-wedlock dilemma that had plagued Dana Iverson and already embarrassed me once.

We compromised. I permitted unmarried young people to volunteer as long as there were capable chaperones who would take the responsibility for looking after the young women. That shifted the responsibility for safeguarding their morals to the Icelanders themselves, which pleased me; and it permitted Heldi to join the colonists, which pleased her.

But she refused to enter herself on the rolls as an unmarried girl. She went as a chaperone.

There were problems in logistics to work out: food, clothing, forage for the animals—a major item. We left all of the details to the Icelanders, who knew far more about them than we did.

Once the project was accepted, the planning went quickly. A couple of hours later our three ships slipped through the slot at Detroit Base with highly unusual cargoes: six Icelandic families with young children, a dozen single people ranging in age from adolescent to young adult, and the first installment of the highly reluctant animal breeding stock that was to follow.

14

According to Lefkir Bonrin, the most successful civilizations are those that are most adept at making virtues of necessities. When food supplies fail, they discover better sources of nutrition in unlikely places. When raw materials give out, they contrive substitutes that work better. I once argued—unsuccessfully; no one argued successfully with Lefkir Bonrin—that the really successful civilization wouldn't have to discover or contrive because it already would have inventoried its potential resources. He smiled and said that this was contrary to nature. No one worked very hard at discovering or contriving or even searching for opportunities without the impetus of stark necessity.

Our next step in the reclamation of Earth would have pleased him. It grew out of our attempt to save the Icelanders, and that certainly was born of stark necessity.

We moved a small colony, complete with animals, to each of the functional Regez Anlf bases. Only Detroit Base was completely outfitted; the colonists at the other bases had to devise their own shelter—but plenty of materials were on hand, and they could have lived without shelter in the protected environment of the base if they chose to do so. We moved forage for animals and food for the colonists from Iceland, keeping Regez Anlf supplies in reserve for future crises. The platforms abandoned by the *Hadda* proved invaluable. We simply loaded them in Iceland, towed them a few kilometers straight up, and floated them toward their destinations. Their automatic controls did the rest.

While we were hard at work in getting the colonists settled, necessity inspired me a second time. Why not, I mused aloud, recruit a few colonists from each of the black tribes? Our bases ranged in size from one to three square kilometers, and each could comfortably house a number of small colonies. Once settled there, the colonists from the black tribes could learn to care for animals and master essential crafts under the tutelage of the Icelanders. When the Unk crisis passed, they could return to their tribes with their new skills and with breeding pairs of the animals that would be most useful to them.

Morl Klun beamed at me approvingly. "Behold—the march of civilization!"

"At this stage, I'm not concerned with civilization," I said. "I'm worried about the economic necessities of human survival."

"It amounts to the same thing," Morl Klun said. "A population that hasn't mastered economic necessities won't be able to support very many poets."

My flush of triumph over this ingenious plan barely lasted overnight. Wiln Marra devoted the evening to his futile efforts to intercept Unk communications. Morl Klun and I observed another passage of the orbiting Unk spaceship, and we tracked it with instruments to learn what we could about it. It was in a near-circular orbit, about twelve thousand four hundred kilometers from Earth and inclined approximately 45 degrees. Morl Klun calculated the orbital velocity at a little less than five kilometers per second.

"It might as well be a million," I told him. "It's a pollutant, and I can't think of a thing to do about it."

"A great pity that all of our weapons are defensive," he agreed. "It'd be a pleasure to shoot it down. I wonder what weapons it has."

That was an unpleasant thought to go to bed with. Morning brought worse unpleasantness. Another of the tribes was missing.

It vanished between darkness and dawn in the same way that John's son and his people had vanished. At sundown on the previous day, Asian time, I had talked with its chief by communicator. Now my signal was not answered. I kept trying, and when, an hour later, there still had been no response, I left for Asia.

I knew what I would find—or what I would not find—but I had to make certain. The village was deserted, but that was as it should have been. The hiding places also were deserted. As with the Detroit Tribe, there were no signs of struggle or flight.

I returned to the village, a picturesque circle of dwellings expertly fashioned by the natives of an indigenous plant they called bamb. When we first encountered it, we thought it was an alien shrub, because none of the references mentioned it. Long afterward we discovered that these large, segmented, enormously strong tubes were officially classified as a grass.

The village's central clearing contained several large fire rings. The fires were burned out, but over each of them the ingredients of a meal were arranged—fish, which we had taught these natives to catch in quantity, and a bread that Morl Klun had devised for them from flour made from the roots of available plants. The food was burned to a crisp, and this was eloquent testimony as to what had happened.

Following my instructions, these natives had taken to their hiding places during the day; but they came together in the early hours of darkness to prepare their daily meal, and the cooking fires had betrayed them. The

Unks silently and invisibly floated overhead and dropped their chemical, after which they only had to land and collect the comatose natives.

I'd neglected to caution the natives about fires.

This native tribe had paid the penalty for my oversight, and that hurt; at the same time, Lefkir Bonrin's principle of stark necessity worked again. The disappearance of a second tribe lent urgency to my argument that each tribe should entrust a few of its young people to the safety of the Regez Anlf bases. I immediately gave instructions to Wiln Marra and Morl Klun by communicator, and before I left Asia, I collected twelve young couples and twice that many children from the remaining Asian tribes and left them at the Asian bases. At the same time, Wiln Marra visited the tribes in the Americas and Morl Klun those in Africa. In two more days, we had achieved our objective: Each Earth tribe—except the two that were missing —had a small colony safely under a Regez Anlf dome.

This sudden influx of inhabitants transformed the bases but not in the way that I'd hoped. The blacks regarded members of other black tribes with deep suspicion and the white Icelanders with hatred. The Icelanders regarded all of the blacks with contempt. Age-old racial suspicions and prejudices seemed to be genetically resurrected and bubbling toward a boiling point. Morl Klun feared that cannibalism might break out among the blacks, or that whites and blacks would soon be fighting pitched battles.

Each base had its own ample water supply and plenty of food. Shelter was no problem in the controlled environment of the bases even where there were no finished buildings, but each small group insisted on its own enclave. The Icelanders took over the buildings; or, if there were none, they laid out their own tiny village, with houses and barns, using rock when it was available within the dome. They were unaccustomed to building with wood. The blacks built shelters out of whatever material was available. These little communities were situated as remotely from each other as possible, and the members of each tried to pretend that the others did not exist. It might have taken years or forever to achieve the communal harmony I hoped for had it not been for one thing: the animals.

The blacks had never seen animals larger than skirls. Young blacks suddenly confronted by a cow for the first time were terrified, then incredulous, and finally fascinated. After a few days of watching Icelanders care for their animals, all of them wanted to try it themselves. There were other exchanges of knowledge: weaving and the making of clothing for basket weaving and skill in cooking over open fires; processing of animal products for skills in foraging and the use of woods. When I permitted small parties to forage outside the domes, the Icelanders had to be taught freshwater fishing by the black tribesmen.

We left the colonists to work these things out for themselves. We members of the RT were still tired from our Iceland ordeal, and the strain of setting up the colonies exhausted us completely. We slept for a day and a night before we emerged groggily from our Detroit Base headquarters to marvel at the community developing there. It was an accomplishment, but one that we could take little pride in; as far as our main problem was concerned, we had merely applied a patch. The Unks' spaceship continued to make its seven-hour orbits, and its visible passes were unseemly blemishes in the night sky. The natives outside the domes continued to hide from marauding flying saucers, and, since they could no longer hunt freely for food, feeding them was going to be a problem in the very near future.

"We've got to do something about the Unks," Morl Klun announced. "If we sit around trying to figure out what they're up to, they'll simply pick off the tribes one at a time as they happen onto them."

"We could easily move all of the black tribes to safety," Wiln Marra said. "Perhaps we should."

"Perhaps we could, as a temporary measure," I said. "Some of them would be willing. They must be getting tired of hiding all of the time. But that only amounts to imprisoning the population of Earth in order to pre-serve it. It's another patch. It might be feasible for a few days or even for an Earth month or two—but what if the Unks don't go away?"

There was a long pause. Then Morl Klun said again, "We've got to do something about the Unks. Up until now, we've been reacting to what they do and desperately trying to keep afloat. Let's make them do some react-ing."

Wiln Marra said, "If only we could monitor their communications—"

"Never mind," I said. "Even if you made an intercept, it might take our computers years to figure out the language. What we need to do is capture an Unk. Then we could take its language and everything else we need to know."

Morl Klun nodded approvingly. "Right. If we captured an Unk, we could find out what they're trying to do, and why, and we could take countermea-sures. So how do we go about it?"

None of us said anything for the next ten minutes.

"We'd have to capture a flying saucer, since they have no ground base that we know of," Morl Klun said finally. "Could we box a saucer with three landing craft?"

None of us could venture a guess. We still knew next to nothing about the Unks or their capabilities, and their behavior had been a total baffle-ment to us. We had to assume that they knew that aliens were present on Earth and that they had all of our bases plotted. They certainly had ob-served our activity in Iceland, because our three landing craft had been parked in the open for days while we worked frantically to stem the plague. They must have been aware of our worldwide visits to the black tribes; they should have monitored our communications, pinpointed the sources, and followed us wherever we went. As far as we could tell, they had done none of that. If anything, they seemed to be avoiding us.

"Is it possible that they're more apprehensive about us than we are about them?" Morl Klun demanded.

"They're certainly apprehensive," I said. "Why wouldn't they be? They don't know what we're capable of any more than we know what they're capable of. That's the stupid weakness in that Regez Anlf regulation. It assumes that any aliens we encounter will want to pursue us, so it orders us to run away—which is as good a way as any to get pursued. When I get around to transmitting another report, I'll point that out to Naslur Rayl. These Unks not only don't pursue, they don't even seem curious about us. Let's go catch one and find out why."

The only thing we knew about Unk technology was that their saucer-shaped ships performed very agilely and their cruise missiles could be fooled. Comparisons with Regez Anlf technology seemed futile, but there was one area in which I was certain that we were far ahead—in biological surveys. If the Unks had had our equipment, they certainly would have pinpointed all of the human settlements on Earth by this time.

This gave me an idea. "Let's do a biological survey," I said.

"Sure," Morl Klun said. "If any of the Unks are AWOL, there's a chance in a billion that we'll find one."

"The Unks may have an Earth base," I said. "They may have taken our missing tribes there. So let's look for it. We're much more likely to encounter a flying saucer if we're doing something mysterious in a routine way than if we're obviously prowling for trouble."

They agreed, and I laid out a survey. We flew parallel courses, and we kept far enough apart to be barely out of visual contact. This permitted us to make as wide a biological sweep as possible without gaps. It also seemed to be as good a formation as any for capturing a saucer.

We flew between the eastern and western mountains, cutting a swathe across the continent's central valley by following a latitudinal line for almost two thousand kilometers and then turning back to fly the next strip. By the time we started our third, I was feeling immensely sympathetic toward Burluf Nori. There is nothing more boring than a biological survey of a planet that is virtually a biological desert. Our instruments recorded nothing at all; unfortunately, the skies were equally bare of Unks.

The course took slightly more than an hour to negotiate. At that low altitude, a faster speed would have made our instruments function erratically. We were flying our fourth strip, and we'd been out almost four hours, when Morl Klun sighted the saucer. He announced the location tersely, and we immediately began the maneuver we'd decided upon. We abandoned it almost at once. Long before we could reach our planned positions—in fact, the instant the saucer's instruments sighted us—it performed an adroit pivot and rapidly disappeared.

It had been traveling at an incredibly fast clip. Suddenly it dipped, seemed to dig into the thin atmosphere and skid, and it was going the other way.

Morl Klun's reaction was a soft whistle. "How did it do that?"

"I don't believe it!" Wiln Marra gasped.

I said dryly, "That answers our question. We couldn't have caught it if we'd had it surrounded by a dozen landing craft. Our craft aren't designed for slick maneuvers in an atmosphere. The Unks' ships are."

"So what do we do now?" Morl Klun asked.

"We continue our survey. As I've already mentioned, this is one thing that we can do and they can't."

It was midafternoon when we passed over the Missouri Tribe. The forest below looked unbroken from our altitude, but the screen registered several glowing blips: the hiding places, showing that the tribe had scattered as planned and was hidden safely. We reached the mountains and turned back, continuing to fly one swath after another. Darkness set in. I called Morl Klun and Wiln Marra and told them that we'd head for home base after we passed over the Louisiana Tribe on our next lap.

We were over northern Mississippi, and I was mentally writing our effort off as a totally wasted day's work, when my screen was suddenly splashed with light. There was large-scale biological activity down there where there should have been nothing at all. I called an order, and our three landing craft began to spiral inward, making refined readings. We floated close to the treetops and then turned away, still uncertain as to what we'd found. A herd of large animals would have been an enormous surprise, but we'd picked up data unlike any produced by human metabolism.

"Do we crash in on whatever it is?" Morl Klun asked.

"No," I said. "We'll land, we'll conceal the ships as best we can, and we'll do nothing overt until we know what's there. Follow me."

Picking a hiding place for a landing craft in the dark is not easy, but the terrain was heavily wooded, and the only real problem was to slip through the trees without causing damage that would be visible from above. I brought my craft to rest and waited until Morl Klun and Wiln Marra had landed theirs nearby.

We gathered to discuss the situation. All of us were tempted to go and snoop—as Morl Klun put it—but we had no portable infrared equipment, and—since there were no lights or fires—I knew that we'd see very little before dawn.

And we might be walking into a trap. If it were one, I wanted to give some thought to making it close on the Unks instead of on us.

We talked, and then we slept. Shortly before dawn, we were cautiously picking our way through the trees in a manner that our American Indian ancestors, if we had any, would have thoroughly approved of. Somewhere up ahead, I could hear voices. They seemed to be talking normally, but distance, and the trees, muffled the sound. I hesitated, and the others gathered around me.

All three of us listened uncertainly, and then I pointed in what I thought was the right direction and moved on. As we came closer, I was able to pick out, and recognize, one particular voice. I focused on it and kept moving slowly. It belonged to John's son.

Dawn had fully arrived in a large forest clearing when I finally maneuvered myself into position, parted the branches of the last obstructive bush, and peered through. What I saw there was so preposterous that nothing in an excellent and highly varied Regez Anlf education had prepared me for it.

The natives were from our missing Detroit Tribe, but I paid no attention to them. They were surrounding, and administering to, the strangest creature I had ever seen. It was monstrous, and in the dim light of early morning, it looked larger than it actually was. Its bulbous body was three meters wide by five or six long and slightly flattened on its back. It was a mottled blue and brown in color with a texture that resembled crinkly leather. It lay on the ground surrounded by legs that seemed to be folded into extruded segments. It possessed a long, thin neck surmounted by a large head whose shape changed from round to flat with the opening and closing of the enormous gash of a mouth that bisected it.

It was eating, and some of the natives were stuffing leaves into the gaping mouth each time it opened. Others were bringing leaves and piling them in front of the beast. Still others seemed to be grooming it—they were pouring an oily liquid on its crinkly hide and massaging it with strangely shaped brushes. The most inexplicable activity was occurring at the beast's rear, where two young males were turning a reel that was taller than they were— to what purpose was not evident.

Morl Klun muttered something and poised himself for a charge into the clearing. I put out a hand to restrain him. All three of us edged sideways in search of a better vantage point. As we peered through the undergrowth again, the beast suddenly tensed itself. The multiple-jointed legs performed a mechanical miracle, raising the huge body a few centimeters. It hunched forward a meter or so and collapsed. In that brief interval, women rushed in to toss baskets of leaves under the body, and the moment it resettled itself, they were at work behind it, removing a mound of excrement. As soon as they finished, the two men with the reel moved it forward—it was on rollers —while they continued to slowly wind up a slender cable that seemed to be coiled under the beast.

The grooming process had reached the creature's neck. It responded by tilting its head to one side and then the other, flexing its neck, and emitting a series of loud clicks of contentment. Then it resumed eating. In front of it, at the edge of the clearing, males were cutting leaves from the trees, and females were gathering them up and bringing them to the beast as fast as they could carry them. The creature seemed to inhale each offered basketful the instant the basket was emptied. The surrounding circle of forest had been stripped of leaves and looked ravaged.

I took in all aspects of the frenzied activity surrounding that grotesquely improbable beast, and I still failed to grasp what was happening. I wanted to blurt questions at someone. An entire tribe of Earth people had been abducted and brought here and put strenuously to work caring for this creature and foraging for it. The first question was why; the second was why they had submitted. Why didn't they simply fade into the forest? We had encountered no barrier that was restraining them.

Then I saw the Unk. It was tall and slender, with body and limbs that seemed as segmented as the legs of the beast. It was attired in a tightly fitting garment with a cape about its shoulders. Its head was narrow and elongated. It clutched a long staff or wand in one hand.

Suddenly it shouted. The word, in English, was slurred but clearly distinguishable: "Faster!"

It pointed the wand.

A woman carrying leaves to the beast suddenly screamed and collapsed on the ground, writhing in agony. Those near her added their chorus of screams and frenziedly rubbed their bodies.

"Faster!" the Unk called again.

The natives moved much faster.

Morl Klun tugged at my arm, and the three of us crept silently away. We put more than a hundred meters between us and the clearing before we stopped to talk in whispers. There was no point in taking chances with an alien life-form's acuity of hearing, and I knew positively that the spectacle we had just been watching would not disappear during our absence. It would be there, in virtually the same place, for the remainder of the day.

"Some of the natives are working almost out of the Unk's sight," Morl Klun said. "It should be easy to abduct one of them—John's son, for example—and find out what this is all about."

"It'd be a waste of time," I said. "I've got a much better idea. I'm going to abduct the Unk and find out what this is all about."

15

I led the way back to my landing craft, where I got a tool kit and began to tinker with my protective suit. I had an idea about the Unk's wand weapon, and I wanted to test it. Morl Klun and Wiln Marra watched for a few minutes, mystified, asking questions; but I didn't care to describe the project until I found out whether it would work. When I continued to ignore them, they began to debate the import of what we had seen.

Obviously the Detroit Tribe had been abducted to look after the beast, but why anyone would go to the trouble and expense of bringing an animal to such an unsuitable planet—Earth's gravity was so cruelly excessive that it could hardly stand—was a subject that demanded facts rather than speculation. I told them so.

"Their objective was to enslave the population of Earth," Morl Klun said. "That's a fact. The rados with a direction signal, Lee Lukkari as a returning deity—"

"That's it!" I exclaimed. I tossed the protective suit aside.

"What's it?"

"The Unks were trying to make use of a pseudo Lee Lukkari. It'd be nothing less than manifest justice to let them meet the real one. I wonder how this particular Unk will react."

I dashed up the ramp to a storage locker, where I kept an assortment of Lee Lukkari costumes that I'd been using on visits to the scattered Earth tribes. The scanty clothing made my plan considerably more complicated, but the idea of wearing it appealed to my sense of retribution. I started over again, this time with a personal field projector that I could wear on my belt, and I told Morl Klun and Wiln Marra to direct their debate at something practical.

"Such as what?" Morl Klun asked.

"Such as what we're going to do with this Unk when we catch it."

Morl Klun dashed off to his own landing craft and returned with a roll of stowage netting. "We'll wrap it in this."

"That'll immobilize it," I said, "but it doesn't answer the question of what we're going to do with it."

"We'll take it to Detroit Base and keep it there," Morl Klun said. "The same goes for the beast and for John's son and his people. The complete disappearance of this troupe will create a considerable mystery for the Unks, and the more mysterious we seem, the more effective our actions will be."

"Is it possible to get that thing up a landing ramp?" I wondered.

"I'm sure we can do that," Morl Klun said. "I'm wondering whether it's possible to get one through the entrance. We'll have to take measurements. But we'll manage."

Wiln Marra said doubtfully, "Maybe it'd be better to find a nice, concealing forest somewhere, with an unlimited supply of leaves."

"Definitely not," Morl Klun told him. "That beast is an important clue to the Unk mystery, and I want both it and the Unk kept safely and securely."

"What are you going to feed it after you get it there?" Wiln Marra asked. "Hauling leaves for it might be a full-time task for at least three landing craft."

"Then we'll teach it to eat something else," Morl Klun said cheerfully. "Or we'll haul leaves for it if we must."

I told them again to aim their debate at something practical. "Do you realize that this is the first time in history that Regez Anlf citizens have gone forth to meet a representative of an alien space power in personal combat? What does a well-dressed Regez Anlf soldier wear? How are you going to arm yourselves?"

"With you to protect us," Morl Klun said, "why would we need arms?"

They decided to keep on their protective clothing, just in case my tinkering didn't work. All I asked of them was that they keep out of sight and avoid contact with my protective field. My own preparations, once I got the personal field modulator modified, were simple. The Lee Lukkari costume offered little scope for concealing an arsenal even if we'd had one. I decided to carry an audio amplifier. When Lee Lukkari spoke, I wanted everyone within a kilometer to take notice. As an afterthought, I wrapped a long cloak about me.

We carefully made our way back through the trees. When we approached the clearing, I motioned the others to keep behind me, and I cautiously parted the leaves of a bush and looked through.

The scene was unchanged. The Unk was seated comfortably in what looked like an inflated chair, and as I watched, it suddenly shouted, "Faster!" and pointed its wand. The natives had learned their lesson; they moved faster.

After a few minutes, I backed away and began to circle.

"What's wrong?" Wiln Marra hissed.

"Nothing," I whispered. "Come on."

I wanted to stage my appearance carefully, both for maximum effectiveness and to give the Unk time to react. I also thought it wise to make certain that there were no other Unks about.

At one edge of the clearing, there was a stack of empty reels as well as several filled with cable. There also was a portable shed that looked like a large box.

"That cable," Morl Klun whispered. "Is it the beast's leash?"

I had no answer, so I didn't try to give him one. I moved parallel to the clearing until I came to the point where it was widest. Again I parted leaves and peered through.

There was another flurry of activity around the beast. Several women had surrounded it and were lifting it by the edges of its body, and others were swabbing its stomach with mops that they dipped in an oily liquid. I waited until they had finished and returned to their normal routine of piling leaves in front of it.

"Don't worry about getting it into the landing craft," I whispered over my shoulder. "If it won't go, we'll pick it up and carry it. It's that light. Are you ready?"

They chorused their assent.

I cautiously parted branches and leaves. When I had cleared a passage for myself, I sprang into the open. Dramatically I flung my cloak aside.

The Unk leaped to its feet. I caught the full, frontal view of its appearance for the first time. Its eyes seemed enormously large for such a narrow face. It stood rigidly, staring at me—but whether with amazement or terror I could not say.

Before it could react further, I tripped my audio amplifier. "I am Lee Lukkari!" my voice thundered. "What are you doing with my people?"

I advanced slowly; the Unk backed away slowly. Suddenly it remembered its wand. It raised it, pointed it at me. My protective field emitted static, and the next moment the Unk was on the ground, writhing in agony. My field had discharged along the stream of electrons, and the effect on the Unk was like a short circuit; it walloped the creature's nervous system.

Morl Klun and Wiln Marra hurried up, searched the Unk quickly for weapons, and then wrapped a length of net about it. It lay helplessly, still twitching with pain.

The natives watched with consternation until they realized that their enemy had been emphatically dealt with. Then they crowded about me excitedly, and I hurriedly switched off my field as some of them tried to embrace my feet. Even the beast seemed to sense that something unusual was happening. It extended its long, thin neck in an arc and tried to look behind it.

John's son had been cutting leaves beyond the clearing, and he had missed most of my performance. Now he came hurrying up to me. "I knew!" he panted fervently. "I knew you'd come!"

"We'll talk later," I told him. "I want to know everything that's happened, but there's no time now. Can you make that—" I pointed at the beast. "Can you make it go where you want it to?"

"It goes only straight ahead and very slowly."

"Then we'll have to make do with it going straight ahead," I said.

Morl Klun went for my landing craft. He landed directly in front of the beast and lowered the ramp under its nose. Long minutes later, when the beast had hunched itself only once and not moved noticeably, we decided to resort to drastic measures. We stopped feeding it and at the same time we piled leaves in a trail leading inside the landing craft, where we stacked more leaves. Morl Klun improvised a small electric probe. The women surrounded the beast and lifted.

It bleated pathetically as the probe touched it. Then it extended its neck and began to sniff at the trail of leaves. Its lurches became rhythmic, and a jerky, torturously slow movement resulted. As soon as the entire body was on the ramp, I raised it so that the beast was sliding downhill instead of laboring up an incline. Wiln Marra greased its sides in case it stuck in the entrance. Finally it slipped through. With a huff of satisfaction it folded its head around a pile of leaves. I closed the ramp.

To my amazement, I discovered that the two males with the reel had followed the beast up the ramp and inside, where they continued to wind in the cable. Wiln Marra started to question them, but I told him we'd wasted too much time already. We loaded as many of the Detroit Tribe as we could carry in the other two craft, told the remainder to hide until we returned for them, and took off for a low-level flight to Detroit Base.

I shared my control room with the Unk. It watched my every move and winced whenever I seemed to be reaching in its direction, but it uttered no sound.

Our landing among the blacks and Icelanders that we'd settled at Detroit Base was a sensation, but we had no time to enjoy it or even to offer explanations. Wiln Marra and Morl Klun left again with two landing craft as soon as the members of the Detroit Tribe were unloaded. They were to pick up the remaining natives and every item of equipment and supplies that belonged to the Unks.

I turned the captured Unk over to Rek. The Icelanders, when they comprehended that this was one of the authors of Mainland Fever, would have cheerfully torn it to pieces, but I quickly made them understand that I would do some tearing myself if anything happened to it.

They carried it away, and I confronted the task of getting the beast out of my landing craft.

It seemed not to know how to back up. The electric probe made it whine and cringe and hunch, but it would not move. Finally I thought of trying a bright light. That worked—slowly. The beast recoiled backward one hunch —and one centimeter—at each flash, and eventually it slipped through the entrance and skidded down the ramp, bleating pathetically. Then it sniffed the fresh leaves that had been cut for it under John's son's supervision, and it forgot its tribulations in an orgy of eating. Later we would have to face the problem of finding food for it, but there were enough trees inside the base to keep it well-fed for days if we didn't mind stripping them.

The two males with the reel were still positioned at the beast's rear. I asked them, "What *are* you doing?"

One of them shrugged. "It—" He gestured at the beast. "It . . . *makes* this." He indicated the cable.

"Makes it how?" I demanded.

He did not know. "We tickle it now and then—like this." He produced an oddly shaped brush and demonstrated. "And it keeps making it."

"So it makes it, and you reel it up," I agreed. "Then what happens?"

"Then someone takes the reels away."

"Who?"

"Anyone."

They explained that an Unk came and cut the cable when the reel was full, and anyone not urgently occupied with something else was ordered to take the reel away. Usually it had been a woman, since there were so few males in the tribe.

I questioned the women. The reel was light, they said, even when it had been wound full, and one of them could lift it. But because of its size it was awkward to carry, and usually two or three worked together. The full reels were taken to wherever reels were being stacked. At dusk, the strange thing from the sky came and took them.

I decided to wait until Morl Klun and Wiln Marra returned before pursuing the question of what it was that the beast made. They would bring all of the Unk supplies and equipment, which doubtless would furnish important clues. I took John's son aside to find out what he could tell me about his tribe's abduction.

He knew nothing at all about it. The tribe had decided that my instructions about hiding did not forbid them to return to their village to sleep at night. They thought they would be safe in the darkness, though they had posted sentries as instructed. They went to bed at their usual time; they awoke in the Mississippi forest feeling extremely ill, and one of the pregnant girls miscarried. There were several Unks there, prodding them to their feet with shocks from their wands and shouting orders. The shocks were administered deliberately as a demonstration of what would happen to them anytime they failed to obey, instantly, whatever they were told to do.

"Cruel," John's son murmured. "Cruel."

The shocks brought on another miscarriage, and Sulette, the first girl to become pregnant, had given birth prematurely. The infant was born dead; probably it had been killed by the shocks. I would have used a stronger word than "cruel."

"There was only one Unk watching you today," I told John's son. "Why didn't you run away?"

That had been tried the first day. The Unks' terrible wands reached out through the forest for a great distance; and then, when the runaways had been returned, the entire tribe was punished with shocks. So none of them had dared to try it again. At first there had been a large number of Unks—sometimes as many as ten—watching and giving orders and inflicting punishment. Later the number diminished, but every Unk had the wand that inflicted pain at a distance, and it was known that even a successful escape would result in cruel pain for those left behind. So they had postponed further attempts.

"Mostly, we were waiting for you," John's son said. There was a note of reproach in his voice. He could not understand why it had taken us so long.

The Unks had charged his people with caring for the beast and feeding it as much as it could eat. If the beast showed any sign of hunger, they would be punished. If it sickened, they would be severely punished. If it died, all of them would die. So the Unks had promised. Once the tribe had been put to work, the natives had no time at all during their waking hours for reflection or conspiring or for doing anything at all except minister to the beast as they were told. The Unks not only did not answer questions; they did not permit questions.

When Morl Klun and Wiln Marra returned, we gave the Icelanders the task of unloading the Unk property. I asked the Detroit Tribe to continue looking after the beast while others prepared housing for them. John's son looked crestfallen. He had rashly assumed that rescue meant escape from that unrelenting burden.

"Tomorrow we'll find easier ways of doing it," I promised him. "But the beast is valuable, and it must be kept healthy. And you are the only ones who know how to do it."

He brightened when I promised that his people would have the pleasure of teaching what they knew to the other colonists. I cut a length of cable from one of the reels, and then my cousins and I went to our headquarters.

While I told them what I had learned, the three of us studied the length of cable. It was dirty gray in color. It looked like a piece of nondescript thick rope—it was slightly larger than a centimeter and a half in diameter—but it was much lighter than any rope we had ever seen.

"Obviously the Unks have a use for it, and they must think it's valuable," Morl Klun said. "There's no point in speculating further. The Unk knows. Let's have a go at it."

The Icelanders were keeping it in a room on the first floor. It was seated on a chair in the corner, still wrapped in the net. It had got over its fright, and now it was darting furtive glances about the room, studying its guards and measuring distances to door and windows as though it were craftily weighing its chances for escape. The net kept it helplessly immobilized, so it had made no attempt—which was fortunate for it. The two sturdy Icelandic youths guarding it were itching for an excuse to lay their hands on it.

It transferred its attention to us when we entered and watched us warily.

"All three of us?" Wiln Marra asked. "Or just one?"

"One," Morl Klun said confidently. "Me."

Regez Anlf psychologists had long contended that the practice of accepting the first person contacted on an outworld as Regez Anlf representative and making his or her eyes the windows through which we viewed that world was sheer idiocy. The process of mind-mating gave us all of that individual's knowledge and understanding, a priceless gift that would have required many years of observation and study even to approximate. Further, it gave the Regez Anlf comprehension of an alien viewpoint—which otherwise might have taken centuries of study to acquire or never have been achieved at all.

But in assimilating all of an individual's knowledge, we also assimilated that individual's ignorance along with its prejudices, its superstitions, and its misinformation. The same objections applied in probing the mind of our Unk. There was no question of mind-mating, of course—Regez Anlf ethics could not be applied to a species that had attempted to exterminate or enslave a world population. We intended to take what we could from this Unk and give it nothing in return. The question was whether all three of us should tap its mind. If we did, all of us would be restricted in our outlooks by the scope of a single alien mentality. We also would have to contend with the same prejudices and misinformation. Morl Klun felt that we should absorb the mental sets of three different Unks, preferably of vastly different status. For one of us to tap the minds of more than one individual was of course out of the question—that would inflict complexes of monstrous proportions on us.

We agreed with him completely. The question was which of us should take on this first Unk, which we'd already concluded was an individual of slight consequence.

"We have to start with what we've got," Morl Klun said. "It's important to learn as much as we can as quickly as we can."

We agreed with that, too, and there were excellent reasons why Morl Klun should go first. The best reason of all was that he wanted to.

"All right," I said. I told the Icelanders to bring the Unk upstairs. It was so light that one of them could have handled it, but both deserved that pleasure. They perhaps squeezed it unnecessarily, and it struggled furiously despite the restraining net. In our upstairs headquarters, it threshed its head about and kept throwing off the probes until Wiln Marra finally rendered it unconscious with an injection.

Morl Klun nonchalantly stretched out on a pad beside it. "Say goodbye," he told me while Wiln Marra was attaching probes and connecting electrodes. "I may never be the same again."

"With you, that's likely to be an improvement," I said.

Wiln Marra threw the switch.

I left the operation to him and went to see how the beast was faring.

It was faring very well indeed. The colonists found it fascinating. It was having all the accessible parts of its body massaged with oil, its head was being affectionately scratched by no less a personage than Heldi, and it was purring contentedly while it continued to eat voraciously and to make the cable that the two patient males from the Detroit Tribe were winding onto an almost full reel. I told Rek to cut the cable and start a new reel as soon as that one was full, and then I went to talk with all of the Earth tribes—an operation that sometimes took hours. I wanted the chiefs kept informed, and—very soon—I wanted to bring all of them together for a meeting. It was important that all of the tribes fully understood the menace and knew what could be done to contend with it. Eventually I hoped that all of them would work together to rid Earth of the Unks.

When I finally returned to our headquarters room four hours later, Wiln Marra was still monitoring his instruments. Both the Unk and Morl Klun were unconscious. "How much longer?" I asked.

Wiln Marra shrugged. "There are some extremely strange patterns. I've often wondered if it would be possible to have a life-form that used its brain only as a computer—to store data—and did its thinking somewhere else."

"That's already true of most life-forms," I said. "Get on with it."

Finally he pulled the switch and began to detach the electrodes. I went to the door and called the two Icelanders. "Carry the Unk downstairs," I said, "and treat it gently. It'll have a headache for a while. If it's able to eat, give it food."

Wiln Marra and I made ourselves comfortable and watched Morl Klun until his eyelids began to twitch and he convulsively clutched his head. He sat up and looked about him dazedly. Finally he spoke.

"I don't believe it," he said.

16

We sat in the comfortable chairs that we used for conferences. The view from the nearby windows was the one I most enjoyed—the sweep of forest covering the ruins of old Detroit, here seen through the turquoise haze of the dome—but today I kept my eyes on Morl Klun.

His chair was tilted far back, and he rested comfortably in it with his eyes closed. Wiln Marra and I had resolutely silenced his attempts to blurt what he had learned. A person coming out of a mind contact has to be handled with care—as he very well knew.

"Answers only," I told him. "Who are you?"

He responded with an unintelligible jumble of syllables—the Unk's name, I supposed, and I was surprised that he could pronounce it. Or perhaps he didn't. "*What* are you?" I asked.

"I'm a farmer," he said slowly. "Maybe not exactly a farmer, but I cultivate, and I feed the harvest to my jerbd, and that's considered farming."

"What are you doing here?"

"Farming," he said simply.

"Who brought you here?"

"The Klniaq."

"What's the Klniaq?"

"It's a—" He paused. "A group, an organization, a—"

"Union?" I suggested. "Guild?"

"No." He shook his head impatiently.

"Marketing association? Syndicate?"

"No. But it's all of that. It's a combine. A combine runs it. I work for it. But not exactly. It's very confused. The combine found this world where jerbdz would flourish, and it guaranteed me a productive site and brought me here with my jerbd, and the combine will handle my gruskm."

Wiln Marra and I exclaimed together, "What's gruskm?"

"That's what the jerbd extrudes. Issues. Excretes. No." He paused. "The jerbd makes the gruskm when stimulated and when its food is right. It—it *spins* it."

"How valuable is the gruskm?"

"Enormously valuable to the Klniaq—the Klniaq gets huge prices for it. I have to take what I'm paid, but I'll do well regardless."

"Why is the gruskm valuable?"

"Because of the demand for it. Because it is unique—there are no substitutes—and because everyone desires it."

"What is it used for?"

"Fabric."

"What's so unique about a fabric made of gruskm?"

"It has the most wonderful softness, and the most wonderful sheerness, and the most wonderful lightness. It is gossamer. It is a mere film of a fabric. Everyone desires it. Everyone is willing to pay high prices for it. It covers the skin so lightly, it brings comfort and warmth and attractiveness, it models the body contours, it's as revealing as the wearer desires. It is the most important item of interworld trade in a vast interworld civilization." Morl Klun opened his eyes and sat up straight. "Does any of that make sense to you?"

"Not yet," I said. "Perhaps it would if we had a sample of this fabric. What are the chances that the Unk doesn't know what he's thinking about? How much of this comes out of his own knowledge and experience and how much is rumor or gossip?"

"He knows. It's an old industry. His father followed it, and his grandfather. It's been his life's work and also that of his brothers and sisters. They're professional ranjerbdz, meaning farmers or herders—more particularly, owners—of jerbdz. He knows."

"All right," I said. "Relax. I'm going to start over." Morl Klun leaned back and closed his eyes. "Where do you come from?" I asked.

We spent the afternoon, the evening, and most of the night questioning him. Then we slept for a few hours, and in the morning we tried again. In the end we had a picture. Multitudes of details were fuzzy or missing, but the full dimensions were there. And, like Morl Klun, we didn't believe it.

The piece of gruskm that I had cut from the reel lay on the table before us, and from time to time we studied it, and handled it, and attempted to divine the source of the fabulous value that impelled the Unks to spread its production through the galaxy at such enormous cost both to themselves and to the inhabitants of the worlds they coveted. We failed to see it as anything more than a worthless length of soiled gray rope.

"It's treated," Morl Klun said. "It's soaked in vats of what must be chemicals. Our Unk doesn't know much about the chemicals, and what he does know is too inexact for a linkage with our chemical terminology."

We abandoned the gruskm and turned our attention to a greater mystery. The Unks had no government, not even in the associative sense through which the Regez Anlf regulated relations between its member worlds and strictly supervised contact with outworlds. How an interworld society could exist, and support an extensive and flourishing commerce, without a mutually agreed upon overriding authority defied our understanding. It was commerce without law, without regulation, without common practices, without collective understanding.

Instead, there were the Klniaq.

They were associations of business interests. They were combines that had achieved interworld monopolies in areas of manufacturing or raw materials. The gruskm combine was the wealthiest, the most powerful. It had existed for centuries of our time. It planned its expansion to meet an ever-increasing demand in future centuries. It seeded potential worlds with destruction to prepare them for their eventual takeover by ranjerbdz, and then it brought them into production as needed.

"What special conditions make a planet eligible for exploitation?" I asked.

"Chemistry," Morl Klun said. "Native plants have to be tested. Their chemistry has to be such that the jerbdz eating them can produce high-quality gruskm. If there are no such plants in abundance, then there must be extensive and maybe expensive experiments to see whether suitable alien plants can be grown on the world. They prefer to use native forage when it is at all suitable."

"There must be other requirements," I said. "Gravity? The jerbd originates on a low-gravity planet. There must be limits to the amount of gravity it can thrive under."

"No doubt. Gravity may influence the quality of the gruskm, too. So the Unks look for worlds with the right chemistry, the right gravity, the right atmosphere, and maybe a long list of other requirements with varying limits for each. Our Unk knows next to nothing about that. He simply went where the Klniaq took him."

Wiln Marra spoke up. "The number of worlds available for exploitation would be severely restricted by even a few limitations. The Klniaq would have to range over an enormous area seeking them. When it finally found one—"

"Wait!" I said. "We're not ready for that. Let's start over. We have a high-tek multi-world civilization. Each world has its own government, but there are interworld business combines, and no doubt each of them attempts to influence and corrupt each or any of the world governments when it seems advantageous to do so. It's a chaotic method of organizing a civilization."

"They grew into it," Morl Klun said. "And then they lacked the intelligence and the wisdom to grow beyond it."

"Obviously," I said and went on, "In this multi-world civilization, there is one low-gravity world where a thread-spinning beast has evolved. Because of the low gravity, it has become a large beast, and the thread—a remarkably light thread—has sufficient substance to be useful in garment making. The garments are introduced on other worlds and become a fad. There's a limit to the amount of gruskm the original world can supply—one jerbd can only spin so much, even when encouraged by tickling, and its appetite requires an enormous grazing area. To increase production, one must raise more jerbdz from infancy and find an equally enormous grazing area for each one. An unlimited demand and a restricted supply make for fantastic prices, and these attract the attention of a Klniaq, which takes over the gruskm business. With its unlimited financial resources, it is able to hire scientists, send out exploring ships, and place the expansion of gruskm production on a sound business and scientific basis. One of the exploration ships finally reaches Earth. When?"

Morl Klun shrugged. "A hundred years before the Regez Anlf came here. Two hundred. Maybe more. This Klniaq is a huge organization with a vision of business futures. It has to find potentially suitable worlds, test them scientifically, and consider what steps are necessary to make the most likely worlds ready for use when their production will be needed. Earth presented a special problem because it was infested with vermin. With intelligent life. The Klniaq wouldn't object to vermin—they're not just potentially useful; they're essential. One of the requirements of a suitable planet would be teachable slaves—a tractable life-form capable of looking after the jerbdz. But a high percentage of Earth's vermin was made up of high-tek civilizations that wouldn't be amenable to slavery or even to having aliens establish a slave economy among Earth's more backward peoples. The high-tek civilizations considered the exploitation of backward peoples to be their own inalienable right. So they had to go."

"Did the Unks start the nuclear war?" I asked.

"My Unk knows nothing about what happened on Earth before he came here," Morl Klun said. "But we're entitled to our own deductions. It's certainly possible that the Unks started the nuclear war. I think it probable. They studied Earth for many years if not centuries. They would know that a nuclear bomb or two at a moment of great political tension would provoke a holocaust, destroy the high-tek civilizations, eliminate much of the undesirable vermin, and conveniently reduce the remainder to a feeble level of survival. So they triggered the holocaust and then went away to bide their time."

"And the Beesee, the Mainland Fever?" I asked.

"My guess is that too many vermin survived the holocaust, and among them were highly capable nuclei who were intent on rebuilding civilization and actually setting about it. A dusting of synthetic plague germs was supposed to correct all of that. Perhaps at that point the false Lee Lukkari appeared to backward tribes all over Earth, presented rados, made gifts of food and other essentials, and promised to announce her return on the rados. Once a cult had been firmly established, the Unks started their plague and left. But the plague worked too well. It almost left the world with no potential slaves at all."

"What about Iceland?" Wiln Marra asked. "The Icelanders are in no position to interfere with what the Unks do elsewhere in the world. Why persist in trying to eliminate them?"

"Superficially, they're still high-tek. They have well-built cities. They operate a fishing fleet. They even have electric lights. The Unks would view them as a potential source of trouble."

I said slowly, "I have difficulty in believing that even a totally unregulated business enterprise could be absolutely without conscience."

"It seems unreal to us because such practices are outside Regez Anlf experience," Morl Klun said. "That doesn't mean that Regez Anlf citizens are innately virtuous—just that we were fortunate enough to arrive at the kind of governments, and to establish the kind of traditions, that prevent such a thing. Look at Earth history—the treatment of native Africans. Or native Americans, for that matter. In Central America, natives weren't amenable to slavery, so they were slaughtered. The history of North American natives is a long history of atrocities inflicted on them. In either case, if the vermin could have been eliminated by a light dusting with a synthetic plague, would those who wanted the land have hesitated?"

"No more than a farmer who wanted to rid his land of insects and weeds would have hesitated to use insecticides and weed killers," I agreed.

Wiln Marra had been listening with a formidable scowl. Suddenly he snapped his fingers. "Just a moment!" He dashed to the reference shelf for a book. "This is the link I was trying to think of," he said excitedly. "The disease malaria was common in warm areas around the world. The black peoples, who originated in the areas most infested with it, developed their own hereditary defense. It was called sickle-cell anemia. Anyone wanting to wipe out Earth's nonblack population and reduce the remainder to a manageable size could have done so with a malaria-type disease. Those blacks with the protective heredity would survive. No one else would. That, I think, is what the Unks tried to do. The fluke of geography combined with their own courage saved the Icelanders. Elsewhere, all of the human and most of the animal population of Earth got the disease. Probably a significant percentage of the black population was supposed to survive and provide a stock of slaves. But as Morl Klun so astutely remarked, it worked too well."

"It must have been a shock to the Unks," I mused. "They returned with a load of jerbdz and ranjerbdz expecting to find a world ready for immediate production of a gruskm crop—and behold, not one of their rados responded, and the only evident Earth population was a high-tek white community. Plus some totally unexpected aliens snooping about—probably they knew that the Regez Anlf left during the holocaust, and they were certain that there'd be nothing here to attract us back. Having no conscience themselves, they wouldn't anticipate that the Regez Anlf might have one. Do you think they've been doing this sort of thing to world after world?"

"I'm certain they have," Morl Klun said. "They've done whatever they had to do to take the worlds they wanted."

"This has got to be stopped," I said fervently. "It's got to be stopped here on Earth, but it's also got to be stopped elsewhere. We'll have to seed the galaxy with Reclamation Teams to correct what the Unks have been led to by their passion for gruskm."

"By their passion for profit," Morl Klun said. "The gruskm is only the means."

I leaned back and closed my eyes. It had been a long night, and it was going to be a longer day. "I was going to bring in all of the chiefs to let them see the jerbd and hear for themselves what John's son and his people experienced," I said. "But it's critically important that we get this hypothesis to Naslur Rayl as quickly as possible. So I'm going to write a report and send it off."

"What do you want us to do?" Wiln Marra asked.

"Study jerbd husbandry," I said.

I told Wiln Marra to observe the animal carefully and see what he could learn from the way the Detroit Tribe had been taught to care for it. I wanted Morl Klun to question the Unk for information that hadn't leaked through during the mind tap. I especially wanted to know something about processing the gruskm.

They left, and I went to my own room to compose a report in unruffled solitude. Before I began, I called Rek in and told him to post a guard that would maintain silence in and around the building and to see that no one disturbed me for any reason at all except a direct attack on the dome by the Unks.

Any hypothesis aimed at impressing Naslur Rayl had to be swathed in facts. I produced a document that was certain to please Lefkir Bonrin when he saw it, and I knew that he would see it the moment Naslur Rayl finished reading it if not before. I researched Wiln Marra's medical inspiration and documented it through a parade of Earth authorities. A percentage of Earth's black population had a hereditary resistance to malaria—that was certain. I delved into the history of the Time of Troubles that preceded the holocaust, as recorded by the Regez Anlf's Earth-born employees: The fires that destroyed major cities—from my perspective, almost certainly Unk arson; the rumors that caused international dissent, racial conflict, military desertions, and terrorism—almost certainly Unk-inspired and Unk-assisted. Much that had been inexplicable in Earth's historical record—the distorted profile of a world bent on destroying itself—suddenly took on an awesome clarity. The first nuclear bombs—alleged to have come from the Chinese—could be traced in retrospect to the Unks. The Unks were trying to gain a world. No Earth nation had anything to gain from the holocaust except a particularly horrible method for committing suicide.

I tried to surround the hypothesis with a sturdy buttress of fact that would prove unyielding even to Lefkir Bonrin's battering. The final report filled a viewing screen twenty-seven times and would be several Earth months en route by faster-than-light transmission—the exact time depending on the position of Regez Anlf ships that could refocus it. To ensure against distortions and technical garbles, I would have to send it twice. But at least the report was finished.

I got to my feet and looked out of a window. It was dark outside, but there was a hint of dawn on the horizon. I had worked through a day and a night without stopping to eat, and I felt famished.

I went to the door, thinking to fix a snack for myself. Outside was a tray with a cold feast on it. Someone—probably Rek—had been solicitous of my welfare while fearing to disobey my orders. I took the tray into my room and began to eat.

Morl Klun came in a short time later. He had heard me moving around. "Finished?" he asked.

I nodded. "Anything new?"

"We've accumulated a lot of jerbd lore. We can tell you more than you want to know, but it certainly isn't urgent."

"I'm going to start the transmission on my report," I said. "Then I'm going to bed. When you feel like doing something, get in touch with all of the tribes and invite the chiefs to that meeting I mentioned. Pick the best time tomorrow, since we'll have to collect all of them and most of the time zones on Earth will be represented. Invite Ira from Iceland, too."

"I'll take care of it," Morl Klun said. "What if the Unks intercept your report?"

"It'd be sheer accident if they did. We haven't transmitted interstellar since the day they arrived. Once they got it, what would they do with it? They'd still have to decipher a code in an unknown language."

"I'll start talking to your chiefs after I've had some breakfast," Morl Klun said.

I finished eating. Then I started the transmission and went off to bed.

Morl Klun awoke me. He had seated himself on a chair beside my bed, and he was gently shaking me. I sat up abruptly; sunlight, softly filtered by the dome, was streaming through the window.

"Sorry," Morl Klun said. "The base isn't under attack, but everything else is, so I thought I'd better wake you."

"What do you mean, 'everything else is'?"

"We've been feeling smug because we have biological survey equipment and the Unks obviously hadn't thought of such a thing. Now they've thought of it. As a result, all of our black tribes have disappeared. I've called each and every one of them, repeatedly. No one answers."

"Then we'll have to run our own survey and rescue them one at a time," I said cheerfully. "I've been thinking that we need a few more jerbdz, and we certainly can find a use for all the Unks we can collect. Let's start right away."

"Unfortunately, we can't," Morl Klun said. "Ira just called. The Mainland Fever has returned to Iceland. Wiln Marra has already left."

17

"It can't be!" I told Morl Klun. "The serum should have conferred immunity on the entire population!"

"But it is," he said. "Or maybe the Unks have contrived some new form of deviltry. Are you coming?"

"You go without me. We have days of grueling work ahead of us, and I can't face that without first finding out what I can about some of the black tribes. I'll get there as quickly as I can."

I went to Iceland by way of South America. I visited the hiding places of the Town Tribe, the West Coast Tribe, and then the South American tribes, and I circled back through Missouri, Louisiana, and Montreal. All of the tribes had disappeared as abruptly and completely as had the first two. None of their possessions had been touched. It intrigued me that the Unks still had no interest in the Regez Anlf communicators. I found all of them, along with the tribes' portraits of Lee Lukkari, and gathered them up. I reasoned that the abductions had occurred at night, and the Unks were not interested in material things—of which they knew that the tribes had very little. All they wanted was live bodies as slave laborers.

I found no other clues worth pondering, but as I skimmed along at low level I made an instrument fix on a flying saucer that was settling into a forest in what had been northern Georgia. My probe in that direction picked up a mass of metal at ground level, and I noted the location. There would be a jerbd there, I thought, and possibly the Louisiana Tribe being broken in as slave attendants—with a group of flying saucers guarding it.

When finally I reached Iceland, I found that I hadn't been missed. The disease was Mainland Fever, but it had infected only the few humans and animals who had escaped infection the first time around and had somehow been overlooked in the confusion when we were administering mass injections. Some of these had lived in isolated locations; others had been too occupied with caring for the sick to claim treatment for themselves.

Wiln Marra, very capably assisted by Heldi, already had everything in hand. The grateful Icelanders served us a lavish meal, and Morl Klun and I returned to my landing craft for a conference.

I squinted at the southern sky, where the Unks' spaceship was shortly due for an invisible daytime passage. It never came as far north as Iceland, and that was some small comfort to us. We didn't have to worry about viewers with super-magnification units watching our every move from space.

"This can't go on," I said bluntly. "The Unks thought they goofed with their first seeding, so they tried again. Now they'll know that Mainland Fever is no longer effective here, and they'll concoct something else. We talked about this before—we're doing nothing but react to what the Unks do, and we've got to turn that around."

"Agreed," Morl Klun said. "How?"

"First, I want to serve notice that Iceland is off limits. Hands off Iceland."

"Splendid idea. How are you going to do it? Even if we had the equipment and materials, we couldn't put a protective field over the whole island. It's too large."

"One of my classmates was a practical joker," I said. "Unfortunately, he also was brilliant. He rigged up something for a prank and almost killed people with it. They threw him out of the Space Academy. I'm wondering whether I could do the same thing on a somewhat larger scale."

"What was it?"

"A projected force field. The effect only lasts for a few seconds, but if it could be timed to collide with a saucer, the results might even be spectacular."

"How are you going to time it?"

"The Unks must be running regular low-level surveys over the island. If I could catch them at it, I'd cure them forever from flying over Iceland."

Morl Klun couldn't understand how one went about projecting a field, but the notion sounded intriguing to him. "What do you need?" he asked.

"A lot of stock parts and a field modulator from one of the spare landing craft."

"Let's go get them."

It took the remainder of the day to assemble the apparatus. I mounted it on top of the building where the Althing met, and I placed the projector on top of a mountain near the town. Its elevation gave me a very satisfactory sweep, but only against a low-level approach from south or southwest. It was my hunch that the Unks would come in low over Iceland's largest town looking for evidence that their second seeding of the plague had been effective. This kind of observation would be difficult at night, so I thought they'd come late in Iceland's long afternoon on the next day.

We moved our landing craft to the country and had them disguised as haystacks so the Unks would have no cause for suspicion. I spent the entire day teaching a picked group of young Icelanders to shoot down flying saucers. They were skeptical that the Unks would come and certain that my machine would not work, but I kept them at it, and two hours before sunset a flying saucer skimmed in low out of the west.

The instruments picked it up long before it could be seen visually, and what followed was a textbook demonstration of what I'd just been explaining to my students. The saucer's image loomed large on the screen, I tripped the projection, and an instant later the saucer collided with it. The projected field, during its brief materialization, was as solid as the mountain that supported our projector, and the results were as spectacular as I anticipated. The saucer crumpled with a flash and an explosion, and the debris fell into the sea.

My young Icelanders danced and cheered. The townspeople rushed excitedly into the streets and called up to us to ask what had happened. I ordered them back inside and quieted my assistants.

"Watch!" I told them. "There's a very good chance that another saucer will be sent to find out what happened to that one."

They gathered around the screen and watched eagerly. An hour later they were still watching, but their enthusiasm had waned somewhat. I was a prophet, and I had proved it; but even proven prophets were fallible.

Then the Unks came—and not in one saucer, but three, which instantly restored me to the pinnacle of prophesy. I let the young Icelanders handle the instruments themselves. In their eagerness they undershot the first ship, and its only damage was a punishing bounce. The other two, flying the ends of a V formation, hit the field squarely and disintegrated. The first ship circled; the Icelanders held grimly to their instruments and got it on the second try.

"Will they send more?" I was asked.

"Not until they've had time to think this over," I told them. "The saucer your first shot missed probably sent back some information about what happened."

I was sufficiently pleased with this performance to set up a second station on the southeast corner of the island. My first crew, now veterans, furnished instructors for a second crew. I was uncertain whether the Unks would try to slip more saucers past this unexpected defense or whether they would consider the loss of four reason enough for leaving Iceland alone for a time. I told my defense teams to expect tedious days and nights when nothing happened and action at the moment when it was least expected, and they promised to remain alert.

"A splendid aggressive defense," was Morl Klun's pronouncement.

"It's no substitute for an offense," I said. "A determined enemy can busy itself elsewhere and try again later. Or it can try something different."

He grinned at me. "I know. You want to rig that thing on your landing craft and go looking for saucers."

"I hadn't thought of that, but it sounds like fun."

"What were you thinking of?"

"I was thinking about that Unk spaceship that's defiling our skies. We can expect trouble of one kind or another as long as it's up there."

"True enough, but it's going to take more than a conjuring trick with force fields to remove it. What did you have in mind?"

"Nothing definite. Just a feeling of indignant determination. The Unks have been playing with us, and I'm angry about it."

"I don't agree," Morl Klun said. "The contrary—they've been ignoring us. That amazes me. They've paid no attention to the bases at all. Now they may decide that we're dangerous and try to take action."

"The ship," I said, "is the key to everything."

"As long as nothing can be done—"

"We'll have to think," I said. "Investigate. Assemble facts. Search for a weakness. I'm tired of seeing it up there. It's an insult."

"It's also a very considerable ship," Morl Klun said thoughtfully.

We sat and stared at each other for the next ten minutes without speaking.

Wiln Marra arrived with Heldi following on his heels like a worshipful pet. The plague, he announced cheerfully, was under control. His most serious cases had been a young litter of pigs. He had miscalculated the dose of serum and given them the amount intended for lambs, and they'd got very sick indeed.

"I'm sure the two of you sat up all night stroking their tails," I said sweetly. "Are you finished here? I'm going back to Detroit Base where I can do some thinking."

He was still concerned about the pigs. Translated, that meant that Heldi was still concerned about the pigs. "I wouldn't dream of tearing you away from such an important problem," I said, still being sweet. "The two of us have some heavy thinking to do, so we're leaving. Be sure and send us regular pig progress reports."

I boarded my landing craft with him looking after me blankly and Heldi looking daggers. The contretemps was my own fault. I'd known since we were children that he did his thinking with his glands.

Morl Klun and I flew back to Detroit Base in formation, and an anxious group of young Icelander colonists surrounded us when we landed. I had already reported to Rek by communicator, and I could only add that everything at home was in splendid shape except for one litter of pigs. Morl Klun and I went directly to our headquarters, seated ourselves in our conference chairs, and stared at the table. An hour later we were still there, still staring, and neither of us had spoken. Wiln Marra came in. He looked at us uneasily, waited for one of us to say something, and finally seated himself in his own chair.

After another ten minutes, he asked plaintively, "What are we supposed to be thinking about?"

"I'm thinking," I announced, "that we should have done some thinking at the beginning. We should have given some thought to Unk psychology."

Morl Klun looked at me with interest. "I've assumed from the beginning that they have one, but I haven't been able to figure out a procedure for thinking about a totally unknown quality. How do you go about it?"

"You go about it by wondering what they're thinking about us," I said. "Since they know all about Lee Lukkari and the Regez Anlf's trading operations, they probably consider it a commercial organization similar to their own Klniaq. They know what products it was trading for, so they certainly know that there's no longer anything on Earth that could interest us. So what do they think we're doing?"

"Ah," Morl Klun said with a superior smile. "It's true that they know the Regez Anlf was here two hundred years ago, and they know all about what it was doing then. *But they don't know we're from the Regez Anlf.*"

I said slowly, "That's true. There's no way they could know that."

"As far as they're concerned, we're a small group of aliens doing some galactic snooping," Morl Klun went on. "Since our ship turned and ran as they approached, and since there are so few of us, and since we've avoided them, there's been no reason for them to consider us a threat."

"Until now," I said. "That enormous ship of theirs may carry a fleet of flying saucers, but they have to notice it when they lose four at a time. They've also noticed the loss of a jerbd, and a ranjerbd, and a group of slaves. And they've noticed the new bases similar to this old Regez Anlf base and the fact that we're using them. So what do they think we're doing?"

"I'd guess that we make no sense at all to them," Morl Klun said. "Maybe they're sitting around a table right now trying to figure out our alien psychology. They certainly won't imagine that the Regez Anlf has fitted out an expensive expedition with no thought of financial return in order to satisfy a moral obligation. As for the disappearance of the ranjerbd and the jerbd and the Detroit Tribe, they may not have connected us with that. We were careful to rake away the marks our landing craft made and to scatter leaves about, and unless they did a really astute investigation, they had to write the whole thing off as an inexplicable mystery."

"They're pretty stupid if they don't suspect us," I said.

"They may suspect, but they can't know. They've seen our landing craft—"

"Of course they have!" I exclaimed. "Landing craft haven't changed much in exterior design over the past two centuries. The landing craft label us Regez Anlf."

Morl Klun scowled. "Not necessarily. You're assuming that these particular Unks have detailed records of what happened here two hundred years ago. I doubt that. Why would they? They see our landing craft as cumbersome, impractical alien ships compared with their saucers. Since the *Hadda* ran off and left us, they may consider us a mere survey team abandoned by our support ship. We're a potential nuisance, but as long as we're avoiding them and not causing any trouble, they've been content to leave us alone. They've had more important problems to worry about—finding slaves and getting the jerbdz into production."

"What are the chances that they'll interrogate the natives and find out all about us?" Wiln Marra asked.

"The Unks never interrogated the Detroit Tribe at all," Morl Klun said. "I see no reason why they would interrogate the others. There's no evident connection between us and the black tribes. On the other hand, they certainly know now that there's a connection between us and the Icelanders.

The picture they have right now *may* look like this: Our mission here is a mysterious one that doesn't concern them. We're not interested in what they're doing, and we won't interfere as long as they leave us alone. Our mission does concern Iceland, however. The Icelanders inexplicably escaped the plague the first time around, and now they've escaped it again, twice, just as mysteriously, and all of that must be due to us. Therefore Iceland is under our protection, and the disappearance of the four saucers constitutes a warning. If they bother us, or Iceland, we'll react drastically. That's how I think they *may* view the situation right now. Of course they'll review that opinion and revise it if we give them any reason to."

"Then let's not give them any reason to," I said. "Let's plan our activities to reinforce that opinion as much as possible. We'll leave them alone if they'll leave us alone."

"You're writing off the black tribes?" Wiln Marra demanded indignantly. "You're going to leave them in slavery?"

"Of course not," I said. "But our actions from now on have got to be in accordance with a well-thought-out master plan. We were fortunate to pull off the rescue of the Detroit Tribe without being caught at it. We can't count on that happening again. From now on, everything will have to be planned carefully."

"Quoth the oracle," Morl Klun pronounced solemnly. "Trot out this well-thought-out master plan. I'd love to see it."

"First," I said, "the starship. While I still consider it an insult and an obscenity, and I would love to try to do something about it, I don't think our resources are up to that. We'll have to wait for inspiration."

"Or a miracle," Morl Klun suggested.

"Don't interrupt the master plan," I said sternly. "As for the Klniaq that owns the spaceship, and the other Klniaq that compete or collaborate with it, and the hundreds or thousands of worlds that support them—they, and their philosophy of mercenary conquest, are properly the business of the Regez Anlf, and the Regez Anlf will have to deal with the Unks sooner or later. The longer it takes the Council to recognize and accept that, the more precarious the Regez Anlf's position will be and the greater the danger to its own worlds. Our duty is to supply as much information as we can and make the threat as clear as possible. These particular Unks are only the vanguard of a ruthless, powerful commercial empire motivated only by greed. Ultimately it threatens to devastate all galactic civilizations in order to exploit the worlds that contain them. The three of us can't begin to deal with a problem like that. We can only sound the alarm. Our proper concern is in saving this world for its own people."

"Agreed," Morl Klun said. "All we have to do is persuade the Unks to go away. Keeping them away will be the task of the Regez Anlf."

"How are you going to persuade them to go away if we can't think of any way to attack their starship?" Wiln Marra asked. "Knocking down an occasional flying saucer won't accomplish much except maybe to reinforce their notion that they should leave us alone."

"The Unks aren't here merely to add another world to their commercial empire," I said. "They're here for profit. So the best way to get them to leave would be to persuade them that Earth is an unprofitable world and should be written off."

"How do we do that?" Wiln Marra asked.

"I don't know," I said.

For another fifteen minutes none of us spoke.

"The black tribes," I said finally. "Our rescue of the Detroit Tribe was done on impulse and a fluke of luck. We can't count on finding another jerbd in an undefended area with only one Unk in charge."

"You're writing off the black tribes!" Wiln Marra said accusingly.

"That's as silly as the last time you said it," I told him. "We have to be realistic about this. We can't rescue them through open warfare. There are too few of us, we're not equipped for it, and we'd probably destroy as many of them as we rescued. We'll have to do it surreptitiously and with careful planning. Before we can even start to plan, we'll have to find out where they are, and that'll take time."

"You're going to let them suffer in slavery—"

"They're suffering," I said. "They may even have a few casualties, but in general the Unks will have to treat them well. There are so few potential slaves on the planet that they can't afford to lose any. We aren't going to write them off, but neither are we going to make desperate attempts to rescue them. We're going to do another biological survey of the planet to find out where all of the tribes are. We'll do it in such a way that the Unks won't know what we're doing. We'll give them no reason to even suspect that the survey is connected with their slaves. We'll ignore the Unks, and we'll encourage them to ignore us. When we've located all of the tribes, the next step will be to learn as much as we can about the circumstances of each one. Then we can consider if or when or how we should rescue it. In the meantime, all of us can try to think of ways to convince the Unks that Earth is an unprofitable planet."

Morl Klun grinned at me. "At least it makes sense to postpone rescuing the black tribes until we find out where they are."

"I suppose it also makes sense to try to think of ways to convince the Unks that Earth is unprofitable," Wiln Marra said. "But I don't think we're going to find any. They studied the planet for centuries, and they already know that it's potentially an enormously profitable world. That's why they came here."

18

Again we flew parallel courses but lower and somewhat slower than we had on our first biological survey. We wanted to map our findings in as great a detail as possible when we did locate a tribe, because we couldn't circle to investigate. We had to present the Unks with the illusion of a totally mysterious activity that had nothing to do with them. For that reason, we flew tedious north-south and south-north laps over North America, ranging from the Arctic to the Gulf coast, even though we were convinced that food and climatic preferences of the jerbdz made it certain that the Unks would locate them in the southern United States or on the west coast north of California.

Several times we glimpsed flying saucers; we ignored them. One trailed us at an extreme distance for several hundred kilometers, but we gave no indication of being aware of it. We had equipped our landing craft to project force fields in the same way that the Icelandic defenses did, and the saucer performing a hostile act would be dealt with summarily, but we would pay no attention to Unks that did not bother us.

By the second day, the Unks' curiosity had become an itch that they desperately wanted to scratch. Three saucers followed us, edging closer and closer. Finally the leader dove on Morl Klun's landing craft as though attempting to force it to land. It collided spectacularly with the projected force field, and the other two fled. We calmly proceeded with our survey without varying our courses an iota. After that we occasionally saw saucers snooping on us from a high altitude, but they never came close again.

As we had expected, the five missing North American tribes were scattered widely across the southern United States. The larger tribes had been broken into compact jerbd-tending units. By the time we had finished with North America, the tedium had become excruciating boredom and our profound sympathy for Burluf Nori had further intensified. We took a much-needed vacation before commencing with South America.

At Detroit Base, we found the colonists highly alarmed about their jerbd. The ungainly creature had become everyone's pet, and the colonists were wracking their imaginations in an attempt to make it comfortable. The Icelanders had rigged a sling for it; periodically they raised its ungainly body off the ground and encouraged it to exercise its legs. As Rek explained to me, in more detail than I cared to know, the creature's inability to stand upright and use its legs meant that the jackknifing limbs never got fully extended. The Icelanders feared that it would lose the use of its legs entirely —hence the periodic exercises.

The Detroit Tribe had been experimenting with its food. The creature would eat virtually anything vegetable, but certain vegetation proved detrimental to it. Its spinners had developed diarrhea—the cable came out a messy smear of yellowish ooze. The creature seemed to be in good health otherwise, but the colonists were deeply worried about this symptom.

The jerbd's leaf diet had been supplemented with fodder brought from Iceland, and when the base's trees became dangerously defoliated, small groups of colonists—both black and white—made nocturnal expeditions to the mainland. I frowned on this; but in a few hours of work they could pack the boats with sufficient leaves to keep the jerbd munching cheerfully through the next day, and they also kept the base supplied with fresh fish. It added a touch of excitement to life at the base, and the danger seemed slight as long as the Unks avoided the base area, so I relented.

I dutifully admired the sling and watched the Icelanders exercising the jerbd's legs. Its feet were curious disks that enfolded my hand and gripped it with painful strength. I conjured up a vision of the beasts—or their arboreal ancestors—gamboling on lengths of their own cable stretched through the treetops on their low-gravity planet.

But I had no more idea than the Icelanders as to what had upset the beast's cable spinning. I suggested that they keep a careful record of what the jerbd ate and that they also should watch to make certain that they weren't accidentally feeding it vines or weeds picked up with the leaves. A couple of days later, Rek told me that the problem was solved. They had caught the jerbd munching on an occasional dandelion leaf or flower from those that now thickly dotted the base's open areas. They had pulled up all the nearby plants, and the jerbd's spinning returned to normal.

"Carry on!" I told him. "Carry" was the operative word—they had to carry leaves and other vegetable matter to the beast for food, and they had to carry away the by-products of manure and cable. I hated to burden them with the chore, but it still seemed important to learn as much as possible about the beast. They managed with more good grace than I expected, and the Icelanders built carts to ease the labor. They also built new reels for the cable. They were delighted to have an unlimited supply of wood to use, and they would have rebuilt the base if I had let them.

We resumed our survey and tediously mapped Central and South America. Again we searched large areas where we knew there was nothing to find in order to convince the Unks that we had no interest in their jerbdz and slaves. We located the South American tribes in eastern Brazil and Argentina, took more time off to visit bases and rest, and moved on to Africa.

Everything seemed to be going well. The Unks' curiosity had diminished. They still followed us occasionally, but it was only for brief periods. It must have been obvious to them that we were performing some kind of survey, and we hoped that the superior officers on their starship were losing sleep in their attempt to figure it out. We continued to fly laps over the continents, even including Antarctica to add to the Unks' confusion, and we carefully noted all the details about the location of a missing black tribe whenever we found one.

Life at the other bases was proving even more boring than at Detroit Base; those colonists had no jerbd to keep them occupied. They had plenty of territory under the domes for pasturing the animals and caring for them and for practicing whatever agriculture they had an inclination for; but the black natives needed more adventurous activities. I finally had to let them venture out in small groups, as I had the colonists at Detroit Base, to look for supplementary forage for the animals and to fish. They were under stern orders to head for the safety of the dome at the first glimpse of a flying saucer and to remain there.

"The problem we face now," Morl Klun announced when we had returned to Detroit Base after yet another boring day of flying survey laps—this time over Asia, where we could fly successions of days without finding anything that would make our instruments flicker—"is that while we're trying to lull the Unks into thinking our activities have nothing to do with them, and we'll leave them alone if they leave us alone, they may be doing the same thing to us. While we're trying to think of something unpleasant that will make them want to leave Earth, they may be plotting something even more unpleasant to drive us away."

"When we were children," I told him, "I used to think you were an optimist. I can't imagine why."

I was too utterly tired out to even be hungry. I politely passed up several invitations to join groups of colonists for an evening meal and went directly to my room. Much later, a gentle knock on my door awakened me. It had been going on for some time when I became consciously aware of it, but it was so subdued that it lacked urgency. I stretched out comfortably and let it continue. It persisted, and finally I responded.

It was Heldi with some of the Icelandic girls. The others were giggling excitedly; Heldi was as coolly dignified as ever.

"We have a gift for you," she informed me.

The situation seemed so odd, and I felt so befogged with sleep, that I didn't know how to react. "That's very kind of you," I said vaguely. "But I already said that I wasn't hungry, and—"

The giggles changed to laughter. Heldi proffered the gift, which was concealed in a fold of coarse Icelandic cloth. I invited all of them in, and I ceremoniously peeled away the cloth.

Inside was a small box of wood. This was not Icelandic. It was something left behind when the original Regez Anlf employees fled Earth—a tiny, rectangular box used for jewelry or other small valuables. I opened it; inside was another piece of folded cloth.

All of the girls, even Heldi, were holding their breaths. I pulled out the folded cloth, and it fell open in my hands, fold after fold, until I could only hold it up before me and stare speechlessly.

It was a garment—a long dress patterned on the ceremonial dresses the Icelandic girls wore for festive occasions. It was ornamented with tiny patterns of exquisitely delicate embroidery, but it was the cloth that was incredible. It was unbelievable. It was almost preposterous, so light and filmy did it seem.

It was gruskm.

"Put the dress on," Heldi suggested.

And I did. I couldn't resist the temptation to wear that billowing softness, couldn't wait to drape it over me. I tore off the rough Regez Anlf worksuit I'd been wearing, and the girls helped me into the dress.

And the feeling was indescribable. The garment's lightness caressed and soothed the skin. It conveyed such a sense of well-being that my exhaustion dropped away from me, and I wanted to cavort and to dance. I suddenly loved my body for the delicious sensory awareness that it gave to me. I wanted to cavort and to dance, and suddenly I did, with the Icelandic girls looking on and applauding.

When I turned, I saw Wiln Marra and Morl Klun grinning into the room. I stopped and demanded, "Did you two know about this?"

"Of course," Morl Klun said. "Actually, they wanted to conduct a scientific experiment. There was some difference of opinion as to whether you're really female, and the dress was a test. I think you passed it."

"This dress," I said, "would even make you feel female. But what—how—"

"Heldi did it," Wiln Marra said admiringly. "She has a most commendable and practical curiosity. She dropped a piece of cable into boiling water, just to see what would happen, and it separated into marvelously fine threads. So she boiled a longer length of it, and these girls wove the threads into cloth. The dress was my idea. It's sheer spun gruskm except for the embroidery. They haven't been able to get the gruskm to take dye."

"I thought you said it had to be soaked in chemicals."

"That was the message the Unk's mind gave me. I'm sure that the Unks do that. Maybe it's a refining process. Your dress is probably gruskm in its crudest form."

"Crude!"

"Well. Over many centuries the Unks will have learned all kinds of refinements in processing gruskm, and it's logical that chemicals would be involved. Perhaps a chemical treatment is necessary to make the thread take dye."

I performed my dance again. "It's sheer intoxication. If this cloth is capable of being refined, I fear for the wearers. The sensation is already like that of a very potent drug."

"At least it gives us a better understanding of what motivates the Unks," Morl Klun said.

"It does," I agreed. "Now we know why gruskm is so valuable."

"We also know that getting the Unks away from a place that can produce it isn't going to be easy," he said.

We finished our survey. We even flew laps over Australia for a day, though we thought we had located all of the missing tribes. The uncertainty came from the fact that the larger groups had been broken up, and we plotted far more jerbd-feeding groups than there had been tribes.

Our misdirection seemed to have worked. The Unks paid less and less attention to us. Locations of intense biological activity were marked in red on the detailed photo map of the Earth that encircled our headquarters room, and we listed every scrap of potentially useful information about each locale.

We still had not thought of a way to convince the Unks that Earth was an unprofitable place for them, and we hadn't managed the beginning of a plan to rescue the captive natives. The only thing we knew for certain was that the Unks had reacted to our successful abduction of the Detroit Tribe and the jerbd by setting up some kind of elaborate surveillance around the areas where the natives were working. Our instruments picked up electronic distortions along with masses of metal—one or more flying saucers concealed on the ground. As time passed and our activity seemed to have no connection with the natives, the saucers were withdrawn. This suggested that the surveillance had been relaxed somewhat, but that could have been illusory.

"The only way we can tell for certain," I said, "is to land and investigate."

We adopted another subterfuge. We visited our bases singly so the Unks would become accustomed to seeing a lone landing craft on a low-level errand. We plotted our routes to occasionally take us past—but not suspiciously near—the jerbd-feeding locations. And we flew in darkness as well as in daylight.

When the Unks had had time to become familiar with that, we were ready for the next step—visiting the captive natives. Wiln Marra flew the landing craft on a night route toward the South American bases. As he passed one of the southern United States locations we had plotted, he dipped into a valley surrounded by hills and hovered just long enough for Morl Klun and me to tumble out.

"See you tomorrow night," I called.

We floated down and took our bearings. This was no Lee Lukkari expedition. We both wore protective clothing and carried equipment that would enable us to deal with anything—we hoped—because we had no idea of what we might have to contend with.

We had a fifteen-kilometer walk ahead of us—except that we did not walk. Personal propulsion has its disadvantages, but there is no substitute for it if ground has to be covered quickly and quietly with a minimal chance of detection. We floated, keeping just above the treetops except where the ground dipped into a valley. When our instruments told us that we were getting close, we slipped down through the trees and floated slowly along the ground, dodging trees and bushes. When we reached the area where we knew natives were being kept captive, we circled it warily and puzzled over what our instruments told us.

There were no flying saucers on the ground. There was some kind of electronic barrier, but much of the biological response came from outside. This made so little sense that we circled the area a second time.

We settled to the ground and faced each other. Morl Klun whispered, "I just don't understand—"

My sudden exclamation cut him off. "Those dudheads!" I whispered. "They've put a protective barrier around the jerbd and left the natives outside!"

"That's nice," Morl Klun whispered back. "It ought to make it much easier to rescue the natives. Or is it a trap?"

"Obviously they value the jerbd much more highly than they do their slaves, which is logical but shortsighted. Their gruskm farming requires both."

"But a mature jerbd may be rare and expensive, and it has to be transported across space," Morl Klun said.

"Slaves will be just as expensive if they have to import them."

It was the wrong place for a debate, so we both lapsed into silence. But the question was so disturbing that I went on meditating it. If the Unks regarded their Earth slaves lightly—had in fact written them off because there were so few of them—it could mean that they intended to import slave labor along with jerbdz, and that offered an enormous potential for future trouble.

As it turned out, more than half the natives were sleeping in a rough camp outside the electronic barrier. They were from our Missouri Tribe, and I found the chief and held a long, whispered conversation with him.

There proved to be nothing sinister about the lack of security. As with the Detroit Tribe, these natives were kept under control by electronic torture. In the early days of their captivity, they had been watched very closely. Those who attempted to escape were treated brutally; the entire tribe received severe punishment after every attempt. Now, even though they knew that the surveillance had been relaxed, they were afraid to try again. The chief used different words, but his message was as poignant as John's son's had been when he intoned, "Cruel! Cruel!"

The chief assumed that my presence meant that rescue was at hand, and I had to gently disillusion him. I was now convinced that the fate of these captives had to be linked with that of all of the others. If we freed a few of them, the others would certainly suffer the consequences. Therefore we had to find a way to eliminate the entire Unk menace. The chief grimly approved of that thought—he and his entire tribe had their own notion of how to eliminate the Unks, and they were willing to start the moment we neutralized the electronic weapons.

In the meantime, they were getting enough to eat, though the Unk food often tasted strange to them. They were worked throughout their waking hours—the jerbd's appetite knew no bounds—and the Unks were vicious. I gave him careful instructions for gathering information that might be useful to us—I wanted to know the duties or functions of various Unks and when they were likely to be present—and then Morl Klun and I faded back into the forest to wait for the dawn.

We remained in the area all the next day, now and then working our way into places of concealment from which we could observe what was going on. The activity around the ungainly jerbd was exactly the same as that we had observed with the Detroit Tribe. The only noticeable difference was that there seemed to be several Unks about all the time.

After dark, when the tribe had been released from its labor, I talked again with the chief. I promised to visit him as often as circumstances permitted and to bring what help I could. Then Morl Klun and I floated back to the place where Wiln Marra was to pick us up.

"It doesn't look as though we'll have much difficulty keeping in contact with them," Morl Klun observed as we skimmed along side by side.

"I suppose that'll be some consolation to them," I said. "I hope so, because I can't think of anything else we can do for them."

"I wonder," Morl Klun mused.

"Wonder what?"

"I was thinking about what you said—convincing the Unks that Earth was an unprofitable place for their gruskm production."

"What about it?"

"If all of the slaves are managed the way these are managed, we'd have very little difficulty in arranging for them to include a few dandelions in the jerbdz' food."

I stared at him. "Yes," I said thoughtfully. "It shouldn't be hard to arrange that. I have a feeling that Earth is going to be a highly unprofitable place for gruskm production."

19

Morl Klun's brilliantly simple idea proved to have tortuous complications when we tried to carry it out.

For one thing, all of the jerbdz were being pastured in thick forests where dandelions grew rarely if at all. It was not a forest plant. The Unks' slaves would have to be supplied with them, which posed the problem of getting fresh plants to them or of finding ways to preserve the plants long enough for the slaves to make use of them. That raised the question of whether the plants would have the same effect when they weren't fresh, and we also had to know how much or how many dandelions, fresh or preserved, the jerbdz would have to eat in order to affect their gruskm production.

One thing we were confident of: We knew where an ample supply of dandelions could be found. They were growing on the former lawns at Detroit Base. But it was now mid-summer and well past the plant's prime growing season, and when we landed there, our shocked eyes saw no dandelions at all.

I went to the reference shelf to learn what I could, and I read with profound interest what my Earth ancestors had to say about this botanical pest. I was surprised to learn of its venerable history as an herbal and fascinated to read of its alleged virtues. It was believed to be packed with vitamins and alkaloids, it had some status as a cult food, and it was long utilized as a remedy for a variety of human disorders. The only one of these that seemed to apply to the jerbd was its claimed laxative effect—which, however, did not seem to affect the beast's bowel functions.

"Found the answer?" Morl Klun demanded when he found me scowling skeptically at the screen.

"I've decided to call it a miracle plant," I said.

I sent Morl Klun and Wiln Marra on dandelion surveys by day; by night we continued with our plan to contact all of the slave groups. Heldi was handed a chore that she resented fiercely. She was asked to experiment with our own jerbd to find out whether dried leaves and roots—this being the form in which we could distribute the plant most easily—were effective, and what quantity would be required to upset the hulking jerbd's gruskm spinning. Her initial reaction was very much what I would have expected if I'd asked her to butcher the creature. Wiln Marra's gentle persistence and his reminders that the beast had shown no other signs of sickness and had in fact liked the dandelions and had eaten them voluntarily as long as they were within reach finally persuaded her.

Once persuaded, she went about the task with the detached efficiency she applied to all of her activities. She first devised a method for drying the leaves in the sun. When that proved to be too slow, she appropriated an oven in the dormitory kitchen. She measured quantities. She made up feeding schedules.

In the end, all of that proved to be unnecessary. A couple of handfuls of dried leaves and roots, fed to the jerbd all at once or scattered through its daily ration of tree leaves, affected the quality of the gruskm as early as the following day. If the dose was continued, the gruskm was completely unusable by the third day and a messy ooze thereafter as long as the dandelion supplement was supplied. The jerbd seemed to relish the dried plants as much as fresh ones.

While these experiments were proceeding, I had to contend with another serious problem: How would the Unks react? We wanted to convince them that gruskm farming on the planet Earth could not be done profitably—that the jerbdz would eventually become sickly or suffer some kind of metabolism failure that would make them unable to produce a usable gruskm. It would not do at all for the Unks to suspect that we were sabotaging their operation. They might then conclude that they could correct their problem by eliminating us. And it certainly would not do for them to surmise that the slaves were helping us. They would react ruthlessly, and there would be horrible suffering among the natives we were trying to protect and rescue.

I formulated a strategy. We didn't want all of the jerbdz to become afflicted at the same moment—that would certainly arouse suspicion. And we didn't want the jerbdz in a certain area to show signs of sickness a short time after one of our landing craft had passed through there. Though the Unks now seemed to pay little attention to our travels, we had to behave as though they were charting every trip we took.

I laid out a schedule. The first jerbd to be afflicted would be the one cared for by the Asiatic tribe that, along with John's son and his people, was one of the first two abducted. Later, as other jerbdz exhibited the same symptoms, I hoped that the Unks would conclude that the beast with the longest sojourn on Earth had become ill first. Otherwise there must be no hint of a pattern, either geographic or temporal.

I showed the plan to Morl Klun and Wiln Marra, and neither of them could suggest improvements. We began packaging the dried dandelions— this was Morl Klun's inspiration—in the fiber bags in which the Unks supplied their slaves with the dried vegetables that were part of their food ration. We collected these bags on our visits to the natives, and later we returned them filled with dried dandelions. The supply would keep each jerbd's gruskm in a fluid state for weeks. I carefully instructed the chieftains as to the role their groups were to play and made certain that they had memorized the schedule. Ten days before the first jerbd was to become sick, we stopped all of our outside activity.

For the first time since our arrival on Earth, I had nothing to do. I wrote another long report to Naslur Rayl, bringing him up to date on our discoveries and what we had planned. Once it had been sent off, I could only wait and try to occupy myself as best I could. The colonies at the bases—all of them—were functioning splendidly. I could observe this every time I glanced out of a window at Detroit Base or walked around the island. The Icelanders had planted a crop of long grass or hay, and it came up luxuriously in the protective environment the base provided. The same thing had happened in all of the other bases. This eased the problem of cutting forage outside the domes or straining Iceland's limited resources. Animals grazed contentedly. There were already some young animals, the delight of all of the colonists. Everything was orderly. There were no human pregnancies, and I expected none. Certainly not at this base. Heldi was in charge, and she sternly supervised the conduct not only of the Icelanders but of the youths from the black tribes as well. They had a name for her that they refused to translate, and they regarded her with mingled fear, respect, and resentment.

Probably Heldi wanted to supervise the conduct of the RT members, too, but thus far she had contained that urge.

I went on walks around the island, looked at both shores, and tried to imagine how things had appeared when two metropolises had faced each other across a watery international boundary, and often, as I had at the beginning, I pictured myself as walking in the footsteps of Lee Lukkari, Ken Jordan, and Dana Iverson.

One night I did the complete circuit by moonlight. It was enchanting until I reached a secluded corner and heard a male voice declaiming awkwardly in Icelandic. It was Wiln Marra, and he was orating about lives dedicated to service. He had an intent audience of one—Heldi. I detoured widely and left them to contemplate the subject in privacy. Morl Klun felt that one of us should speak to Wiln Marra—the way that Heldi followed him about was not only embarrassing, but we feared that it was also laughable and might undermine our status in the minds of the colonists. But I was having a similar problem with a disciple of my own, Rek, who followed me devotedly whenever I let him, and I understood that phase of the problem. My concern was that Wiln Marra would, at any moment, start following Heldi, and I told Morl Klun to handle that possibility in whatever way he saw fit.

Time passed, and the day came when the first dose of dandelions was to be administered. We were confident that the slaves would follow instructions meticulously. Our schedule was worked out to produce the precise effect that we wanted. The only thing lacking was a prognostication about the reaction of the Unks.

"How long do you think it will take?" I asked Morl Klun.

"How long will what take?" he asked innocently.

"Don't try to play stupid!" I snapped.

"Well." He sat down opposite me and crossed his legs. "When I first had this notion about dandelions, I thought I'd solved all of our problems. Then I began to wonder. I'm still wondering. We know so little about the jerbdz. This messy gruskm may be a common complaint. Maybe every ranjerbd has a medicine or pill in his kit—one dose, the jerbd's cured. You see what I mean?"

"I do," I said reluctantly. It had been a beautiful idea.

"In which case there won't be any reaction at all. The ranjerbdz will administer the appropriate medicine, go on administering it as long as necessary, and gruskm production won't even be affected. Not significantly. The other extreme would be that messy gruskm is something highly unusual. In that case, the Unks certainly aren't going to leap to the conclusion that Earth is unhealthy for jerbdz and pack up and leave. They've been visiting and studying Earth for centuries. Probably they have volumes of scientific reports concerning almost anything on Earth that could conceivably affect the jerbdz. They may even have analyzed Earth's plants, in which case they'd know immediately what's causing the problem. If they haven't any explanation for it, they'll observe the symptoms carefully and send off a report asking for advice. And higher Klniaq headquarters will send them a scientist or jerbd doctor who will study the situation some more. No, I'm afraid we haven't solved a thing, but we may be able to learn something about the Unks. Unfortunately, we won't know what it is until long afterward when we can interview the natives again. I only hope we haven't gotten them into trouble."

The tribes were to keep their bags of dandelion leaves and roots concealed among the food bags but not hidden. If discovered, they were to say that these were a favorite food, and they'd been gathering them for a feast. If challenged, they were to demonstrate the truth of their claim by eating them. We had provided them with choice dandelion recipes from the same source from which I had obtained my dandelion information. I doubted that the resultant foods would be tasty, and I was skeptical about the nutritional claims for dandelions, but I was certain that the plant wouldn't hurt them. That was to be the foundation of their defense—*they* ate dandelions. They wouldn't feed them to the jerbdz because dandelions were their own favorite food, but—since it was a common plant—the jerbdz might have picked up some on their own. And what if they did? The natives ate them, and they weren't harmed. Why should dandelions harm the jerbdz?

It seemed like infallible reasoning; but if the Unks were angry enough, and suspicious enough, they certainly would inflict punishment whether they considered the natives innocent or not.

That day passed, and the next. The first jerbd should have begun to show alarming symptoms, but there was no way that we could know for certain. We still didn't want to jeopardize our chances for success, however minuscule they might be, by giving the Unks any basis for suspecting that we were responsible, so we remained at home.

More days passed. The second jerbd should have been showing signs of the same illness. And then a third. And a fourth.

Above us, the Unks' starship held its orbit and made its regular passes, and I went out to watch when it appeared in our night sky. I wondered again whether the Unks had magnification units that would enable them to scrutinize the base. It wasn't likely, but it was a possibility. I told Wiln Marra to restrain himself during his nightly courting of, or being courted by, Heldi—the Unks might be watching. He stared at me speechlessly.

More days passed, and suddenly the Unks reacted.

They attacked the domes. All of them.

They wasted no time on scientific analysis, and—as we learned later—they never suspected the natives for a moment, didn't even bother to question them. They knew that an inexplicable catastrophe of that magnitude could be due only to the machinations of the other aliens on the planet, and they hit the source as hard as they could.

They surprised us completely. The colonists were going about their usual peaceful routine. A small group had left for the mainland to scout new locations for leaf gathering, this being difficult to do at night. Wiln Marra had left with Heldi on a medical circuit of the bases—he was holding regular clinics for colonists and animals as well as classes to train medical assistants for each base. Morl Klun and I were enjoying a leisurely breakfast and wondering, as we did daily, whether our dandelion campaign was having any effect. Suddenly explosives were rattling off the dome's protective field.

Our first concern was for the scouting party. Morl Klun leaped to a window and swept the upper reaches of the Detroit River with his binoculars. Fortunately it had already reached shore and hidden its boat. For the moment, it had the protection of the forest.

More explosions rattled above us. There were at least ten flying saucers circling high overhead. While Morl Klun studied their maneuvers and tried to determine what sort of explosives were being dumped on us, I called Wiln Marra.

He already knew about the attack. He had been approaching Andes Base when bombs began breaking on the protective field there. Now he was lying back and watching the attack develop.

I talked to all of the bases, one at a time. Each of them was under attack by a small squadron of three to five saucers. Detroit Base had been singled out for special attention—further evidence that the Unks, whatever their mental capacities might be, were not inobservant.

"Are you through taking inventory?" Morl Klun asked impatiently.

"Anything nuclear?" I asked.

"Nothing as yet. I need an extra hand here."

After our success in projecting small force fields, we had planned and rehearsed a maneuver to convert the base's massive field into an attack weapon. We had succeeded in bouncing it as high as a kilometer. There was an element of danger—during the bounce, the dome was defenseless, and a saucer might slip in under the field. But the time interval was never more than a few seconds—too brief an interval for the Unks to figure out what we were doing—and we would not use the maneuver when saucers were positioned to take advantage of it.

The timing was important. I scanned the low-level approaches and gave Morl Klun an all clear. He was watching the circling saucers. "They dive slowly," he said.

"Or cautiously?" I suggested.

They seemed to be regrouping. Finally one peeled off into a dive, and the others followed. "They're gaining confidence," Morl Klun observed.

"We'll soon fix that," I said.

We bounced the field. The leading saucers abruptly encountered an invisible solid where they expected nothing but air, and the results were thoroughly satisfactory. Pieces of three smoldering saucers blanketed the Detroit River from Belle Isle almost to the lake, and the remaining saucers decided that they had urgent business elsewhere. Moments later, they had passed beyond the range of our instruments.

"I wonder why they haven't used nuclear weapons," I said. "Do you suppose they haven't got any?"

We weren't concerned about the bases. Regez Anlf defenses could handle nucleonics. We were worried about Earth. This world had suffered enough, we thought, without the Unks starting another ordeal by radiation.

"My guess is that they haven't got any," Morl Klun said. "Theirs isn't a military expedition, you know. They're a supply mission for slaveholding farmers on worlds that are all but depopulated. Their weapons are intended for terrorizing backward populations."

"They might send for better weapons," I suggested.

"Would a business organization spend money to equip itself for that level of destructive warfare? Not without a specific purpose—such as triggering the nuclear war on Earth when the Regez Anlf was here. It's much cheaper for the Unks to get what they want by chicanery and foul play. I think we've achieved the ultimate stalemate. We haven't any attack weapons, so we can't drive the Unks away from Earth. The Unks' weapons are useless against our defenses, so they can't drive us away. Their jerbdz are vulnerable to our trickery, but we can carry that only so far before they retaliate against their slaves, which is an area where we're vulnerable. This could continue indefinitely. Fortunately, they haven't grasped that our most vulnerable area is Iceland, and they don't know that we won't attack their jerbdz because of our concern for the slaves. Until they find that out, it's a stalemate."

I said slowly, "Iceland certainly is our most vulnerable area. If they decide to bomb the island from high altitude, there won't be much that we can do about it except mount a permanent patrol. They won't send saucers over if one of our landing craft is in the air."

"I think the three of us would get rather tired of daily eight-hour shifts patrolling over Iceland," Morl Klun said. "If we do that, it's all we'll have time for. Also, it would put us back in the position of reacting to what the Unks do. That noble plan about making them react to us won't be worth much if we try one thing and then back away."

"Do you think we ought to keep feeding the jerbdz dandelions?"

"Certainly. We also ought to perform research and find out whether anything else has an adverse effect on them. The stated purpose was to make the Unks think that Earth is an unprofitable place to be. We should be working on the next step."

"I think," I said, "that one of your ancestors was a pendulum. One moment you're casting gloom on all of our good ideas, including your own. The next moment you're waving flags and making battle slogans. What'll it be tomorrow?"

"I don't know what I'll be thinking tomorrow," he said, "but I'm pretty sure the situation with the Unks will be one day older and still a stalemate."

The scouting party returned in a state of high excitement. It had watched the attack and cheered itself hoarse when we brought down the saucers—until pieces started falling dangerously near, which had given it a more sobering view of warfare. Rek wanted to know whether the foraging party could go out that night, and I told him yes. We already had rehearsed the necessary precautions, and I knew that the attack would give them urgency.

That night I treated myself to a long bath, lolling in the hot tub while I reviewed our strategy. I decided reluctantly that Morl Klun was right. We certainly had confused and mystified the Unks. In all of our confrontations we seemed to be overwhelmingly powerful, even though we never deigned to attack first. But it was less than a stalemate, because sooner or later they were bound to figure out that we were ignoring them because we had no choice. We could react forcefully when attacked; otherwise, the only action we could take was on the level of the dandelion trick. I watched another passage of the Unks' starship that night and reflected that as long as it was there, our own efforts would never be anything more than a holding action.

Wiln Marra returned at dawn, and he gave us a brief report on conditions at the other domes, of which he had visited three. "The natives weren't even frightened," he said. "We should rig some of the other domes so we can bounce the protective fields."

"Could we rely on the natives?" I asked. "One slip—"

"It's time we started to rely on them for a lot of things," Wiln Marra said. "We have these spare landing craft. If we suddenly put all of them in the air, the Unks would be confounded. They've never seen more than three at a time. Anyway, it's the natives' world. They're willing to fight for it, and we should teach them how."

"It might be a way to tilt that stalemate," Morl Klun said. "Right now, it's the three of us against all of the Unks, and—judging by the size of that starship—they're rather numerous."

I had no doubt that we could teach the young Earth natives—black and white—to pilot landing craft and use other machines with ease. Youths of the Detroit Tribe had taken readily to powered boats. But in a time of war, I mistrusted their instinctive behavior. We of the Regez Anlf had grown up with the kind of technology we were using. We adapted it to our needs almost without thinking, whether it involved projecting force fields or playing games with the Unks' cruise missiles or short-circuiting their electronic wands. We couldn't rely on the natives to achieve fluency overnight with a technology that was both years and light-years beyond their experience. In a war situation, their errors could be disastrous both for them and for us.

"Any action at all involves some risk," Morl Klun said. "Doing nothing also involves some risk. The Unks may not be content to sit on a stalemate. If you want to nudge them before they nudge us—"

"I'll think about it," I said. But I had already thought about it. Putting all of our landing craft into the air might startle the Unks, and it certainly would make them more wary, but it wouldn't disturb the stalemate.

Later that night, I returned to our headquarters room for a book. One corner was bathed with red light from our instrument section. I thought for a moment that one of us had failed to throw a switch; but it was the message alert from our trans-space communicator.

I ripped out the message with a shout. Morl Klun and Wiln Marra dashed in while I was reading it.

"Don't tell me Naslur Rayl has actually spoken!" Morl Klun exclaimed. "Is the Regez Anlf coming?"

"Do you want it to come?" I asked.

He grinned. "Now that is a leading question. I would like to tidy this mess up all by ourselves, but the way things are going—"

"Are they actually considering rescuing us?" Wiln Marra demanded.

"They're certainly considering it," I said.

"They can't do that! We won't let them. Our charter says explicitly that no one sets foot here without our permission."

"Shall I tell Naslur Rayl that he's welcome to come to Earth but we won't let him land?" I asked. "Or should I just suggest that the Council go soak its collective heads?"

"Tell him the Earth situation is perfectly under control and suggest that the Regez Anlf concern itself with Unk activities elsewhere," Morl Klun said.

"But is the Earth situation perfectly under control?" I asked. "I've been thinking about this stalemate of ours, and I've decided that it isn't a stalemate. A stalemate is a situation in which further action by either party is impossible. All we have is an occasional pause while both we and the Unks think about what we're going to try next. That's no stalemate."

Morl Klun sat down disgustedly. "So the Regez Anlf is coming to bail us out."

I shook my head. "Wrong. Naslur Rayl expresses indignation at the infamous manner in which the *Hadda* abandoned us. He congratulates us on the courage and resourcefulness that are sustaining us in our lonely vigil on a planet surrounded by enemies. He implores us to send regular situation reports. And he informs us that the Council will shortly be considering ways and means of succoring us."

"*Succoring* us!" Wiln Marra exclaimed indignantly.

Morl Klun's face relaxed into a grin. "Oh, well. If the Council has to consider ways and means, all of us are likely to die of old age before the Regez Anlf takes any action at all."

20

Like the others, I didn't want to be rescued—because we of the RT did not need rescuing. It was Earth's tiny surviving population that was in danger, and it enraged me that Naslur Rayl and the Council should already have forgotten why we had come here. The grand commitment to rebuild a world had somehow slipped into a cowardly mission to smuggle the three RT members off a hostile planet. That was the way I read his message.

I also was infuriated that he would break his long silence with a brash request that I send regular situation reports—which of course I had.

But I understood only too clearly what had happened. At first, Naslur Rayl had been overwhelmed by the political implications of what was taking place. *He* had sent the RT to Earth and thereby got the Regez Anlf involved in this messy entanglement. It would cost a lot of money to extricate us, the galaxy would never be the same again, and a lot of politicians of dubious mental capacity would consider all of that to be Naslur Rayl's fault. A politician can meditate long about a problem like that without doing anything at all.

Eventually, in response to repeated nudges from Lefkir Bonrin, Naslur Rayl had become aware that history would form its own independent judgment of what had transpired, and the politician who had sent an RT to Earth and then abandoned it there was going to get very short shrift from historians. Hence the belated promise that ways and means would be considered, which actually promised nothing at all.

I lay awake until morning without deciding anything. Finally I went for a walk in the hope that the bright freshness of the base would revitalize me. Things had returned to normal after the attack. Loads of leaves had arrived from the mainland during the night. Rek had a crew of mixed Icelanders and blacks at work in a new vegetable garden. He had discovered that jerbd manure, combined with the special hothouse qualities of the base's dome, had an unbelievably potent effect on vegetables. Not only did their sizes magnify, but their flavors were marvelously accentuated. I congratulated him with perhaps more enthusiasm than was actually necessary, and now he had to be restrained from converting the entire base into a production line for vegetables.

Heldi had her own work force producing gruskm cloth. She was determined to create a complete outfit of gruskm clothing for me, and a gruskm jacket and trousers would be ready in another day or two. The Icelandic girls had some difficulty in sewing the flimsy cloth—it was a slow, tedious process—and efforts to dye it still had not been successful. It emerged streaked and blotchy. Colored embroidery had to be done with Icelandic wool yarn.

The unfinished jacket and trousers were displayed for my approval, and I responded as ecstatically as my mood permitted. My mind was still occupied with the perfidiousness of politics and the frustrations of fighting a war with defensive weapons, and the fact that these items of clothing were priceless did not excite me. I had no place to wear them.

Heldi took me aside and rather diffidently inquired as to whether there was some other item of clothing I would like made for me. I suggested that all of the young women working for her might like their own festive gruskm gowns. The suggestion was received with indifference; they had no place to wear them, either.

This gave me an idea. I went back to headquarters and composed a message for Naslur Rayl: "Reclamation proceeding on schedule. Please rush clothing patterns in latest Dfolma styles for females, all common sizes." Dfolma was the Regez Anlf fashion center.

I sent it off. Then I left copies for Morl Klun and Wiln Marra and returned to my meditations. I went down to my own favorite place by the river and watched the choppy waves and for a time thought about the Earth that had been instead of the Earth that was or would be.

Morl Klun came along later, waving his copy of the message. "Are you insane?" he demanded.

"Less so than I was yesterday," I said. "It's a sign of emotional growth to be slightly less insane with each passing day."

"Naslur Rayl will think you've found a new way to produce a vacuum in your head. He's got a crisis on his hands that certainly has him pickling his fingernails, and you're asking for clothing patterns."

"It'll give him something different to think about. He needs it. For that matter, so do we."

"Sure. Clothing patterns?"

"Why not?"

"I know. You're going to frighten the Unks away from Earth by dressing all the females in Regez Anlf styles. It might even work."

"Do you have a better idea?"

"I do. We can end the Unks' gruskm farming overnight by arranging to have all of the jerbdz die. Some poison on the food—"

"No. I've thought about that. The Unks would suspect what had happened. They'd punish the natives. Probably they'd exterminate them, since they'd have no use for slaves until they imported more jerbdz. And when they did, they'd bring in alien slaves to look after them and thus solve all of their problems. Have you paid any attention to our pet Unk lately?"

"He's eating well and gaining weight. He delivered what probably passes for an Unk smile during the bombing attack. He didn't seem the least concerned that the bombs were as likely to destroy him as us, so you can take note that the Unks aren't cowards."

"Would we be likely to pick up anything new if you tapped his mind again? Or if Wiln or I did?"

"I'd say no chance at all. His guards watch him closely, and they'll report anything that seems unusual, but I doubt that we're going to learn any more from him than we already have. Maybe we should try to take another prisoner."

"How do we go about finding one with a broader background and more knowledge than a ranjerbd?" I asked.

He shook his head.

"I suppose there's only one answer," I said. "We'll have to go up to their starship and get one."

He stared at me. "Now I know you're insane."

"Of course. If we weren't insane, we wouldn't be here. One thing I do know—we haven't been giving that starship the attention it deserves. We should have studied it intently from the moment it arrived."

We moved our instruments back to the roof of the office building, and— as quickly as I could—I appointed an official astronomer at each of the other bases, and I trained these youths in the rudiments of simple visual and instrument observation. I was determined to learn as much about the starship as possible with the equipment and assistance available to us.

Whatever else could be said for the Unks, they—or their instruments— were damned fine navigators. They had laid on an orbit with a precision that would have done any Regez Anlf captain proud. Morl Klun said I was making deductions much too long after the fact; after all, the Unks had been up there for months of Earth time, and they'd had ample time to refine whatever their original orbit was. I asked him to explain why they would bother. They had no intention of becoming a permanent satellite. The ship would move on the moment its Earth mission was completed. Why, then, this flawless circular orbit? I wondered whether it had something vital to tell us about the Unks. Were they superbly capable or merely fussy about details?

I also wondered why the Unks had chosen that particular orbit some twelve thousand four hundred kilometers up. Since the ship functioned as a supply depot, one would have thought that the Unks could have saved considerable fuel and flying time for their saucers by moving in closer. If they were concerned about their defensive posture, just in case an alien ship caught them there, their orbit was much too close. The position made no sense.

In one respect the Unks were space primitives. They had no equipment comparable to the Regez Anlf cargo platforms. Everything was being ferried down by their flying saucers, and these, with their limited capacity, had to be extravagantly inefficient cargo ships.

I supervised my crew of astronomers, tabulated their records, and studied these as much as time permitted. Wiln Marra continued to make the rounds of the bases conducting medical clinics. Morl Klun was teaching the colonists techniques for defense just in case the Unks decided to attack again. All three of us were involved in regular contacts with the captive tribes. Wiln Marra attempted to deal with their medical problems, and he coped as well as he could with the difficulty of conducting surreptitious medical clinics in the dead of night for slaves under surveillance. Morl Klun and I were still attempting to baffle the Unks with dandelions, and we worked out another schedule whereby the dried roots and greens were fed to the jerbdz intermittently. We hoped that a gruskm diarrhea that came and went would be more mysterious than one that seemed permanent.

But I knew, now, that this would not drive the Unks away.

As I watched the occasional visual passage of the Unk starship, I wondered what the Unks aboard were doing and thinking. I considered the ship an unspeakable pollutant in the night sky. Probably the Unks thought the same about us, but they had learned, at the cost of a number of saucers and crews, to leave us alone.

That is—those Unks in charge of the jerbd project had learned to leave us alone, as had the pilots of their flying saucers, and all of them were probably devoting some of their waking or even sleeping hours to an attempt to devise appropriate tortures for us. I was no longer interested in them.

It was the crew of the starship that I was wondering about. I doubted that those individuals gave any thought at all to us. If they did, we were only a vague nuisance that had somehow upset the gruskm production schedule. We certainly weren't regarded as a menace. No one safely and comfortably orbiting the planet at that distance would give much thought to an Earthbound foe that lacked the means of getting into space.

"Our main weapon," I announced one night to Morl Klun and Wiln Marra, "will have to be psychological, since we haven't got anything else."

They were standing attendance on me through a sense of duty, since neither of them thought my observations were likely to accomplish anything. "I suppose you're going to knock a starship out of the sky with psychology," Morl Klun said sarcastically.

"Don't be silly," I said. "You don't use psychology on a ship. You use it on the ship's crew."

"That's no different from trying to attack the ship," Wiln Marra said. "The ship is up there, we're down here, and we have no weapons. The crew is up there, we're down here, and how do you practice psychology on someone you're not even communicating with?"

"Perhaps if we could arrange to feed the crew dandelions—" Morl Klun began.

"What's the crew's mental state by this time?" I asked.

"Torpid," Wiln Marra said promptly.

"My thought exactly," I said. "They can't be expecting any threat from space—didn't our starship run away when they approached? And they aren't expecting any danger from Earth. If we had a weapon, we would have used it long ago. So the crew has been there all this time in that perfectly trimmed orbit, the ship flying itself, nothing to do, no threat of any kind. It's time that we constituted ourselves a threat."

"Sure," Morl Klun said. "Do you have anything in mind besides the dandelions?"

"She said 'psychology,' " Wiln Marra said. "I'd love to introduce plague, or even an aggravated itch, among the starship's crew, but there's no way to do it from this distance. I'm just the team's med tek. Kera is its technician. You're the psychologist. Why don't you suggest something?"

He had nothing to suggest. I did, but I wasn't ready to mention it—not yet. We continued to take turns watching the starship through a telescope, and I continued to wonder about the mental state of its crew. Later I went over the accumulated records and statistics and isolated one possibly interesting fact: Flying saucers came and went frequently when the starship was on the day side of the planet; they never approached it from the night side. Perhaps this meant nothing; perhaps it only meant that the Unks were not nocturnals, and neither were we.

Days passed with this uneventful routine. When my mental state became as torpid as I assumed that of the starship's crew was, I went for a walk, admired the peacefully bustling community the base had become, interrupted the jerbd's voracious eating to scratch its unlovely head, and then returned to headquarters.

I was returning from one of these walks when my glance fell on the shelf where I had lined up my collection of rados. I had acquired them in the early days of our contacts with the native tribes, and they had startled us by emitting the fake Lee Lukkari's message when the Unks arrived, but I hadn't given a thought to them for weeks.

Now they inspired a thought. I opened a window and called down to Rek to grab Wiln Marra before he took off. He was about to leave on another tour of the bases. He came galloping up the stairs, and I gave him one of the rados.

"Just curiosity," I told him. "The native tribes were to press this button when the rado informed them that Lee Lukkari had returned. It certainly activates a signal that would have led the Unks to the natives for an efficient slave raid. I'm wondering whether the Unks are still listening for such things. On your trip south, find yourself a nice, lonely place and leave the rado there with its signal turned on. Then watch from a distance and see if anything happens."

"It'd be easy to ambush any saucers that come to investigate," Wiln Marra said.

"Of course it would. But then they'd never investigate another rado. Let's first see what their reaction is before we consider how to make use of it."

He reported later that a flying saucer had dipped down just under thirty minutes after he'd turned on the signal. Then others had come, and they seemed to be searching the entire area. He'd slipped away unnoticed, or so he thought.

This was interesting, but all it meant was that we could set a trap and knock off a saucer or two whenever we felt like it. We could do that once, but—unless the Unks were far more stupid than we had any right to expect —the trap would never work a second time. As far as ridding the planet of Unks was concerned, it had a slight nuisance value and nothing more, and I filed it with our other discarded ideas.

There was only one thing to be done. I knew it, I had known it for some time, but it was fraught with so many uncertainties that I had to push myself toward it reluctantly.

Finally I went to see Heldi. I told her bluntly, "Morl Klun and I have a mission to undertake. If we succeed, we may rid this world of Unks. If we fail, we may not be back."

She studied my face gravely. "And—Wiln Marra?"

"I don't want him to know about it," I said. "If I tell him, he'll insist on going along. I don't want to risk the life of Earth's only doctor on a wild gamble. If we fail, it'll be up to him to keep Earth's population alive and healthy until help comes from outside—and help may be a long, long time in coming."

"What do you want me to do?" she asked.

"Keep Wiln Marra occupied. Be ready to invent an important errand that will take him away from this base overnight. Can you do that?"

"Of course," she said. She smiled at me. We were allies. Then she said soberly, "You're prepared to die—for us?"

"I have a job," I said. "I'm prepared to do it."

Convincing Morl Klun was not so easy. "That starship," I told him, "has been polluting our sky long enough. I've decided to get rid of it."

"That's nice," he said. "Another psychological weapon?"

"A very good one that we've had all along. Our landing craft are highly capable limited-range spaceships, but the Unks don't know that. They've never seen them operate above the atmosphere. I'm going to pay them a visit."

"You're going to fly up to the starship?" he demanded incredulously.

"Yes."

"I agree. It's a psychological weapon. If they happen to notice you, they'll be surprised. Then you can fly down again. What will it accomplish?"

"How can I tell before I get there?"

"You're refusing to tell me because you know I'll disapprove."

"I'm refusing to tell you because I don't know myself. I want to do a test run."

"When?"

There was no point in holding back. I gave myself the final push. "Tonight," I said.

21

Wiln Marra was away on an African visit, so there was no need for Heldi's wiles. Morl Klun and I took a landing craft and lay in ambush for the starship. When it rose above the horizon, I began to climb in its path. I wanted to check our timing and at the same time see whether such an approach alarmed the ship's crew. We ascended almost twelve thousand kilometers with no sign of our being noticed.

A Regez Anlf landing craft has mediocre virtues for horizontal atmospheric flight, but its vertical characteristics are unequaled. A climb is like reversing gravity to make it push instead of pull—you zoom upward. I topped off our ascent and began to drop away as the starship passed overhead. Up to that point, Morl Klun had watched the entire maneuver without comment.

"Think you can manage it?" I asked him.

"You mean—to actually make contact with the ship? Of course. But to what purpose? If we had a bomb, there might be some point to this. We could stick it to the side of the ship or maybe even smuggle it on board."

"It'd take more than one bomb for a ship of that size," I said.

"I suppose so if they have any damage-control system at all," Morl Klun said glumly. "So what are you going to do?"

"Smuggle a psychological bomb aboard."

"That's nice. What form does a psychological bomb take?"

"You're looking at it," I told him. "Me. In my Lee Lukkari costume. It's time that Lee Lukkari called the Unks to account for maliciously impersonating her."

"No." He shook his head. "It's a fiendishly clever idea, and it's a great pity that it won't work. The Lee Lukkari impersonation was a gimmick used by Unks directly in charge of the Earth operation. Most of the crew won't have heard of her. You think all you have to do is go into your Lee Lukkari act, and they'll die of remorse. What do you do when they don't?"

"Look for openings and take advantage of what I find."

"I don't like it."

"It'll be a lot more fun than sitting around waiting for the politicians to appropriate rescue money."

"So you think you're going aboard the ship. What do I do? Drop a few thousand kilometers and start spreading nets for you?"

"You park immediately under the ship and wait for me—or wait to see what happens."

"What if you can't get in?"

"I've thought about that. If our Regez Anlf experience means anything, spaceship hatches have high-quality latches but no locks. They always can be opened from either side. For emergency procedures, or for repair crews working outside the ship, an accidentally locked hatch might spell disaster. Also, the last thing any starship is worried about is someone sneaking aboard in space. It's a well-known fact that they almost never encounter pedestrians. I won't have any problem getting in."

"But why go alone? Take me with you. Or Wiln."

"No. The world's only doctor is irreplaceable, and one of us has to be left in charge in case something goes wrong. And you'll be much more useful as outside support."

"I don't think that's a compliment," Morl Klun said glumly. "So I'm to park underneath the starship, and you're going aboard without so much as one small bomb to help out, and—"

"I'm the bomb," I said.

"I can't even claim to be your backup bomb, because I have no idea what you think you'll be doing. I can only hope that you don't turn out to be a dud. When does this exciting maneuver take place? Tomorrow?"

"No. I have some equipment to get ready."

"I should hope so," he said fervently.

It took me three days. When I was finally ready, I passed the word to Heldi. She worked her wiles, and Wiln Marra came to me and asked, with obvious embarrassment, if I minded his making an overnight trip to the African bases.

"Why should I mind?" I asked. "You know your job, and I assume that you're doing it."

"Well—we talked about the black population having some immunity to malaria because of sickle-cell anemia. I would like to do some tests to see whether any of our black colonists have it. Any kind of anemia should be curable."

Heldi exceeded my expectations. I had expected more sick lambs. "All I ask is that I know where you are in case we need you," I said.

I packed my equipment with care, and Morl Klun and I took off at midday so as to position ourselves for the most advantageous night ascent. The maneuver actually was a very tricky one. It meant putting ourselves in the same orbit as the starship as inconspicuously as possible. If we reached orbital height too soon, even an unalert ship might detect us. Too late, and we would experience the same high risk in overtaking it from behind. Morl Klun handled the landing craft as though he had been practicing that particular operation for weeks. We were a thousand kilometers below and just the right distance ahead of the ship when we reached orbital speed, and from there it was only a matter of nudging the landing craft into position.

Finally we were drifting a mere twenty meters below the enormous, looming hulk. "Close enough?" Moral Klun asked.

"Any closer and they'll hear us breathing."

He turned and looked at me. "Are you really certain—"

"I'm not certain of anything except that I'm going to do this. When I come out, catch me if you can. If anything erupts, play it as it happens and don't take silly risks."

"You know I wouldn't do that," he said sarcastically. "Not with the splendid example our commander sets. Silly risks? Not in this RT."

"I never gamble for more than the agreed stake," I said. "*I* am the agreed stake. If I'm lost, I'll guarantee that the Unks will pay dearly for it. Losing you, too, would be too great a price. Now behave yourself."

I left him seated at the controls and glowering at me.

There was no point in opening the main hatch and ramp. I reached a small upper hatch with one bound, flipped the air lock shut behind me, and then slipped out. There I was in space with nothing between me and oblivion except my scanty Lee Lukkari costume—plus a carefully selected assortment of Regez Anlf protective devices. I wore a small backpack, designed to be as inconspicuous as possible, and in it I carried as much equipment as I thought I would need.

A Regez Anlf protective field keeps everything out—absolutely everything. But it also can be set to keep everything in, including enough atmosphere to enable one to pass from one ship to another. I pushed off gently and floated toward the vast shadow. Behind me, the landing craft looked like a parasitic midge sneaking up on a super-gigantic insect.

I reached the starship and slowly rose along the vast, curving side. My first concern was to learn what I could from the outside, but there was little to be discovered there. I drifted high up the side of the ship and then down again, looking for observation ports—I'd hoped that they would give me some clue as to how many deck levels the ship contained—but I found them only at the two hatches I encountered. When my air began to fail, I breathed from the oxygen reserve I carried and vented the dead air as a jet to move myself along the side of the ship. Eventually I reached a hatch that was far enough from Morl Klun's station to direct attention away from him. I studied the recessed mechanism, folded out a handle, and turned it a full circle.

The hatch, forced by pressure from the air lock beyond, popped open. I stepped in, pulled it shut, and secured it by rotating the inner handle. The air lock's inner door had an automatic lock that released when the hatch was secured. I pushed it open and paused to test the air. The Unks we were familiar with thrived in Earth's atmosphere, but I did not know how many species I might have to deal with or which of them the ship was designed to accommodate best. I found the ship's air to be breathable though a trifle lean on oxygen; the Unks must have found Earth's atmosphere exhilarating.

I was in a darkened cargo hold. The vast room, lit only by streaks of emergency luminance, would have been recognizable to anyone familiar with spaceships. It was empty, and its only alien feature was an odd, link-like track on the deck that suggested an automatic cargo-handling system. The tracks converged on what must have been a trans-deck conveyor, but I chose not to get involved with a mechanism I might not be able to control. Nearby I found an emergency 0-gravity tube lined with a coarse mesh for hand- and footholds. I propelled myself upward. As quickly as possible, I wanted to put distance between myself and the hatch I had entered.

I emerged in a corridor softly lit by the dully reddish glow of recessed lamps, which surprised me. We hadn't suspected that our captive Unk's vision might be tilted toward the infrared, and it was a bit late now for me to be pondering the effect that might have on my mission. I moved at a loping run, taking long, soaring leaps in the low gravity. I found another 0-grav shaft and ascended to the next deck, where I resumed my rush toward the distant rear of the ship.

Then I saw my first Unks.

I heard them at the same time. I'd had a tap from our captive to make me reasonably fluent in the Unk language, but this distant conversation reached me only as a confused babble. I slowed my pace and watched them move toward me with the loose-jointed walk so characteristic of our own Unk. Their flapping work togs looked dullish gray in the red-tinted light. They were intent on their conversation, and they turned aside without noticing me and vanished through a door, closing it after them.

As I approached it, I became aware of a subdued jumble of sound. I opened the door a crack and peeked into an informal messroom. Some twenty Unks were eating in a mood of relaxed joviality. They sat on mats in groups of five, legs jackknifed around large, deep, circular trays that were heaped with fist-sized brown balls that looked like bread.

I couldn't have asked for a more auspicious moment for Lee Lukkari's first appearance. I took a moment to check my equipment; then I flung the door open and stepped through.

At the same instant, I triggered a piercing shriek from my amplifier. "I am Lee Lukkari," my voice bellowed in my best Unk accents. "Where are the miscreants among you who have profaned my character and enslaved my people?"

I repeated that three times, moving first one way and then the other and leaving a trail of overturned food trays and rolling food balls as the diners recoiled from me. Then I departed abruptly, swinging the door shut behind me and busying myself with the latchment for a moment before I moved on along the corridor at a loping run. I glanced over my shoulder once and saw the latchment still glowing red hot, and I heard the scream of the first Unk who tried to open the door. I intended to teach them to use caution in trying to follow Lee Lukkari anywhere.

It was a corridor of large rooms. I glanced into one used for recreation, saw only three Unks playing a game that filled the air with spinning hoops, and hurried on. The next door opened into another messroom. There were three eating groups of five, and all fifteen Unks retreated to the bulkheads as Lee Lukkari thundered her accusation. I heat-charged the latchment as I left. I managed two more performances before the first door had cooled enough for the Unks to began to cautiously venture into the corridor.

I was ready for act two of my performance. I stood waiting as the throng edged toward me. It began to surge confidently as more doors cooled and the numbers of Unks increased. Then, as the vanguard came closer, its leaders had second thoughts and tried to hold back. A voice in the rear snarled angrily—an officer, urging action from a place of safety. The crowd edged forward again. I waited until the leaders came to an uncertain halt ten paces from me. For a long moment I held a dramatic pose with all eyes fixed upon me. Then I vanished.

The Regez Anlf personal force field can be set so that light waves curve around it—a fact we had discovered at the Space Academy when we subjected our equipment to the thorough testing exercised by students everywhere. The apparent invisibility was imperfect, but in the dimly red-lit corridor the illusion was more than adequate.

I vanished. I quickly leaped aside, leaving the Unks to stare rigidly at the place where they'd last seen me. I backed away with gliding footsteps and turned at the first intersecting corridor. The crowd of Unks hadn't moved.

A short distance along the side corridor, I found another 0-grav tube. I propelled myself up two levels. There I turned back, retracing my steps and heading for the bow of the ship. I met no one, perhaps because I'd had the good luck to arrive during a meal break.

Alien minds evolve their own unique, drastically varying perspectives, but I believed that certain situations must have an intrinsic universal logic that would overpower such distinctions. My invasion of the Unks' starship could not have been successful the day of its arrival or during the first month—or months. Enough about the unexpected complications of the Earth situation would have trickled down to the crew to produce uneasiness, and uneasiness means alertness. But I reasoned that the Earth mission had been planned as a short, routine stop, and it now had dragged on for uneventful month after uneventful month—and this was not a military crew. Discipline would be lax; boredom would be perpetual and unalleviated.

The sudden appearance of Lee Lukkari had to be a terrifying experience to the Unks. The aftereffect of her sudden disappearance would be worse. So would the reaction of the ship's officers when told that Lee Lukkari had made speeches at several messes and then disappeared while more than half a hundred crewmen watched her.

For a time, at least, attention would be focused far behind and below me —there would be a futile search, and there would be an attempt to obtain a coherent statement of what had happened from an excitedly babbling mob. I hoped for enough time to find the ship's control room unhindered, and that same exercise of logic told me that I'd find it in the extreme forward part of the ship.

I did—eventually. I searched that level, and the next, and then the next, and suddenly there it was—a vast, plushly furnished arena with its ceiling—

an enormous sweep of the curving bow—crowded with instruments. A cluster of viewing screens looked upon dark space or dark Earth. There were two enormous, curving observation ports.

The room was empty. That was the culmination of my logic—I had hoped that it would be. A starship that's been in a stable orbit for months, with a capable autopilot to correct the unlikely error, doesn't need a watch. On a ship run with military discipline—and all Regez Anlf ships were—it would have had one anyway. The Unks' commercial starship did not.

I closed the door and secured it. Then I turned to the banks of instruments. Logic, combined with intrepidity—or rashness—and a considerable amount of luck, had brought me this far. What I accomplished here depended entirely upon luck.

The instruments were as strange as hieroglyphs in an unknown language. Their labels, their numerical gradations, were jumbles of nonsensical marks. The functions and operating principles of the controls were a total enigma. Our captive Unk's mind had been no help. He had never seen a spaceship's control room.

Somehow I had to understand the controls and do it quickly. I could only hope that they, too, had an intrinsic logic that overpowered alien distinctions.

The ship was locked in orbit. Therefore the functioning instruments, the ones that were blue-lighted, were reporting physical conditions—velocity, shape of orbit, distance from Earth. Or they were monitoring conditions within the ship—pressure, temperature, constitution of the ship's atmosphere.

Connected to those functioning controls, I knew, would be an orbit control computer, the robot pilot that automatically maintained the orbit. It would make minute, highly exact adjustments the instant they were required.

The empty control room was testimony to the Unks' confidence in that robot control. And why not? They'd been in orbit for a long time with no computable error. Before that, it would have functioned equally well on other orbits around other worlds, automatically performing any necessary adjustments with chemical jets designed for close-orbit maneuvering. With an orbit laid on perfectly and checked occasionally, nothing very serious could happen. At twelve thousand plus kilometers, the orbit was far enough from earth so that even the unthinkable malfunction could be quickly corrected the next time anyone thought to check.

But there would certainly be some kind of backup alarm system, I thought, as I continued to study the controls. If the ship wandered significantly off course, a signal would bring the crew on a run. I also had to assume that there would be backup controls elsewhere in the ship.

My object—so wildly impossible that I hadn't mentioned it to Morl Klun —was to take control of this starship and crash it. This was the only effective way of getting it out of Earth's sky. Mere sabotage—the wrecking of vital controls or machinery—would have the opposite effect. It would keep the ship where it was. My problem was to significantly change the ship's course without setting off an alarm.

What would happen—I mused to myself—if instead of attempting to power the ship out of its orbit, I simply instructed the robot control to follow a new orbit? If the change were slight, the computer would automatically adjust to it, and there would be no alarm. Another slight change of orbit, another adjustment. If I had sufficient patience and a monumental amount of luck, it might work.

But first I had to figure out how to do it.

With most orbital control arrangements, the operator would punch the figures for the desired orbit into the computer and add any necessary instructions. To change the orbit, new figures would have to be supplied with new instructions or even a sequence of instructions. No amount of blind fumbling could have solved that arrangement.

But the Unks' design engineers had achieved a brilliant simplification. I wondered afterward if they had been forced to do so because their starship crews were stupid.

A three-dimensional projection showed the assigned orbit in blue, the actual orbit in white—when I entered the control room, the two lines were overlapped—and, as I quickly learned, any area of deviation in yellow.

And the assigned orbit was manually adjustable.

It required only a moment's experimentation for me to release the set that froze the adjusting knobs. I made the assigned orbit minutely smaller. The yellow deviation warning flashed on, and the robot control began to adjust to the smaller orbit.

I was beginning to enjoy myself. I perched on the edge of a superbly comfortable pilot's lounge and went to work. I was oblivious to the passage of time. I can only guess that two hours went by, with my making one small orbit change after another in rapid succession, before something aroused the Unks' curiosity about what might be happening in their control room. Or perhaps it was only a routine inspection visit.

Someone tried the door and was knocked unconscious. More time passed before someone else made the attempt with the same result. A short time later, I heard riot and consternation beyond the door, and what must have been the ship's main alarm system went off with shrieking honks that bruised my eardrums.

With the ship fully alerted, I no longer had to proceed cautiously, and I had been studying the controls in anticipation of that. I now began to dismantle them, experimenting with each one as I did so. And I gave the robot control an assigned orbit so close to Earth that Mount Everest would have flinched on each passage. That set off another alarm, but it was hardly noticeable in the hubbub already taking place.

By then I knew that there were no backup controls. I continued to take apart the control boards, and another hour may have passed, or perhaps it was only minutes, before I finally punched or pulled or disconnected the right combination of things, and one of the ship's main drives caught with a frenzy of vibration that reached all the way to the bow. I don't know how long we accelerated toward Earth before the technicians disconnected the drive manually—perhaps only seconds, but it was enough.

My work was done, and I wanted out before the ship hit Earth's atmosphere. There I made my first miscalculation—what I had thought was an emergency escape tube turned out to be an empty stowage compartment. Outside, the Unks were reaching over an accumulated pile of bodies to batter in the control-room door with clubs. When they seemed about to succeed, I placed myself just inside the entrance and turned my protective field up to full power.

The door yielded, and the first of the rushing Unks ran headlong into my field. They recoiled, screaming, with clothing and flesh shredded. Blood sprayed over those behind them. In a twinkling the corridor outside the control room was empty except for twitching bodies. I closed the door as well as I could in its wrecked condition, clamped a heat device on it, and decided that I could take justifiable pride in my performance. Certainly it had vastly exceeded my expectations.

It was time to consider how to save myself before my luck ran out completely. The starship was headed for Earth. If I could get out, and if Morl Klun had managed to keep up with it, he'd be waiting to rescue me. These were large "ifs." Failing either of them, it made little difference whether I hit Earth with the ship or without it.

I found an 0-grav tube and descended to the level I'd entered on. I moved from cargo hold to cargo hold. Each had its own service hatch—and the inner doors of all of the air locks were secured. Perhaps someone had taken an obvious precaution on learning that there was an invader aboard. I applied all of my Regez Anlf gadgetry to the locks, but I could not spring one.

The starship was screaming through Earth's atmosphere now, and I was certain that Morl Klun had been left far behind. I continued to work my way along the cargo deck in a futile quest for an open air lock. Some of the compartments were loaded with strange-looking bundles and bales and cartons, and I could have gleaned an important education if I'd been willing to take time to snoop. But there was little time left and no indication that I had any future need for more education.

I had reached the midsection of the ship when the scream of the atmosphere became deafening beyond all description. There was nothing more for me to do except sit down and wait for the crash.

22

The Unk starship was built in self-contained segments, and those segments were scattered across a wide swath of Siberian steppe. Some smashed into mounds of compressed metal. Some ripped open and spilled their contents, which smashed into many smaller mounds, equally compressed.

My compartment ripped open.

But a Regez Anlf protective field does not smash. It simply takes gargantuan bounces. Fortunately for me, it proved to have unsuspected qualities for protecting its wearer during high-velocity impacts. I survived, but my condition could have served as a medical textbook illustration demonstrating how to set every possible kind of broken bone on the same body.

Morl Klun, knowing I was still aboard the starship, followed it down as best he could until he'd pinpointed the crash area. He'd already alerted Wiln Marra, wrenching him away from Heldi and the sickle-cell anemia research. The two of them ferried in rescue workers from all of the bases and from Iceland to sift through the rubble. They were looking for me, but along the way they piled up quantities of usable salvage and unceremoniously buried a lot of dead Unks.

They also rescued some survivors, all of whom were indignantly bleating jerbdz. The strange creatures were fortunate either in the way their capsules landed or in their anatomy, or both. They had to be freighted away immediately to areas where their favorite food supplies existed in readily accessible quantities that could match their appetites.

Morl Klun eventually deduced that I had been thrown clear of the wreckage. He instituted an electronic search and picked up the glow from my force field kilometers from the point of impact. I was taken back to Detroit Base, worked on extensively by Wiln Marra, and immobilized for healing. The massive chore of mopping things up fell on Morl Klun and Wiln Marra.

The jerbdz were a serious problem. Except for Iceland, where the natives had their own animals to look after, most of Earth's population was already intensively occupied in tending and feeding jerbdz. We had learned with our own jerbd that its care could be organized on a much more efficient basis than that used by the Unks, but the Unks remained in control of their little jerbd enclaves and of their slaves, and their flying saucers were still flitting about. On the first day after the crash of the starship, it seemed that I hadn't changed a thing.

On the second day, flying saucers and Unks began to vanish. Before the native slaves quite realized that they were free, Morl Klun or Wiln Marra arrived on the heels of the fleeing Unks, checked each tribe's physical welfare, gave food and medical attention when needed—and then persuaded the natives not only to continue looking after their jerbd but to accept responsibility for another. Some tribes were moved to locations where jerbd food was more easily gathered. All were given better tools and an improved organization. In the end, they were able to care for two jerbdz with less effort than one had required under the Unks.

During this period of frenzied activity, I was lying suspended in a sling similar to the one used on our Detroit Base jerbd—except that Wiln Marra had designed it himself to minimize the effect of gravity on my broken bones. I had nothing to do other than watch the activities of the base through a window and think, and I did a lot of thinking about the Unks.

"Where did they go?" I demanded when a very tired Morl Klun hurried in to see how the patient was progressing.

He didn't know. For the moment, he didn't care. "They panicked when they found that the starship had vanished," he said. "I don't know whether they're aware that it crashed or they think it ran out on them. If the latter, they've picked a refuge for themselves, and they'll plan to hide there until the ship returns or another shows up."

"We've got to find out where they are and clean them out," I said. "This planet will be polluted as long as a single Unk is at large."

Morl Klun grinned. "We'll find out where they are as soon as we get our housekeeping—or jerbdkeeping—organized. Cleaning them out is something else. All of our weapons are still defensive."

"I want to be able to report to Naslur Rayl that every Unk in the system is either dead or captured," I said.

"That appeals to me, too. The *Hadda* turned tail and left us, so we three wiped out the entire invasion force ourselves, starship and all. I like that. But first we'll have to find them."

The Icelandic girls had set up their dressmaking salon just below my window. Rek had fashioned dressmaker's dummies for them in graduated sizes, and these stood in a row displaying the girls' experiments in dress designing. Some of them demonstrated genuine talent, but the designs took shape with torturous slowness. Sewing the gruskm required meticulous stitches, each one inserted with care, because the cloth was so filmy.

When I tired of that scene, I looked across the common at the antics of the jerbdz—Detroit Base now had three—and the efficient conveyor system that brought food to them. Fishers came and went, the base's flourishing gardens were tended, and the Icelandic animals, all of them pets, received their share of attention. Off to one side was the gruskm factory, where the cable spun by the jerbdz was converted to thread in vats of boiling water. Thread was accumulating in such quantities that Morl Klun had to design large spools for storage and a special winding mechanism. The Earth natives were not yet aware of it, but the foundations for an industry were being laid one faltering touch at a time under my Detroit Base window.

Periodically Heldi marched in to exercise my mending limbs. She manipulated me with such tender concern and such overwhelming competence that I resolved to hit her as soon as my arms had healed. Rek paid me touchingly humble visits, like a faithful pet coming to pant at the master's bedside, and I resolved to hit him, too. I also wanted to hit Morl Klun, for dashing about so cheerfully while he did my job, and Wiln Marra, for confining me in his silly sling.

Time passed. I was up and haltingly about when Morl Klun tracked down the refugee Unks. It seemed a fitting retribution that these aliens who had made refugees of most of Earth's population should meet the same fate. Not surprisingly, they had selected a forest refuge to conceal themselves and their saucers. The exact location surprised me until I had reflected about it. It was in the mountains of southern India, close to the point of the Indian peninsula. Not only was there ample concealment and a ruggedly inaccessible terrain, but the land formation was one easily identified from space. A rescue expedition would have no difficulty in finding it.

"It was my mistake," I told Morl Klun on one of his visits. "I thought eliminating the starship would solve all of our problems. But you can take it for certain that the Unks have filed a detailed report on everything that's happened here. They're confidently waiting to be rescued, and their sponsors will conclude that nothing less than a substantial military force will be needed to restore order. We got rid of a ship. We'll get a fleet in return. There'll be two rescue expeditions converging on Earth, one from the Regez Anlf and one from the Unks. I want no part of either of them."

Morl Klun stared at me. Then he sat down heavily. "That little accident that you got into on purpose has caused a personality switch. I'm the one that's supposed to go about spreading gloom and proclaiming consternation. But you can relax if you're worried about two rescue expeditions converging here. My understanding of our captive Unk's thinking convinces me that Unk headquarters is a lot further away than Regez Anlf headquarters. So we're likely to be unwillingly rescued by the Regez Anlf long before any Unk military expedition can show up here. Is that good or bad?"

"Bad," I said. "Bad thinking on your part. The Unks may be able to stage a rescue without holding political debates first, which means that they're already on their way while the Regez Anlf is still debating. And while the Unk headquarters may be a long, long way off, the Unk fleet may have been holding maneuvers a couple of star systems away while hoping to receive a distress call that would give it something to do. It could arrive tomorrow. If it gets here before the Regez Anlf, we'll be in deep trouble. Especially all of the natives living outside the bases will be in deep trouble."

"A choice between humiliation and catastrophe," Morl Klun said cheerfully. "But since we don't know what's going to happen, or even if anything is going to happen, I'm in favor of carrying on in our own blunderingly resourceful manner. The best way to dampen the spirits of an Unk rescue expedition would be to leave it no Unks to rescue."

A careful survey of the Unks' refuge convinced Morl Klun that the Unks were safe from any weapons in our arsenal. The huge block of mountains rose abruptly from the western coastal plain of the Indian peninsula. These heights resembled nothing so much as a vast, inaccessible fortress, with densely forested slopes, steep escarpments, and a honeycombing of deep clefts and gorges. Our old reference books referred to the rich variety of trees in the rampant tropical forests, to the area's inaccessibility, and also to the cool climate and natural beauty that once made these hills—as they were called—popular summer resorts. The beauty, the climate, and the inaccessibility still remained. The Unks probably had hidden their saucers as we once hid our landing craft, by drifting among the trees and burrowing in as deeply as possible. Probably they had found caves for themselves. If they had weapons and the will to fight, it would be difficult for an army to dig them out.

I was now able to walk a bit, and I wanted to see this mountain redoubt for myself. Rek and Heldi fashioned a special seat harness for me, and Morl Klun piloted the landing craft. The natural beauty of the area gave me little pleasure as we floated along awesome escarpments and Morl Klun pointed out their invulnerability.

"If they didn't have their saucers," Morl Klun said, "we could safely let them rot here. Eventually they'd go primitive or starve. The saucers make them capable of unpredictable mischief."

"Mischief," I said, "isn't a word I'd apply to them. Any species that casually goes about trying to decimate world populations is not mischievous by any definition. Could we disable the saucers?"

"Easily, if we had weapons designed to do that. But the Regez Anlf weapons—"

"Are defensive. So our only ploy would be to tempt them to attack us, and they're not about to try that again. If they come out at all, it'll be for sneak attacks, and the only things they can attack with confidence are unprotected native settlements."

"Or Iceland," Morl Klun said. "They lost their laboratory when the ship crashed, but I've been wondering—perhaps they already had an Earth base here stocked with supplies. Including unused bacteria."

"You're being your cheerful self," I said bitterly.

We floated low over the area on the chance that the Unks might try to shoot down the landing craft and reveal what sort of weapons they had, but the bait was ignored.

"You brought down their starship with psychology," Morl Klun said. "Why not try smashing their saucers the same way?"

"It's a thought. I might do that."

He turned on me in alarm. "Wiln Marra said your brain miraculously escaped damage. I'm going to suggest that he reexamine you."

"Psychology is a very good weapon," I told him. "Let's go back to base and figure out a way to use it."

Our morosely uncooperative captive Unk was still sullenly watching for an opportunity to escape. I'd almost been tempted to give him one so I could watch the result. He glowered at us, and Morl Klun and I studied him distastefully.

"Tell him," I suggested, "that our superior weapons have shot down his starship."

Morl Klun did so. The Unk made no response. Obviously he didn't believe us, and there was no reason why he should.

"Ask him if he would like to see the wreckage," I said.

There was still no response.

"Tell him," I said, "that the only other Unks left alive on this world are fugitives. We have no reason to kill them unless they make it necessary. We've treated him kindly enough. We'll also treat the others kindly—if they surrender. Wouldn't he enjoy having fellow prisoners of his own species? We're going to show him the wreckage of the crashed starship, so he can see it with his own eyes and examine it with his own hands. Then we want him to record a simple message that we'll broadcast to the Unk hiding place. We want him to tell his brethren what he's seen and advise them to surrender before we lose our patience and exterminate them."

The Unk still had no comment. Morl Klun took him away, well guarded, to examine the fragments of the starship that were smeared across the Siberian steppe. The Unk's large, staring eyes were as inexpressive as ever when he returned, but he finally was willing to talk. He recorded the short message we asked for. Morl Klun listened to it carefully, over and over, and found nothing wrong with it. He recorded his own preface and postscript, concluding with an exhortation to the Unks to surrender now, and live, or prepare to die. The following day we returned to the Indian mountains and slowly flew zigzag and spiraling routes over the Unk hiding place, blasting echoes from the crags with the amplified message. There was no response.

"I wonder," I said finally.

"Wonder what?"

"Do you suppose the Unk is able to play tricks with intonation that negate everything he's saying?"

"I think I would know it if he is."

"Just in case, let's go at this thing differently."

We visited the Unk a second time. "Tell him," I said, "that a single prisoner is far more trouble to us than he's worth. If the refugees don't surrender promptly, we'll find a scientifically interesting manner to dispose of him. We might drop him at the same velocity that the starship crashed at just to see whether he'll break into the same number of pieces. We want a pitch from him that's both persuasive and sincere."

The Unk heard this threat as impassively as he'd heard everything else, but he readily agreed to record another appeal, and he worded it himself.

We returned to India the next day and played it; the Unks remained hidden.

My convalescence had progressed to the point where I was permitted a long walk around the island. Rek trailed after me; he was afraid that I'd collapse and lie unnoticed for hours amidst all of the bustle that now filled the base. We had reached the island's tapering western point when a youth from the Detroit Tribe caught up with us, shouting and gesticulating wildly.

I was wanted immediately.

I returned to the headquarters building at a speed far faster than the one the doctor had prescribed and rushed up the stairs. Morl Klun and Wiln Marra were both there, eyes intent on a scanner I had rigged to follow the monotonous revolutions of the Unk starship.

"The fleet is arriving," Morl Klun said.

I sank into a chair. "That's nice. Which fleet?"

"I've counted twenty-seven ships and that's only the beginning."

"*Which* fleet?" I demanded again.

"I don't know," he said. "They don't look like Unk ships. On the other hand, my Regez Anlf signals are either not received or ignored. Maybe it's neither."

<h1 style="text-align:center">23</h1>

"Here we go again," I said resignedly. I hurried to the communicator and alerted all of the bases. Then, while Morl Klun and Wiln Marra continued to monitor the screen and take notes, I wracked my imagination trying to think of advice that might be useful to the black tribes. There was no way that they could act for their own safety without abandoning the jerbdz, and I was convinced that the ungainly Unk beasts were destined to play a large role in the future of Earth.

But the jerbdz were not more important than people. I decided wearily to sound an alert in as calm a manner as possible and wait to see what developed before ordering the tribes into hiding. I had called more than half of the tribes, and Morl Klun had tabulated a hundred and twenty-three ships, when our trans-space communicator screen suddenly flickered to life.

Naslur Rayl's face glowered out at us. "Where's Kera Jael?" he demanded.

I was almost angry enough to refuse to answer.

When I finally presented myself, he hit me with an avalanche of idiotic questions. Who were my great-grandparents? What was my father's father's middle name? Who were the members of my echelon at the Space Academy? It finally dawned on me that he was asking me to prove that I was Kera Jael.

Long afterward, I learned what had happened. My request for clothing patterns had been the trigger that launched the greatest Regez Anlf fleet ever assembled. Politicians, traders, outworld specialists, scholars—anyone professing the faintest qualifications was called upon to analyze my message, and the unanimous conclusion was that the three members of the Reclamation Team had been taken prisoner by the Unks. There was no other way to account for the message, this parade of non-experts thought, than as an attempt to disguise an appeal for help in an ordinary commercial message. In high alarm Naslur Rayl shut off the ongoing political debate and took full responsibility upon himself. While he girded for action, he turned my message over to a panel of cryptographers in the hope that they could decipher what had happened and what it was that we needed. The cryptographers worked right up to the moment of my face-to-face conversation with Naslur Rayl, having been brought along on his ship so that they could hand him their conclusion as to the *real* meaning of "Reclamation proceeding on schedule. Please rush clothing patterns in latest Dfolma styles for females, all common sizes," the moment they had one. I never heard what they finally decided.

When Naslur Rayl learned that my request for clothing patterns had been nothing more than a request for clothing patterns, his reaction taxed the communicator's facility for showing faces in living color. His became several shades of red and purple simultaneously. I then altered all of them to a single shade of purplish black by demanding to know why his fleet had violated Earth's approach zone without the consent of the RT commander.

This brought him dangerously close to incandescence. Finally someone at his elbow pointed out to him that it was only his own order that he was violating. He controlled himself and managed to ask, with a semblance of politeness, for permission to orbit his fleet. I pointed out that the RT had totally vanquished the Unknowns who had invaded Earth, and also destroyed their starship, and his fleet would be much more useful elsewhere.

He continued to glare at me apoplectically. He was incapable of speech for so long that it became embarrassing to both of us before an assistant humbly asked if I had a suggestion. At the same time, Morl Klun, from somewhere behind me, was demanding to know what I meant by "totally vanquished."

I told Naslur Rayl, "Since we're expecting a retaliatory invasion by a fleet of Unknowns, I'd suggest that you launch reconnaissance probes and establish a defensive perimeter to screen this system. I'll call you back in thirty minutes and give you a recommended plotting." I cut the com link.

Morl Klun protested, "It won't take thirty minutes to work out the coordinates. I can give them to you now."

"Quiet," I said. "I need time to think. With a hundred and twenty-three ships up there—"

"It's almost three hundred now."

"We ought to be able to find some kind of use for three hundred ships before we send them off chasing Unks. Get those coordinates ready and keep quiet."

I made Naslur Rayl wait the full thirty minutes before I called him back. "Two things," I told him. "First, here is the deduced axis of probable approach for the Unknown fleet, based upon the best information we're able to obtain. A twenty-degree spread will certainly cover it."

"Thank you." He nodded absently. "What's the other thing?"

"How many ships in your fleet?"

"Eight hundred and forty-seven," he answered.

I squared my shoulders. I'd used three of the thirty minutes to throw on a dress uniform. With a chair concealed behind me I was able to stand straight enough, but I still was pale from my medical ordeal. I hoped he would read that as a sign of fervor rather than the aftermath of a long convalescence.

"As Acting President of Earth's Council of Tribal Organizations," I declaimed, "I formally petition that before departing this system, the entire fleet perform a ceremonial night orbit. It will be an event that will live for generations in the memories of Earth's peoples as a tangible and dramatic symbol of Regez Anlf power and achievement."

Naslur Rayl echoed weakly, "Acting President of Earth's Council of Tribal Organizations?"

"It's the superior governmental unit on the planet," I explained sweetly.

"I'll consult the admiral," Naslur Rayl said.

The screen went blank. I backed into the chair that had been supporting me and took a deep breath.

"Why do you want a ceremonial night orbit?" Wiln Marra demanded.

"You heard me. It'll be an event that will live for generations in the memories of Earth's peoples as a tangible and dramatic symbol of Regez Anlf power and achievement."

"I understood that the first time. Why do you *really* want a ceremonial night orbit?"

"Watch and see," I suggested.

Naslur Rayl's image appeared again. "The formal petition of the Acting President of Earth's Council of Tribal Organizations is granted. The entire fleet will begin forming at once for a ceremonial night orbit."

I pushed myself to my feet. "In behalf of the Council, and in behalf of all of the peoples of Earth, I thank you," I said. I cut the com link again and turned to Morl Klun and Wiln Marra. "No politician can resist the old patriotic squeeze. Remember that."

"Sure," Morl Klun said. "Why *do* you want a ceremonial night orbit?"

I smiled and looked suitably mysterious.

For the next twenty-four hours, the eight hundred and forty-seven ships of the Regez Anlf fleet filled Earth's night sky. The term "ceremonial orbit" is misleading. They were not orbiting; they were performing close-in maneuvers that paraded the entire fleet back and forth against the backdrop of space to produce the effect of brilliant stars moving in spectacular patterns. I had not exaggerated: It *was* a tangible symbol of Regez Anlf power and achievement, and I felt certain that no one who witnessed it would ever forget it. It *was* an event that would live for generations in the memories of Earth's peoples. Few worlds in the galaxy had been fortunate enough to witness such a spectacle, and none in the Regez Anlf sphere of influence had ever seen one of such magnitude.

I advised all of the Earth tribes and all of the colonists at the bases to enjoy this remarkable display that was both a gesture of friendship from the Regez Anlf and a warning to their enemies. Everyone on Earth stayed up all night. It was an overwhelming experience that mere words could not do justice to.

In the mountains at the southern tip of India, all of the Unks stayed up all night, too. I ensured that by cruising over their hiding place and blaring a new recording at them. "Our fleet has arrived," the recording told them. "Look up, and you will see it. It is ready to attack. One hour after dawn, if every last one of you hasn't surrendered, the fleet will melt these mountains and you along with them."

We did not have to wait out the hour. The moment the first rays of dawn struck the mountains, the Unks marched out to surrender.

The history of Earth's Reclamation Team did not end with its vanquishment of the Unks. The work toward a prosperous Earth with a harmonious and growing population has endured into our old age with one discovery or achievement following another. There was genuine adventure in all of that, year after year; but I fear that historians will write that Earth's great period of adventure ended when the Regez Anlf fleet left. The fleet's subsequent annihilation of the Unk fleet and its curbing of the Unks' reprehensible planetary exploitations belong to Regez Anlf history and not to that of Earth.

We turned the captured Unks over to Naslur Rayl and gave his technicians enough Unk materiel for years of study. I permitted no one else to land. I told Naslur Rayl that Earth had solved its own military problems and had no need of a Regez Anlf garrison. When he saw the remnants of the downed starship, he agreed with me.

The only Regez Anlf representatives we were prepared to welcome were commercial ones. I informed Naslur Rayl that Earth wanted to finance its own rebuilding. He was immensely sympathetic. I modeled my gruskm garments for him, and he was astonished at the filmy cloth.

He also was in a hurry to get on with his war. When I asked for a contract giving Earth the exclusive right to supply gruskm to the Regez Anlf for the next hundred years, he called in an aide, told her to give me what I wanted, and hurried off to a military conference.

The aide was suitably impressed, so I asked for an exclusive contract for two centuries and got it. I also, as a wry postscript, repeated my request for clothing patterns and got them, too. Later, when the Regez Anlf had freed world after world that the Unks had converted to gruskm production, Naslur Rayl came storming back to Earth and accused me of fraud. He even threatened to abrogate the contract if we refused to renegotiate it.

We stood firm. There are things that a politician can and cannot do, and abrogate is a "cannot." I told him that the liberated worlds already had a gruskm market in the Unk empire, and they could resume supplying it the moment peace was restored. Earth had nothing but the Regez Anlf, and the Regez Anlf had an obligation both to Earth and to itself.

Naslur Rayl fulminated further and ended by telling me I was a disgrace to the Regez Anlf. Lefkir Bonrin, who accompanied him, chuckled dryly and observed that I was nevertheless a credit to both of my great-grandmothers; and he reminded Naslur Rayl that he had warned him at the beginning that my particular combination of genes might be explosive.

The contract was honored, and gruskm profits financed the rebuilding of Earth—aided in small part by a Regez Anlf treasure trove from Ken Jordan's trading days. He had buried ingots of precious metals at Detroit Base, and one of Rek's gardening ventures dug them up.

Wiln Marra eventually married his faithful Heldi—but only after they succeeded in convincing themselves and each other that they could marry and raise a family while dedicating themselvs to lives of service.

Rek despaired of his plodding courtship and found an Icelandic bride. I liked him immensely, but I didn't want a human-sized pet constantly underfoot. We made him the official Regez Anlf representative for Iceland, and he bore his distinction with dignity and did good work.

Morl Klun and I finally married. He likes to explain that we had learned to tolerate each other and no one else could tolerate either of us, but the truth was that we had been in love since we were children and we both tired of concealing the fact. The New Earth was our achievement in a different sense from that of Wiln Marra, and we wanted to reinforce the genetic strains that made it possible.

Descendants of my two great-grandmothers were obsessed with the thought of someday returning to Earth. Some of our descendants, we feel certain, will be obsessed with the thought of someday returning to the Regez Anlf and walking the ground that Morl Klun and I have trod. Perhaps there will be a future Regez Anlf cruiser captain among them. We hope so. It is, after all, a family tradition on the Regez Anlf side.

Morl Klun and I also hope that most of our descendants will remain to garner their Earth heritage on a world our hands have healed and their hands will raise again to greatness.